Being a poor sleeper, I've been making up stories for years now to try and exhaust my mind, and get some much needed sleep. It doesn't always work as the stories then demand to be written! I write mainly Historical romances, but I've also written Contemporary romances, Romantic Intrigue and I've also tried my hand at Futuristic and Time Slip romances. I live on the beautiful island of Anglesey in North Wales, with my wonderful husband, Colin. By day I'm an Environmental Health Officer, where I get to meet lots of interesting people – all grist to the writer's mill.

http://carolinestorer.blogspot.co.uk/

@CarolineStorer6

The Roman's Revenge

CAROLINE STORER

Harper*Impulse* an imprint of
HarperCollins*Publishers* Ltd
1 London Bridge Street
London SE1 9GF

www.harpercollins.co.uk

A Paperback Original 2015

First published in Great Britain in ebook format by Harper*Impulse* 2015

A catalogue record for this book is
available from the British Library

ISBN: 9780008147990

Automatically produced by Atomik ePublisher from Easypress

Printed and bound in Great Britain

Thanks so much to my lovely editor Charlotte Ledger for all her help and support in getting this book ready.

I would also like to thank all the readers who left fabulous comments on my debut book "The Roman" and who asked when the next book is out...this book is for you.

And finally...to Colin, my fabulous husband who always encourages and supports me.

CHAPTER 1

Ostia – Port of Rome, Italy – June AD 80

"Magia, calm yourself, please. You will make yourself ill."

"Ill? Of course I am ill, I am *sick* to the stomach. How could he do this to us? He can't make me go. I refuse to go. I *won't* go I tell you. He can kill me, I don't care."

Livia worried her bottom lip, her insides churning with tension as she realised Magia was on the verge of hysteria, and had been ever since they had boarded the ship just over an hour ago. Although she had tried to calm her, nothing seemed to help, and it was fast proving a futile exercise, as every time she said something it just seemed to make her *tire-woman* even more agitated.

In a fit of panic she cast her eyes around the deck, trying to find someone who might be able to help. But there was no one. Everybody was far too busy loading up, and preparing the mighty *trireme* for its long journey to Alexandria. A journey she, and Magia, had only found out that morning they would both be making. Breaking her gaze away from the busy scene before her, she tried once more to calm the old woman.

Lifting her hand, she placed it on Magia's arm in a gesture of comfort, and lowered her voice, as if she were talking to a young child, and not a woman old enough to be her grandmother. "Magia, *please* try to understand if there was anything, *anything*, I could have done to stop this, then I would have. But Flavius decreed it, and I had no choice. *You,* of all people should be able to understand that. Now let us go down to our cabin and rest awhile. It has been a long, tiring day."

If anything, the words seemed to inflame Magia even further, and she slapped Livia's hand away, her eyes wild with rage. Under normal circumstances, Magia, a slave, would have been flogged for striking her mistress; but Livia realised these weren't normal circumstances, so she chose to ignore the outburst. But as she stood there feeling utterly helpless, she wished with all her heart she could do *something* about the mess the two of them found themselves in.

Metellus could see the old woman was clearly upset and angry about something, as she gesticulated and shouted at the young woman who was on the receiving end of her tirade. And the young woman seemed powerless to do anything about it, if the anxious expression on her face was anything to go by.

He couldn't make out what the woman was saying, the noise from the dock side, as well as on board the *trireme* was deafening as the ship was loaded for its imminent departure. But he was intrigued nonetheless, and he moved away from the stack of wooden crates which partially obscured him, and leaned against one of the wooden masts on the open deck. Crossing his arms over his muscular chest, he deliberately relaxed his stance, made his face expressionless and watched the exchange between the two women.

He knew who they were of course. News of the arrival of the beautiful *patrician,* and her *tire-woman,* had spread around the ship like wild-fire. The fact she was also the daughter of a Senator – although he didn't know which one yet – had heightened the gossip even more; and as he watched them, he couldn't help but wonder why on earth she was on her way to Alexandria. The gossip had been remarkably lacking on that score!

As he watched her, he had to acknowledge the sailors hadn't

exaggerated her beauty. She was indeed one of the most beautiful women he had ever seen, and he felt his body harden in response. She was enough to steal *any* man's breath away with her pale skin, clear and unblemished and unadorned by the powders and paints so often favoured by the rich women of Rome. His eyes were drawn to the rich mahogany of her hair which was a perfect foil for her wide spaced hazel eyes.

His gaze moved over her small straight nose, down to the fullness of her lips. Lips so tempting, he had to fight the urge to walk over to her and taste their sweetness, regardless of the older woman standing there shouting at her.

Reluctantly he tore his gaze from her face, and took his fill of her tall slim body, the thick silk of her *stola* unable to disguise the fullness of her breasts, and the irrational thought of how well they would fit together flashed into his mind as temptation clawed at him like a hungry beast. Something inside him jolted into life, feelings long supressed came to the fore, and he had the powerful urge to go over to her and kiss her anguish away. He imagined her without clothing. Naked. Writhing beneath him, her back arched in wanton abandonment, the ultimate in temptation, and he felt desire slam into him – hard.

As he watched her take the brunt of her *tire-woman's* verbal attack her small white teeth worried her lower lip, and a frown appeared, a frown which momentarily spoilt the perfection of her heart shaped face. She stiffened, her back ramrod straight as she listened to the older woman, shaking her head at something the woman was saying, and Metellus's eyes were drawn once more to the thickness of her hair, swept upwards off her face, so the abundant waves swung backwards and forwards across the slimness of her back. He wanted to wrap his hands in its thickness, test the weight of it, pull her forward and…

Metellus shook his head, annoyed with himself, and his wayward thoughts. There was no place for a woman like her in his life. Not yet anyway. Not until he'd had the revenge he had sought, and planned, for years now. Fifteen long years in fact, ever since his father had been arrested and taken away in the dead of night by Nero's Praetorian Guard. And as he remembered that fateful night, his hand lifted subconsciously, rubbing the thin scar which marred his left cheek.

He'd been nine years old when he had been awoken by the shouting and screaming coming from inside the main part of their villa. Running out of his bedroom, into the *atrium,* he saw his father being clamped in irons by four burly soldiers. Furious, he'd charged at them, demanding his father's release, but his strength had been futile against the sheer strength and number of the guards surrounding his father. Instead, he'd been thrown across the room like a rabid dog, where he'd hit his face against a sharp edge of one of the many marble statutes that lined the *atrium.* He'd been knocked unconscious, and the only thing he had to show for his attempt at trying to save his father was the scar.

A loud scream jolted Metellus out of his dark thoughts, and his eyes widened in surprise when he saw the old woman rush past him, her hand holding her cheek, a red mark clearly visible. It was obvious the *patrician* had slapped her, and bemused, his eyes swivelled from the *tire-woman* who was running towards the open hatch, and the sanctuary of the cabins below, back to where the younger woman stood.

He saw the glaze of shock in her eyes, as she stood there unmoving, until she finally blinked and refocused on the present. It was only then that her magnificent hazel eyes focused on him, seeing him for the first time as he stared at her.

Their eyes locked, the force of her gaze as powerful as a punch in the stomach, and for several long moments they looked at each other. He lowered his eyes to her mouth, saw the trembling of her bottom lip, and had to fight the urge to stride over and kiss her senseless. There was something about this woman that pulled at him, tested his resolve and demanded that he do something… anything…

Instead he raised an enquiring eyebrow. It had the desired result, when he saw hot colour suffuse her cheeks as she realised he had seen *everything* that had happened between her, and her *tire-woman*. Her eyelids fluttered, before she looked away, but not before he saw disbelief cloud her expression, as if she couldn't quite take in what had just happened between them.

But then, as if she couldn't control herself, her eyes once more sought his, as if she were unable, unwilling, to look away. She blinked several times, before her gaze lowered, taking in his tall muscular build, weighing *him* up as if he were a slave to be bought in the local market. When she realised what she was doing, her eyes snapped back to his, and this time she was bold enough to meet his gaze face on, her expression challenging.

Metellus took the challenge she offered, and stepped forward, closing the distance between them. Immediately he saw the boldness of her gaze disappear, to be replaced by uncertainty, fear even, her face losing all colour as she stiffened.

"May I be of assistance? Your slave seems...troubled," he said, unable to keep the mocking tone out of his voice, as he came to stand next to her, so close, that her delicate scent, the slightest hint of roses, and something else, teased his nostrils and he felt his body harden once more. He watched, as hot colour once again surged into her face, and her magnificent eyes fell from his.

"No. No thank you. She will be fine once we set sail," the woman said, her words stiff, brittle, refusing to meet his gaze. Then she turned her back on him, effectively dismissing him.

Metellus grunted to himself. What had he expected? True to form the woman had dismissed him out of hand. But he didn't expect anything different. A *patrician* wouldn't have looked twice at him, dressed as he was in a coarse, threadbare tunic of dark green. He would be beneath the likes of her. Spoilt, and feted, daughters of Senators did not mingle with men who worked on-board a ship.

Metellus frowned. Although he knew her to be the daughter of a Senator, equally she could also be married. An irrational burst of jealousy hit him as he contemplated the thought of her with another man. Annoyed with himself, and his fanciful musings, Metellus stiffened, and with one last look at the woman's rigid back he walked away.

Livia gripped the wooden railings, staring sightlessly down at the busy dockside, her stomach clenching in anguish before she closed her eyes in mortification. *Was he still watching her?* She dare not turn around for fear of encountering his mocking gaze once again. *Go away*, she wanted to shout. *Leave me be. Can't you see I want to be left alone? To lick my wounds in peace.*

The day had been an unremitting nightmare so far; and after Magia's hysterical outburst a few minutes ago, the fact that a complete stranger had seen her slap her, had been the final straw.

Livia shivered as a gust of wind blew in off the sea. She wasn't exactly pleased about being here either. If she had been told yesterday, that the gods had decreed she would have to board a ship at Ostia harbour, and set sail to Alexandria to marry a man she loathed, she would have thought they were jesting.

But the gods hadn't been jesting. She really *was* here waiting for the *trireme* to set sail for the Egyptian city, *and* she was on her way to marry a man she had once threatened to kill if he laid his fat, sweaty hands on her person ever again.

She bit back tears which were in imminent danger of falling. She had to be strong – for both of them. There was no point in her becoming hysterical like Magia. But she couldn't blame her *tire-woman*; the poor woman was elderly, and fully deserved to live out her days in relative peace in Rome, not find herself on the way to an unknown city, and an unknown land, halfway across the Empire. But like Livia, she had been given no choice. Livia's brother – her half-brother actually – Flavius had seen to that – again!

This was the second time Flavius had meddled in her life, had effectively sold her to the highest bidder. The first time had been nearly four years ago when Livia had just turned sixteen. Flavius had been instrumental in persuading their father that a marriage between her, and the elderly Senator Faustus Grattus Galvus, would increase their father's standing in the Senate. Livia, being a woman with no worth apart from her body, had had no choice, no matter how much she had protested at the time, and within a week she had found herself married to a man old enough to be her grandfather.

She shuddered, blocking out that period of her life which had made her so unhappy. And now, it was as if history were repeating itself, but instead of being a young girl of sixteen, she was a widow of twenty, on her way to marry another rich and powerful man for no other reason than to increase the political standing of the *Drusii* in the cutthroat arena of the Senate. Flavius, having reached the age of twenty-eight had recently been appointed *quaestor*, and was doing everything in his power to work his way up to gaining a place in the Senate, knowing full well that competition for the coveted seats was fierce. If it meant marrying his sister off to the highest bidder then so be it…

Naïvely, she had thought that her second marriage could have been a love match, someone she could have chosen rather than the men of her family, but that had been a foolish dream; a dream which would never have been allowed to happen as she well knew now.

She shook her head. She didn't want to think about what lay ahead. Opening her eyes, she spent a few more minutes staring sightlessly ahead, until she risked turning to where the man had been watching her. Thankfully, he had gone, and the breath she hadn't even realised she had been holding, hissed out of her lungs in relief.

The stranger had unsettled her. Not because he had seen her slap Magia. It had been the only way she could stop the older woman from becoming so hysterical, that she was fast becoming a danger to herself. No, it had been the mocking expression in his grey eyes as he watched her, judged her, and found her wanting, that had

7

grated on her already stretched nerves. Maybe, if he knew what she had endured today, he might not have judged her so badly.

But if she were also honest with herself, he had also unsettled her in the only way a man could. Never in all her twenty years had one man made such an impact on her in such a short space of time, and she wondered who he was.

Slave? No, not a slave, for a slave wouldn't have been so bold as to approach her; and a slave definitely wouldn't have looked at her with desire in his eyes as he had done…and he wouldn't have looked at her as if he'd wanted to devour her.

No *definitely* not a slave. She didn't even think he was *liberti* either. Again a freedman wouldn't have been as bold as he'd been, she was sure of that. That only left merchant or sailor. She favoured sailor, as his threadbare tunic and powerful body were evidence of a life of hard work, whereas merchants tended to be rich older men, content to let others do the hard work.

Livia shivered as she remembered the few brief moments their eyes had met, and the words he'd spoken to her. His voice had been a low husky rasp which had sent tremors of desire through her. She had never felt such an attraction to a man before. It had been visceral and instantaneous and she had been acutely aware of the height and power of his body.

And although he was big, he carried muscle rather than excess flesh, and he carried it well.

Very well indeed. She could see the many hours spent working on the ship had honed his body to the peak of physical perfection, if the width of his shoulders were anything to go by. His skin was a deep golden bronze, testimony to his work outside. His hair, a deep dark brown, almost black like a raven's wing, had lifted with the breeze which blew in off the sea, and Livia had wanted nothing more than to run her fingers through it and feel the strength of him as she pulled him into her arms…

She had to acknowledge he was one of the most physically perfect specimens of manhood she'd ever seen. He even rivalled

8

the gladiators she had seen perform in Rome's arenas.

Mesmerised by his physical beauty, her eyes had been drawn to the one thing that marred his perfection – a scar which ran across his left cheek up into the hairline of his dark brown hair. But even the scar didn't detract from the handsomeness of his face, rather it added to it, giving him a hardened, tough look which made her heart beat faster. Temptation had clawed at her, a powerful urge, that made her want to step forward and reach out her hand to stroke the hard planes of his face, to feel the strength of his body for herself.

But she hadn't of course. Dutiful daughters, and half-sisters, of one of Rome's most powerful families didn't do rebellious things like that. To do so would be to ruin her, and her family's reputations. And the reputation, and standing of the *Drusii* amongst Rome's elite, was the one thing which had been drummed into Livia from the moment she had been born.

So she shook her fanciful thoughts away. Thinking about handsome men, and how their bodies would feel against hers as they kissed her, was the thinking of young, foolish girls. And Livia was anything but foolish. Livia was practical, and dutiful, which was why she was on-board this ship, and on her way to marry someone she detested.

But for a moment she could dream couldn't she?

CHAPTER 2

The door to her cabin flew open with such a loud crash as it slammed against the wooden wall, it caused Livia to jump in shock. Trembling with fear, she lowered her hands; hands which had been clamped over her ears in the vain hope of drowning out the noise of the storm that had been raging for hours now, and the even more pitiful screams of the slaves trapped in the galley below.

She was about to get up from where she had sat huddled on her bunk to close the door, when eyes widened, and her breath hitched in something approaching fear, as she met the shadowed silhouette of the mocking stranger she had seen on her first day on board the ship three days ago.

Only this time, there was no trace of mockery on his partially shadowed face as he stood there.

Water streamed down his face, and his wet hair was plastered to his skull. His jaw was clenched so tightly, Livia could see a nerve pulsing there. His muscular chest rose and fell with exertion, the force of the storm raging outside obviously so fierce, he'd used every ounce of his strength to make his way to her cabin.

Once again Livia's impression of him was of raw hard power, all broad shoulders and bulging biceps. His soaking wet tunic clung and moulded every muscle and sinew of his massive body, and she could even see the delineations of the slabs of hard muscle of his stomach through the thin material. Instantly she became aware of his potent masculinity.

As he stood silhouetted in the doorway of her cabin, filling the space with his height and breadth, Livia stared at him, unable to break eye contact, as if she were some small forest animal awaiting its fate at the hands of a much larger beast. She stiffened when he stepped into the cabin, his bulk shrinking the space with the full force of his presence.

Finally, she was able to see his eyes for the first time as he stepped in from the relative darkness behind him, and Livia couldn't stop the tremor that shook her when she met his piercing gaze. A gaze, she noticed, which bored into hers with no emotion whatsoever evident in their grey depths.

His face was an inscrutable mask, and she realised with a jolt, he seemed to be fighting his own internal battle, as if he were somehow questioning his own reasoning as to why he was here in her cabin.

"Come with me. It is your only chance of staying alive," he finally said, his voice rough as he stepped further into the cabin. He held his hand out towards her, the gesture forceful, demanding her attention, his open palm commanding a response from her.

Livia hesitated, unsure what to do as she weighed up his words. Her reluctance to go with him must have annoyed him, because she saw his lips flatten in irritation, and anger blazed in his grey eyes at her perceived resistance.

"If you do not come with me you will drown. Now give me your hand. Up on deck you will have a far better chance of survival."

"But what about Magia? I…I can't leave without Magia," Livia pleaded, her eyes going to where her *tire-woman* lay comatose on the other bunk.

She saw him frown, before he looked away from her to where the old woman lay on her bunk bed.

"What ails her?" He demanded, his words clipped, harsh.

"She has been suffering with the sea sickness. She has been so

11

very ill and I have been looking after her. When...when the storm started she fainted and I cannot rouse her."

The man's frown deepened, and the nerve twitching along his jaw line pulsed harder as he gritted his jaw, making the scar on his left cheek stand out even more before his eyes once more impaled hers. "I can't take you both," he bit out, "I need all my strength to fight the storm."

"But I can't leave without her! Please, I beg you. Help her," Livia pleaded. She couldn't leave Magia. The poor woman had been petrified from the first moment she had set foot on the *trireme*, and had been a virtual recluse in their cabin ever since. And if that wasn't bad enough, she had suffered from such terrible sea sickness Livia had spent the whole time on board the ship tending to her. She couldn't leave her; her conscience just wouldn't let her.

The man stood staring down at her, before he nodded abruptly, "Come up on deck with me first, and I will return for her," he said, his voice demanding, as he stared at her with a dark brooding look on his face.

Livia looked up into his harsh face for a long moment. Realising she had to trust him to return for Magia, she nodded in acquiescence and uncurled her body. As she stood up, she placed her left hand on the cabin wall to steady herself. The ship was rolling so much, she was in serious danger of falling flat on her face.

"Give me your hand."

Livia looked up in surprise, but seeing the closed look on his face she didn't protest, and she held out her other hand. She was immediately aware of the smallness of her hand being enveloped in his much larger one, felt a jolt of awareness shudder through her when the flesh of her hand met the flesh of his. And even though his hand was as wet as the rest of him, the heat emanating from his skin where it touched hers was enough to make her look up at him in wonder.

He didn't seem to be affected by *her* touch, as all she saw on his face was bland indifference. But then all thoughts of his touch disappeared, and her breath escaped on a gasp when he pulled her forward so she came within touching distance of his large body.

"W...what are you doing?" She squeaked, trying to pull her hand out of his firm grip, when she saw he was trying to wrap some rope around her waist with his free hand.

He yanked her hand back, and trapped it in his strong grip, carrying on with his task, his face grim. "I'm tying the rope around your waist so you don't get washed overboard. Now be still woman."

His rough command halted her movements, and she watching in stunned fascination as he tied the rope first around her waist, and then around his own, and Livia couldn't help noticing how the rope cut into the tunic he wore, emphasising once more the sheer strength of his body.

"No matter what happens on deck, stay as close to me as you possibly can."

Lost for words, all Livia could do was nod her head, but she wasn't even sure if he had seen her gesture, as he had already turned to walk out of the cabin.

A series of lightning flashes illuminated the lower deck as Livia followed in his wake, before he started to climb the wooden steps leading up to the top deck of the ship. Livia squealed in shock when a deluge of icy cold water crashed down through the open hatch, soaking them both. Shivering with cold, and trepidation, she couldn't help but wonder if she was doing the right thing. *Did she really have a better chance of survival up on the top deck, there at the full mercy of the raging storm?* Rather hysterically, she realised, she didn't have much choice about it as she was irrevocably joined to the man by a thick rope.

As they climbed up the slippery steps, Livia heard the huge timbers of the ship creak all around them as the vessel fought against the forces of nature. The noise was so frightening, it was as if the ship were screaming its own protest about being battered by the storm.

Once she reached the top rung of the ladder, a hand was thrust down towards her. "Take my hand, and don't let go, or you will be washed overboard."

She placed her hand in his, the smallness of hers lost once more in the strength of his, as she allowed herself to be pulled up onto the deck of the heaving ship. Once she was standing on the deck she was unprepared for the force of the wind as it tore through the thin silk of her gown, the lashing rain saturating the fabric so it moulded against the slimness of her body, hampering her movements. Icy tentacles of cold speared her, and her teeth started chattering. She turned to where the man stood, his free arm holding onto one of the wooden masts as he used every ounce of his strength to stop them both being swept overboard.

He pulled her roughly into his body, so they stood fused to each other as he used the thickness of the mast as a makeshift shelter. Shock coursed through her as she realised how close they were, breast to breast, hip to hip, thigh to thigh. If it had been any other situation she'd found herself in, she would have been mortified at the intimacy of their embrace.

But this was survival. Pure and simple.

Deep in her heart, even though she didn't want to acknowledge it, she knew he had lied to her. There was no way he would be able to go back and fetch Magia. The sheer ferocity of the storm would make it a suicide mission, and if she was brutally honest with herself she didn't want him to release her. She knew her only hope of survival lay with him. Tied to him – literally.

As the howling winds screamed above their heads, the storm raging all around them, Livia burrowed deeper into the solid strength of the man who held her. She had never been so frightened in all her life as wave, after wave, of ice cold water crashed over them time and time again, battering them both with its intensity and ferocity.

"If we get washed overboard, you must kick out as hard as you can. If you don't, you will drown. Do you understand?"

Livia heard his words shouted above the cacophony of noise

which swirled around them, as the storm lifted the huge ship higher into the night sky before a great swell rolled in once again from the dark depths of the ocean.

"Yes!" She shouted, just before another deluge of icy water washed over her, choking her, salty water filling her mouth and nose, threatening to suck the very life out of her lungs.

The crest of the wave passed beneath them, and the massive ship dropped like a stone, and water once again cascaded down the length of the deck. Then, as if things couldn't get any worse, another massive wave tore through the ship, and this time the stranger's strength wasn't enough to protect them as they were washed along the length of the ship, powerless and totally at the mercy of the mighty storm.

Livia screamed with terror as they were tossed into the air like leaves blown about by the wind. For a moment she felt free as she flew through the air, but the feeling came to an abrupt end when she fell into the freezing cold sea, salt water once again filling her mouth, rushing down into her already tortured lungs.

She felt herself being pulled up, against the force of the water, and then she remembered she was still tied to the man. The rope tightened as he pulled her towards him, his arm wrapping around her waist as he lifted her above the crashing waves, enabling her to draw in a vital breath of air. For a moment she felt safe in his arms, but it didn't last long as another wave washed over them.

"Kick!"

The order permeated her frightened subconscious, and she did as he ordered, trying her best to kick as hard as she could, even though the fabric of her silk gown clung to her, hampering the movement of her legs.

She didn't know how long they stayed in the water, both of them kicking frantically against the massive waves. The blackness of the night overwhelmed her, and she wondered if she would die tonight wrapped in the arms of a total stranger. A man whose name she didn't even know! And with that thought, she felt the urge to laugh, as a feeling of hysteria consumed her. But when a dark shape shot out of the ocean and hit her, striking her on the temple, she mercifully felt herself slipping into blessed darkness.

It was the groans which woke her. A slow, painful, awakening, she did her utmost to fight, the pounding in her head so severe, she never wanted to open her eyes again. She didn't want to wake up; didn't want to face the all-consuming fear she had felt when she had been thrown into the icy waters of the ocean. She wanted to sleep forever, safe in the cocoon of her dreams—

"Shh. Lie still or you will injure yourself." The whispered words soothed her fear, as they permeated her foggy mind. Comprehension dawned, when she realised the moans she had heard, were in actual fact her own.

She tried to open her eyes, but her eyelashes seemed to be stuck together, and she felt a moments panic at the thought of never being able to see again. Then, as if she had somehow managed to communicate her distress, she felt cool water trickle over her face washing away the salty residue. She flicked out her tongue, eager for the cool water to assuage her dry throat moaning again, this time in relief.

"Quiet now. Can you open your eyes for me?"

She recognised the voice as being the man who'd taken her from the cabin. Opening her eyes she blinked at the brightness which assaulted her pupils. It was several moments before she was able to focus on the shadow of a man next to her. She couldn't see any of his features as the fierceness of the sun above her cast his profile into shadow. For several seconds she lay there letting her eyes adjust to the brightness, until she was able to make out his features.

He was leaning over her, a frown of concern on his face, and instinctively Livia raised a trembling hand up to his face, tracing a finger across the thin line of his scar. She saw the pupils of his eyes dilate at her feather light caress, saw the grey of his eyes darken at her touch.

"What is your name?" She heard the huskiness in the tone of her voice and swallowed hard, winching at the soreness in her throat. It felt as if she had swallowed a cup of metal shards. Then she saw him frown, obviously taken aback by her question, before he leaned back on his haunches, the movement causing her hand to drop away and fall back down onto the ground.

For several long moments he looked down at her, and Livia wondered whether he was going to ignore her question, but then he replied, "Metellus. My name is Metellus."

Livia smiled slightly, and closed her eyes once more, turning her head away from the searing brightness of the sun. "Metellus," she whispered. "Thank you. Thank you for saving me."

CHAPTER 3

The next time Livia woke, her headache was still there, but not as painful as before.

Again the intensity of the bright sunlight caused her to blink, and for a few minutes she had to let her eyes adjust to the brightness. As she lay there, she could see she was sheltered under the shade of a tree whose leaves danced above her in the slight breeze.

She was content to watch the branches sway high above her head for a moment, sunlight bouncing off the leaves in bright bursts of colour, their movement's hypnotic. She didn't know what type of trees they were, as they were nothing like the pruned ornamental ones which grew in the *peristylium* and *atrium* of her family home.

Thinking of her life back in Rome caused tears to clog her throat. Not because she missed it, but because she knew without a shadow of doubt that Magia was dead. She swallowed hard, blinking away the tears that fell. She lifted her hand and wiped away the dampness, but the small movement was enough to cause a blinding pain to crash through her head, and she gasped out loud.

For a long moment she closed her eyes once more, and lay still, letting the pain subside, content to listen to the wind blow through the branches of the trees overhead, before she stretched her hand out, encountering the softness of wool under her fingers. The fabric protected her skin from the abrasiveness of the sand beneath, and she felt a warm glow flow through her at the kindness of the person who had taken the time to shield her from the elements.

After a few more moments of rest, she forced her eyes to open once more. This time the pain wasn't so brutal, and she moved her head, until she was able to look around her.

She was in some sort of makeshift camp, high up on the shoreline, to her right she saw the beginnings of a large forest. Draped over the branches of some of the trees she saw several red woollen cloaks drying in the breeze. She recalled seeing the cloaks being worn by a small unit of soldiers who had boarded the ship the same time as she and Magia had. They, like her, had been on-route to Alexandria. Livia shivered, wondering where the men were, and whether they had survived the storm.

Supressing her dark thoughts, she turned her face to the left and saw three wooden barrels lined up next to each other, acting as a makeshift table on which some wooden utensils had been placed: several bowls, spoons and a comb. Next to the barrels there were two small wooden chests, their lids open but she couldn't see what was inside them. Her eyes were drawn to several swords propped up against one of the barrels, their metal blades glinting in the sun. Again she recognised the swords as belonging to the soldiers who had been aboard the ship. Their presence reassured her somehow, as they seemed to offer protection against an uncertain future.

Apart from that, there was nothing else, and her gaze shifted beyond the camp, taking in the long sandy beach which seemed to stretch for miles and miles in both directions from where she lay.

In any other situation she would have relished the chance to be on such a beautiful beach, taking in the iridescent blue of the sea and sky around her. But this was different. Could they – she didn't know how many of course – be the only ones inhabiting this vast expanse of emptiness? If they were, then they would have a difficult time surviving. An uninhabited island meant only one thing – there would be no water.

Metellus! Instantly her brain assimilated the fact that he wasn't here, and a panic filled her, and heedless of the pain in her head, she shot upwards into a sitting position, fighting back the nausea threatening to engulf her, as her eyes scanned the vast stretches of sand before her.

Where was he? She lifted a trembling hand to her forehead, shocked to feel sweat pouring off her brow, and as she moved her fingers trying to sooth the pain in her head she felt a large lump. It was obvious she was still suffering from the effects of whatever had knocked her out, and she should really lie back down and rest, but her mind was racing.

What if Metellus was injured? Dead even. And, ignoring everything her brain was screaming at her to lay still and rest, instead she sat up, forcing herself up on her knees. The world spun for a moment, and she took a deep calming breath before she stood up. Her legs trembled with the exertion, threatening to buckle under her as she took a tentative step forward. But determination, and an inbuilt desire to survive, propelled her forward. She stumbled, and had to reach out a hand to hold onto one of the wooden barrels to prevent herself falling, before she felt stable enough to try again.

She had to find him. She *needed* to find him, as a feeling of dread came over her at the thought of being the only person alive on the island. Looking down towards the shoreline, at the vast expanse of sandy beach, she could see he hadn't walked on it as there were no footprints in the sand. That left only one other option – he must have gone into the forest behind her. Turning, she fought the nausea welling up inside her, and walked towards the relative darkness of the forest in front of her.

Metellus paused to wipe the torrent of sweat off his brow, his chest heaving with exertion. For a few moments he stood unmoving, his head bowed, before he lifted up his makeshift wooden spade and continued digging. The "spade" was the same piece of wood which had crashed out of the darkness on the night of the storm, and had knocked Livia out. It was also the same piece of wood which had saved their lives as it had afforded them the much needed buoyancy to stay afloat during the raging storm on that fateful night.

But now, it was being put to a more practical task, helping Metellus dig the holes he needed to bury the dead bodies. Dead bodies, which had been washed up on the shore in ever increasing numbers over the past five days since he had been attending to Livia…

For a moment he hesitated in his digging, leaning his forearms on the plank of wood, as he remembered how close to death she had been. The bump on her head had been the size of a duck egg, and he wondered if she would ever wake up from the unconscious state she had fallen into.

The days had seemed endless as he'd tended to her, wiping away the fever which had consumed her, and when this morning, she had awoken and asked him his name he had felt an overwhelming sense of relief. It was a turning point he hoped, one which would mean they could leave this part of the island and try to find food and water. As each day passed, their small reserve of fresh water diminished, and now there was only a quarter of a barrel of water left. But at least they had some water, and he had thanked the gods when the one barrel had been washed ashore intact.

Because of Livia's incapacity, he hadn't been able to explore any further than the periphery of the forest, as he couldn't leave her alone just in case she woke up to find him gone. But the time was approaching when they *would* have to leave, and Metellus had even considered making a wooden sleigh of some sort so he could drag her along.

But, with the gods on his side, he prayed he wouldn't have to resort to that just yet; the lump on her temple had decreased substantially and he was praying she would soon be well enough to walk. Hopefully, with one more day of rest, they might be able to leave.

A grim look came over his face. Before he could return to Livia, and their makeshift camp, he needed to get this grave dug and bury the two bodies which had been washed ashore that morning. So with a renewed sense of urgency, he carried on digging the grave, and once he had finished burying the men, he offered a prayer to Pluto the god of the underworld, and headed back to the camp.

But his steps faltered when he saw the empty space on the red woollen cloak he'd used as a bed for Livia. Frowning in frustration, he glanced down the wide expanse of beach, but there was no sign of her. That left only the forest, and his fists clenched in anger, when he realised how much danger she had put herself into.

He threw the plank of wood onto the ground with a muttered curse; and with a grim expression on his face he charged into the undergrowth.

Livia realised she had made a monumental mistake going into the forest. For a start she hadn't a clue where she was going, and secondly, she may well now be lost, although she was sure the beach was behind her - somewhere.

She'd lost track of how long she had been here – perhaps no more than an hour – but it was soon becoming the longest hour of her life. She realised she had no choice but to abandon her search for Metellus and try to find the beach, and their camp. So she stopped walking and turned round to make her way back.

A sudden gust of wind came in off the sea, causing the trees behind her to sway and groan as if in protest. The noise was eerie as it blew through the trees, and Livia shivered in fright, afraid of the forest, and what could be lurking deep within its dark depths. She immediately thought of wolves. Would the island have wolves? Again she shivered, and then, as if she wasn't already scared enough, a disembodied voice came from behind her causing her to squeal in fright.

"What in the name of Hades do you think you're doing, woman?"

"Metellus!" Relief flooded through her, and Livia spun around, but not before a sudden wave of dizziness came over her causing her to stumble. She would have fallen into a tree trunk if it hadn't been for Metellus reaching out and catching her, and Livia couldn't help the shudder of awareness that assailed her when she felt the warmth of his hands on her arms. He was so near, she could feel his breath on the side of her neck, and heat curled in the pit of her stomach, as warmth spread through her whole body. She became aware of his strength, his raw power, a power which seemed to overwhelm her, causing her heart to pound, as much as the pounding in her head.

She had never been aware of a man as much as this one in her whole life, and for some reason it unsettled her, unnerved her, and with a blush of mortification she straightened and pushed him away.

"I am well now. Thank you," she said, trying to control herself, before she saw Metellus frown down at her and his hands dropped away as he took a step backwards, breaking the contact between them.

"I asked what you were doing in the forest, Livia."

Stiffening at the harshness of his voice, she looked him square in the face, her tone cool, "I was looking for you, I…I thought you may be hurt or something." Her words trailed off when she saw him raise an eyebrow in disbelief; and now she'd said the words aloud, she realised how stupid they sounded. Here he was, the most physically perfect specimen of manhood she had ever seen, and one who looked none the worse for wear after their ordeal, and *she* was concerned about him!

She realised she must look, and appear such a fool, but thankfully he didn't say any more on the subject.

Instead he said, "The camp is back this way. Shall we?" Not waiting for an answer he took her arm and guided her back through the dense forest, and back to their temporary home.

For a few minutes they walked in silence, their pace slow, so Livia didn't exert herself too much. Trying to break the tense silence between them she asked, "Where had you been before… before you found me?"

For a long time he didn't answer her, and she wondered if he had heard her question. She glanced up at him, about to repeat her question but the words died in her throat when she saw the dark brooding look on his stern face. He was staring down at her, watching her with an intensity that was unsettling.

"I was burying the dead," he answered eventually.

"Who?" She whispered, stopping dead in her tracks, her breathing laboured as his words sank in. Her hand reached up to her throat in trepidation. "Magia?"

He shook his head, his mouth twisting, "No, not Magia. Some of the sailors, and soldiers who had been on-board."

She turned away from him, lest he see her tears, as she thought of her *tire-woman*. Poor Magia. How she had hated every moment she had been on-board the ship. If Livia could go back in time she would have; if only to persuade her brother to leave Magia behind. She should have protested harder, insisted the older woman remain in Rome, but Flavius had been adamant. She was to accompany Livia and nothing would dissuade him. And even though she had tried so desperately to get him to change his mind it still didn't stop the powerful upwelling of guilt assailing her none the less. For several minutes she said nothing, just carried on walking thinking of Magia.

But realising she had to be strong - this island demanded it - she wiped away the salty tears, and when she had composed herself, she asked, "Are there any other survivors?"

She saw the shake of his head, and her stomach dropped. Swallowing hard she whispered, "How…how many men have you buried?"

"Thirty so far. They have, unfortunately, been washed up on the shore these past five days."

Livia gasped, her eyes widening, "Thirty! Oh those poor men." Then the full implication of his words sank in, "We've been here *five* days?" At his slight nod she turned to stare with sightless eyes out towards the sea, as they had now come to the edge of the forest and she could see their camp in the distance. She whispered, almost to herself, "I hadn't realised I had been so ill."

Then the ramifications of what he just told her slammed into her, and a wave of heat suffused her whole body. If she had been ill for five days then he *must* have tended to all her needs. A shiver went through her as she realised what *that* involved. He'd been responsible for seeing to all her bodily functions. The thought of him touching her, washing her, tending to her was too much to bear, and she closed her eyes for a few seconds as she tried to deal with the enormity of what had happened to her since the shipwreck.

When she had composed herself to some degree, she risked opening her eyes and relief replaced embarrassment. Metellus had left her standing there, and was walking towards the camp. Whether walking away from her was a deliberate action on his part she wasn't sure, but she was relieved that he'd given her a few minutes to compose herself, and thankfully he'd said nothing about tending to her for the past five days.

It was only later as she sat on her woollen cloak, sipping a much needed bowl of water, that Livia realised Metellus knew her name. She frowned, trying to remember if she had told him who she was, but after several moments of quick thinking she was convinced she hadn't. She lowered her bowl to the sandy ground, and glanced over to where he sat leaning against a fallen tree trunk, one knee bent, his arm draped over it in an attitude of maleness that seemed unique to him somehow.

"How do you know my name?" She asked hesitantly.

"I asked the captain who you were," he said, looking across at her with a closed expression on his face, his grey eyes giving nothing away. "You are Livia Drusus. Daughter of Senator Augustus Drusus. Sister to Flavius Augustus—"

"Half-sister in actual fact." Livia said interrupting him, her chin lifting in defiance as she heard the scorn in his voice. "You know my family?"

She saw Metellus hesitate, his eyes narrowing, before he answered her question, "All of Rome knows of your family."

Again Livia heard the veiled sarcasm in his voice but said nothing, keeping her thoughts to herself for the moment.

"The mighty Senator Drusus's reputation goes before him. How is he by the way?"

Again the sarcasm, and Livia stiffened before she answered, her tone curt, "He has been ill recently—" She stopped short, realising her mistake, when she saw Metellus frown as he seized on that piece of information like a lion pouncing in the arena.

"Ill? I have heard nothing. What ails him?" He demanded, his body stiffening as he stared intently at her.

Livia shrugged, knowing she had been caught out. She had been sworn to secrecy by Flavius to say nothing about her father's illness; and now here, hundreds of miles from Rome, on a deserted island she had given the secret away! She released a deep sigh, and finally answered his question, "He has had a seizure of sorts. The whole of the left hand side of his body is paralysed."

Metellus's eyes narrowed further, as he assimilated her words, and an ominous silence fell between the two of them. She wondered what he was thinking, but his face was a tight, closed, mask giving nothing away, and she couldn't help the shiver of unease which coursed through her. *Why was he so interested in her family? It made no sense...*

"Your brother—" he paused, a small smile twisting the corner of his mouth, before he continued, "Or rather your half-brother, is I presume, taking over your father's business interests?"

Livia hesitated, unsure whether to answer his question. She could plead ignorance of her brother's affairs, but the way in which he was watching her, with an intensity that was frightening, made her tell the truth. She nodded slowly, "Yes."

Her one word answer made his mouth twist in derision, "I

thought so," he said more to himself than her.

Livia stiffened, "You seem to know a lot about my family. Have you been to our villa to do business with my father and brother?" She asked, knowing in an instant, that if she had seen him at their villa, she would have definitely remembered him!

"Visit your villa?" Metellus barked, his grey eyes boring into hers, "The affluent, and extremely well connected *Drusii* consorting with the likes of *me*? I don't think so, Livia."

The words were meant to hurt, to put each of them firmly in their social places, and they were was not lost on her.

Livia knew her father, and now, most probably her brother, had more enemies than friends; as everything they did, and had done over the years, had been for political, and financial gain.

And for what? So her father could lay on a bed paralysed, unable to walk and talk? Dribbling like a baby as he was fed by the slaves. Had it been worth the hatred he had accrued for himself over the years? And now, her half-brother was treading the same path, emulating their father, as he too became obsessed in his quest to become one of Rome's elite, to become one day, one of the most powerful and influential Senators of Rome.

And as the only female offspring from her father's loins, *she* had been nothing but a pawn to be used and bartered in the political arena. It had been that way ever since she had come into womanhood, and why she had been on her way to Alexandria, to an arranged marriage with a man she detested.

Then, as if he had the power to read her thoughts, Metellus interrupted them by asking, "So why were you on the ship? Have you displeased your family so much they were compelled to send you half way across the Empire?"

Livia stiffened even more, and she looked up into his closed face, his fathomless grey eyes as cold as a dark winter's night as he watched her. For some reason a sense of foreboding came over her, making her feel vulnerable, and she lifted her chin, unwilling to tell him her reason for going to Alexandria. "Is it any concern of yours?" She asked, the words acting as a shield to protect her fragile ego.

She saw his eyes narrow, "Not really. You are right. You are no concern of mine." Then he stood up and walked away, dismissing her.

CHAPTER 4

At his words Livia sat up, feeling cut to the bone, dismissed like she always had been by the men of her family. Piqued by his blatant disregard for her, she snapped, "Well, if I am no concern of *yours,* why did you rescue me in the first place? You should have left me to drown, along with all the others."

Her words had the desired effect, as he stopped mid-stride and turned to face her once again, his eyes hooded as he stared down at her for a long moment. Then he smiled – a wolf's smile – and the knife Livia hadn't been aware of him holding, tapped against his thigh.

"A good question. One I'm not sure if I have an answer for," he shrugged, before his eyes narrowing and he said, "Maybe you aroused my curiosity? Maybe it was greed? The promise of a fat reward if I saved the precious daughter of one of Rome's finest perhaps? Let's hope your brother has enough money to pay me. My price is very high as he – and you – will find out."

Livia gasped as a sharp pain pierced right through her. Is that all she really meant to him? Monetary gain?

Pain, was replaced by anger, and in her iciest tone she said, "And what will you do if he refuses to pay anything for me? Take me back out to sea and drown me? *You* have made a big mistake if you think my father, and brother, care one jot about me."

And with those final words, she stood up and walked over to the farthest part of their makeshift camp. She sat down on the hot sand, her knees bent as she stared out to sea, wishing she were anywhere else but here, on a deserted island, with a man who detested everything about her, and her family.

As Metellus watched her walk away, he cursed himself. He had gone too far he realised, but there was no going back. She didn't know it of course, but he had blatantly lied to her. He hadn't saved her for any monetary reward. Far from it – he was richer than them by far.

It was common knowledge that the *Drusii* fortune had been virtually wiped out last year, when Mount Vesuvius had erupted, destroying all their vast areas of farm land in, and around, Pompeii and Herculaneum. Land, which had once been used to grow grapes for wine, and olives for the much coveted olive oil, and which now laid buried beneath tons of solidified lava and mud. The eruption had even destroyed the two small ships they had moored in the port area of Pompeii which were used to convey their goods to Rome. And if there was no money coming into the *Drusii* coffers it would mean they were at risk of failing to meet the 100,000 *denarii* threshold that Senators were obliged to have in order to keep their seats in the Senate.

And because Senators were barred from trading in commerce, such as shipping, the *Drusii* wealth had been their land. And apart from a small farm near the port of Brundisium, Metellus knew that most of their land holdings had been lost when Vesuvius had erupted.

Metellus's mouth tightened, as he wondered if the eruption had contributed to Livia's father's sudden decline in health. It would seem to be the logical answer.

It would also explain why Flavius had been so active in recent months, taking over most of his father's business affairs. Business affairs that had included borrowing vast sums of money from merchants and the moneylenders of Rome.

It was obvious they had fallen on hard times since the eruption. Metellus also knew Flavius, in an attempt to swell the family's coffers, had taken to gambling. Unfortunately for him, he wasn't very good at it, and he wondered if Livia knew of this latest development as she sat there in her tattered silk gown? He very much doubted it.

So, to answer the question she had thrown at him. He hadn't rescued her for a monetary reward. He had in fact rescued her for two reasons.

The first reason was easy enough to answer. Revenge.

Metellus's jaw tightened as he remembered the *exact* moment he'd found out who she was, when the captain, two days into the voyage, had told him Livia was the daughter of Senator Augustus Drusus. Metellus had taken *that* bit of news like a blow to the stomach, so much so he'd had to restrain himself from barging into her cabin and demanding if the captain spoke the truth.

Instead, he had held back his shock and anger, and had thought long and hard about how he could use Livia to exact revenge against her father. Livia's father, who, through his lies and innuendo's had spread rumours throughout Rome which had implicated Metellus's father in a conspiracy to murder Nero. That his father was innocent was immaterial. The damage had been done. The Emperor Nero, already on the verge of madness, had believed outright the information provided by a high ranking Senator. Metellus's father, a low ranking merchant – albeit a rich one – had no chance of pleading his innocence. Within two days of his arrest, he had been tried, found guilty of treason, and executed.

And now, fifteen years later it was as if the gods had handed him the very tool for his revenge on a golden platter. Here, on an uninhabited island, he had at his mercy the daughter of his sworn enemy.

Metellus's mouth twisted as he contemplated the second reason for rescuing Livia. In short, he'd rescued her because he wanted her. He had from the first moment he'd laid eyes on her, and the desire for revenge had battled with his desire to possess her body.

Sexual hunger kicked him in the gut with the force of a wild horse. He wanted her with a primitive force which refused to go away. She was pure temptation with her wide hazel eyes, her full mouth that begged to be kissed, and a body made for his enjoyment.

He should feel hatred for her, but instead he felt desire.

Angry with himself for allowing his emotions to rule his head, he cursed under his breath. He needed to be stronger, fight the feelings he felt for Livia, feelings which were threatening to overtake his rational thoughts. He hadn't come this far to allow it all to filter through his fingers like a handful of sand. *Livia Drusus was the daughter of his sworn enemy, and therefore fair game in his planned revenge.*

Metellus sighed, his eyes staring out at the expanse of blue sea in front of him. There was just one major flaw in his so called plan for revenge. He had no idea whatsoever *how* it was going to happen. He just knew it *had* to…

It was the reason he'd been feeling so unsettled ever since he'd found out who she was. *And* it had been the excuse he had used to persuade himself to burst into her cabin and on the night of the storm and rescue her.

He hadn't wanted her to die; he'd wanted her to survive so she could be the conduit in pursuing his plans for revenge against her family. But as the storm had raged around them, his plans for revenge had been suspended. Because it had then become a matter of survival – pure and simple. Life or death.

And the gods had decreed they should live. They had been given a second change, and he'd vowed to himself he *would* leave this island, and return to Rome, and fulfil his desire for revenge against the *Drusii*. And nothing was going to stop him…

"We are going to have to leave here soon."

Livia looked away from the tranquil scene in front of her, and turned to where Metellus stood behind her. It had been several hours since she'd last seen him, and she had been sitting on her makeshift bed watching the ebb and flow of the waves as they lapped along the shoreline. Lifting her eyes to meet his, she saw he was watching her with hooded eyes once again, his face giving nothing away.

"Why? Aren't we safe here?" She kept her voice neutral, not wanting to inflame his, or her anger, again.

Metellus's mouth thinned, "We are safe yes, but we have virtually no food supplies left, not to mention we are in danger of running out of water."

It was obvious she had managed to say the wrong thing again, and she felt hot colour steal over her face, "But how can you be sure there is food and water anywhere else on this island?"

"I can't. But it is a gamble we have to take if we are to survive."

When she said nothing more he carried on, "We will break camp in the morning." He then walked over to one of the wooden chests, and took out some black twisted strips.

"Here," he said, handing over one of the strips. "Eat."

Livia took what he handed to her, a frown of confusion on her face, for some reason loathe to take the offensive looking substance off him. Wrinkling her nose she asked, "What is it?"

"Salted meat."

Her face screwed up with displeasure, but before she could say anything more Metellus bit out, "I realise that it is not what you are used too. But we are not at one of your father's elaborate banquets now. You haven't eaten for days. So do you eat it, or do I have to force it down your throat?"

Livia bristled at his sarcastic tone, and her small jaw clamped shut. Reaching out her hand she snatched the salted beef out of his hand, biting a small piece off, her mouth twisting at the sour taste of it, but she refused to look away from him, her eyes defiant. His, she noticed, were still unreadable as he watched her.

"When you've finished, you will need to sleep, as we will be leaving early in the morning."

Effecting a mocking salute at him, she retorted, "Yes sir!"

Livia realised she'd gone one step too far, when he strode across to her and grabbed her hand, pulling her upwards so she fell against him. Hard. He then sat down on one of the barrels, and Livia couldn't stop the yelp of surprise as she tumbled full length onto his lap, instantly aware of her softness colliding with the hardness of his body.

"This is no joke, Livia," he snapped. "This is survival, yours and mine. If you don't want to live, then stay here, but *I* am leaving tomorrow. But if you decide to come with me, you will have to carry your fair share of equipment. I will not tolerate any feminine antics from you. Do you understand?"

Livia nodded, refusing to answer him, but her nod of acquiescence was enough to appease Metellus, as his face softened and he continued speaking, "If I tell you to do something, you will do it. This place is not going to lift up its hands in supplication and make things easier for you, just because you are the daughter of a Roman Senator. We have to be constantly on our guard. It's going to be tough, and we may not survive anyway. Do you understand?"

For some reason, Livia felt like crying, hurt by his words, but she bit her lip. *Was she that selfish? That shallow?*

Not wanting him to see her tears, she turned away, trying to pull her hand out of his grip. But he didn't let go, and if anything his grip tightened, giving Livia no choice but to look up at him.

"Do you understand?" He repeated, his tone demanding an answer.

"Yes." She whispered, trying once again to break free.

But still he refused to let go of her hand, and she looked up at him, his inscrutable gaze once again bearing down on her. For several long seconds their eyes battled with each other, until hers widened in alarm when she saw his head lower, as inch, by slow inch, his mouth came closer until it met the softness of hers.

"Oh!" She gasped, her eyes closing, as his firm lips pressed against hers. It was a kiss like no other. And when his free hand lifted to cup the soft skin of her jaw, he exerted enough pressure she had no choice but to open her mouth. She sighed as his mouth took hers, with a hunger which frightened her with its intensity.

It was everything she'd ever imagined a kiss would be, and her heart soared, her other hand lifting and gripping his broad shoulder. The movement bought her closer to his body, and her softness moulded to the hardness of his. It reminded her of the time aboard the ship when they had been as close as they were now. Then it had been about survival, but now it was about pleasure. Their pleasure.

She felt an unfamiliar, but powerful pull of attraction for this man as his tongue demanded entrance to the softness of her mouth, and she acquiesced, allowing it to enter, to mate with hers, unable to stop her low moan of desire. Never in all her life had she been kissed with such passion, and she opened her mouth wider, glorying in the pleasure his mouth and tongue was bringing her, and as the kiss deepened in its intensity, this time it was *his* moan of desire she heard.

His hand loosened its hold on hers, and settled on the full curve of her hip, pulling her forward. She clung to him, as if she'd somehow lost the ability to stand, feeling every hard plane of his body imprinted against hers.

Her breasts pressed against his chest, her stomach moulded the hardness of his lower groin, making her painfully aware of his erection. Heat pooled in her lower belly, causing a melting sensation to flood through her when his hands slid further around her back moving downwards to cup the softness of her buttocks.

She didn't know how long the kiss lasted – a minute, an hour, eternity – but she only became aware of its ending when Metellus pulled away, and her hands; hands which had somehow entwined themselves in the crisp dark hair at the nape of his neck, fell away.

"Oh!" She said again, whether from disappointment, or shock, she couldn't say, and she blinked, trying to adjust to the present as she watched him move away, his bearing now stiff and rigid.

"That shouldn't have happened. Rest assured madam, it won't again."

The words were harsh, guttural, insulting even, and before Livia could say anything, Metellus strode off towards the seashore.

She stared after him, a frown of frustration creasing her brow as she worried her lower lip, aware it throbbed from the force of his kiss. She knew, if she were able to see them, they would be kiss ravaged, red, full, wet and glistening. As she stood there watching him walk away from her – again – she had to bite back the urge to shout after him; to demand he return and explain what had just happened between them.

But she didn't. Instead, she watched as he walked away from her wondering how on earth she was going to cope for the next few days – weeks even. Cope, not only with his ever changing moods, but rather worryingly with the growing desire she felt for him. This stranger who had rescued her, a man whom she knew nothing about, but with every instinct she possessed screaming at her, telling her that *he* seemed to know an awful lot about her, and her family. And what he *did* know, he didn't like, or trust, one bit.

CHAPTER 5

Dawn couldn't come soon enough, Livia thought, as she lay there watching the black night turn to a dusty pink, bringing with it another day.

A new day in which they would head out, and try and survive the unknown perils inflicted on them by this remote island. She turned, and bit back a small groan as her muscles protested in anger at the hardness of the sand beneath her thin cloak.

She'd hardly slept at all last night, tossing and turning, trying to find a comfortable position, lying there, hour after hour listening to the alien sound of another person sleeping next to her. It had guaranteed a sleepless night. Metellus, on the other hand had slept the whole night through if his deep, even breathing was any indication!

"Are you awake?"

His words startled her, and her eyes swivelled to where he lay on his makeshift bed. She couldn't see his features, because he still lay on his back. *How on earth did he know she was awake? Was the man cursed with some sort of magical powers?* She was tempted to ignore him, but she remembered his orders yesterday, about their survival, and how she had to obey his commands, so she thought better of it. "Yes. Yes I am."

"Good. Let's get started. I want to break camp and head off as soon as possible."

And with those brief words, he rose, and started packing their meagre possessions away. Livia sighed. Today was going to be a long day. A very long day indeed.

Several hours later, Livia was wishing she had stayed abed as she took one more agonising step forward. Every muscle in her body screamed out in protest and she lifted a shaking hand to wipe the sweat off her face. They had been walking for the best part of the morning, and she didn't know if she could take another step. Her head pounded, as she desperately fought back a wave of nausea.

"Metellus! Could...could I beg a little water please?" Those were the first words which had been spoken between them since they had arisen and broken camp. Metellus had been remarkably tight lipped since they had set off. No doubt he was still regretting kissing her yesterday…

Thankfully he stopped walking, and glanced across at her. His countenance was stiff and unyielding and Livia couldn't help but notice that he looked more like a soldier than someone who toiled aboard a ship. He was wearing one of the red cloaks, obviously to protect his skin against the blistering sun. Strapped to his waist was one of the soldiers' swords, and his bare muscled arms glinted with sweat from his exertions. Livia shivered at the masculine image he portrayed, as he stood watching her. He looked ready for battle rather than walking across endless miles of sand…

But when he saw her face he frowned, and dropped the make-shift sleigh he'd been dragging behind him, and walked over to her. With gentle fingers he lifted her chin. Something shifted in his eyes as he frowned down at her. "Are you ill?" he asked, his voice uncharacteristically soft.

"No not ill, just—" The words ended abruptly, when she fell forward, dropping the cloaks and some utensils she had been carrying, before everything went blank.

With lightning reflexes Metellus lunged forward, reaching for Livia just in time, so she fell into his arms and not onto the hot sand. He wrapped his arms around her. She felt so slight, so fragile, her bones as delicate as a bird he'd once held in the palm of his hand. Her arms flopped down by the side of her body, and Metellus lifted her higher so he now held her against the hard wall of his chest.

With an unconscious movement he dropped his chin until it rested on the top of her head, the gesture one of protection as he tried to ignore the press of breasts against the hardness of his muscles. But their fullness tempted him, so soft, like a plump cushion that he wanted to lay his head on and savour the sweetness of them with his mouth and tongue—

"Hades!" He cursed, annoyed with himself for once again falling under the spell of attraction he felt for this woman.

He lowered her to the ground, his movements gentle, and once he was certain she was a comfortable as possible he looked up at the sky. The sun was at its zenith, and they had been walking during the hottest part of day. What had possessed him to allow her to walk for so long in the heat? It was obvious she wasn't strong enough to cope with the gruelling pace he had set since early that morning.

He had to get her out of the sun; so once again he lifted her into his arms, and walked back up the shoreline so she could at least benefit from the shade of the trees. Once he had lowered her onto the sparse grass which grew there, he ran back down to where he had left their supplies.

He untied the barrel of water from the makeshift sleigh of branches he'd made, his fingers fumbling with the leather strips which had been used to secure it; strips he'd taken from the sandals of the dead soldiers he'd had to bury. As he worked at the knots he cursed himself once more. He had been so preoccupied with trying to find out whether or not there was any life on the island, he had dismissed Livia out of hand.

And if he was honest with himself, he had deliberately blocked her out of his subconscious, trying to forget how good she had felt in his arms last night when he had kissed her. It was a kiss he had wanted to forget, and he had to some extent, but it had been at her expense!

Once he had the barrel upright, he opened the lid and reached for the small wooden bowl floating inside. Scooping out some of the precious water, ignoring the fact they had so little left, he walked back up to where Livia lay. She was still unconscious, her breathing rapid and shallow and he dropped to his knees. With shaking hands, he once again trickled water into her mouth, like he had done on the five days previous when she had lain unconscious.

The coolness of the water trickling down her throat was like ambrosia from the Gods and Livia flicked out her tongue, tasting the sweetness of it, desperate for more.

"Not too much, or you will make yourself ill."

At Metellus's whispered words, Livia opened her eyes and saw him kneeling over her. Concern was etched on his face, reflected in the darkened grey of his eyes.

"What…what happened?" She asked, aware of the huskiness of her voice as it rasped past her dry throat.

"You fainted."

"Oh."

"It was my fault. I should have realised you were still too weak to walk so far."

"Oh."

Metellus lips quirked, "Is that all you can say?"

Livia watched in fascination as a small dimple appeared on the right hand side of his face, and she was aware her mouth had opened in shock. Had he *really* just smiled down at her? She must indeed be ill! But before she could say anything to his last question, Metellus stood up and went over to where a small sapling grew. She watched as he stripped off several long branches, aware of his muscles rippling and bunching with the effort it took, until he came back to her, holding the branches up above his head like a slave carrying an ostrich feather parasol.

She realised what he was intending, and a warm glow flowed through her. His kindness was rather surprising, considering all that had happened between them so far.

"Thank you. The shade will help. You are most kind."

Her words were met with a bark of harsh laughter and she saw his face close. Once again she'd managed to say the wrong thing.

"'Kind' is not a word often used when describing me, Livia Drusus. You had best remember that."

Livia stiffened at the sarcastic tone, and turned away from him. There was no reasoning with the man, "Yes. How stupid of me to forget," she snapped, and made to stand up, not wanting to give him any excuse for her delaying them.

"Don't move," he ordered, "We will stay here for the rest of the day. Tomorrow, when you are rested, we will set off and try to make a full day of it." Then he turned, and walked back down to where he had left their supplies.

Livia leaned back down on the grass and closed her eyes, willing the gods to send a ship to rescue her. Now!

Once again, Livia woke up early, and this time, before Metellus could ask whether she was awake or not, she got up. Out of the corner of her eye she saw that Metellus was still asleep. She saw with a start, that the woollen cloak he was using as a blanket had slipped down to his waist, revealing the broadness of his naked chest, and his naked body.

Totally naked body she realised, her eyes widening, when she spotted his thin woollen tunic lying next to him. Her mouth went dry at the sheer beauty of his body as her eyes tracked the vast expanse of his chest, the hard muscles bronzed to a dark golden brown; muscles so well delineated, Livia had the urge to run her hands over them to see if they were as warm, and as hard to the touch as they appeared.

Once again she couldn't help but acknowledge how handsome

he was. It was a shame his tongue wasn't as pleasing as his body. And as she thought of his tongue, and remembered the kiss they had shared, her eyes lifted to his face…and met his inscrutable gaze once more.

Hades he was awake! Awake and watching her, his face expressionless, closed. Livia's stomach dropped as if someone had just punched her – hard – and she pulled in her lower lip in consternation, annoyed with herself for having been caught staring at him again. She looked away and walked over to where the water barrel stood. Taking a small cup of water she sipped from it slowly, ignoring the trembling of her hands.

As she drank the water, taking an inordinate amount of time in doing so, she heard him get up, and the slight sounds of fabric rustling as he put on his tunic caused her to shiver in longing. Breathing in deep, she tried to shake away the mental image she had at the thought of the fabric of his tunic sliding over his naked body. She had just about managed to do so when she felt his presence behind her. She stiffened, battling the urge to turn to face him, to bury her head in the strength of his chest. He was so close, tension radiated between them as she felt the warmth of his breath on the exposed part of her neck.

"Could you pour me some as well?"

"Yes." Her voice, she noticed sourly, sounded like a squeaking mouse, and she felt heat crawl up her body. *Why did this man make her feel so self-conscious? She was a woman of Rome, a widow even, not some simpering girl in the first flush of youth!* With shaking fingers she poured out some water before thrusting out her hand, waiting for him to take the wooden cup. She quivered when his fingers touched hers, and she pulled away, her movements abrupt before she stepped away from him, breaking the tension which seemed to be there every time he came within touching distance. She walked back to where she had slept, picked up her red cloak and folded it with jerky movements before doing the same with Metellus's.

She really had to control her emotions more when she was around him. She was fast becoming a liability to herself. Hadn't Metellus made his feelings plain enough yesterday? She would do well to heed his warning…

Thankfully, the rest of the day passed without mishap. She was able to keep pace with Metellus this time, partly due to the shade provided by the branches of the tree he'd cut down for her, and which he'd tied to the makeshift sleigh so it draped over her as she walked; and partly due to the fact he'd slowed the pace down considerably.

Livia didn't know how much ground they covered that day, but it must have been many miles. She noticed that the terrain up ahead had changed, the sandy beach coming to an end in about another half a mile or so to be replaced by a rocky coast line.

"Does the change in terrain mean anything?" She asked, when they had stopped for the day, and made camp.

Metellus frowned, staring at the rocky outcrop ahead of them. "I don't know. But I pray to the gods it will mean we can soon find some food and water."

"Do you know where we are? The island, I mean…"

Metellus shook his head. "Not really. The storm was so fierce, the ship could have been blown anywhere. But, if I were to hazard a guess, I think we may be on one of the Greek islands. But like I said, I'm not sure."

"Have you been to any of the Greek islands before?"

Metellus grunted, and shook his head, "No. I'm just a humble merchant that's all. This would have been my first trip. I recently took over the family business from my uncle. We sell wine to Africa and then import papyrus paper back to Rome. This was my inaugural voyage. Not a good start was it?"

Livia lifted her eyebrows in surprise. She hadn't thought him to be a merchant. Rather, when she had seen him on the deck that first time, she had convinced herself he was just one of the sailors.

"Looks can be deceiving, Livia."

She blushed, when she realised he had read her thoughts – again. She shrugged, a small smile playing on her mouth. "Yes, I realise that. But like you say, looks can be deceiving."

That evening a companionable silence fell between them, as they ate their small ration of dried beef. As Livia chewed on a small piece of meat, she couldn't help but remember the food back home at her father's villa, and for the first time in days she felt real hunger, and her stomach growled out in protest. Loudly.

So loudly, that Metellus looked across from her and smiled, "Me too. I'm so hungry I could eat anything."

Livia laughed and smiled across at him. "I must remember to recommend this to my father's cook when I get back home," she said, lifting up the piece of dried meat.

Her words had the effect of a splash of cold water, when she saw the smile leave Metellus's face.

"Ah, yes. Your father. The great Senator Drusus. How could I forget?"

Livia's face drained of all colour at the harshness of his words, and she watched him get up and walk away from her, breaking the easy companionship which had been there moments ago.

What on earth had her father done to cause his displeasure? It was obvious there was bad feeling between the two of them, but for the life of her she couldn't think what. She was desperate to find out, but she knew with a certainty Metellus wouldn't tell her what it was. It was best to keep her thoughts to herself. For a while at least. Now was not the time to challenge him about the past. She was wise enough to *know* that.

CHAPTER 6

"What is it? A fort?"

Metellus didn't look away from the awesome sight before them, but shook his head at Livia's questions. "I'm not sure," he said slowly, "If it is a fort, it's one I've never seen the likes of before. For a start it's only got one wall," he said nodding to the wooden structure – complete with parapet walls and a watchtower - which acted as some sort of barrier. It was about ten feet high and had a massive door in it. But as a defence it was worthless, because it was only one sided. The rest of the settlement was open, and he could see a myriad of huts and buildings behind it. He also saw people rushing about, shouting at each other. And if he was correct, they were shouting about them!

He knew they had been seen, as heads had popped up on the parapet wall with regular frequency only to disappear back down quickly. He could hear them shouting in Greek, which made his earlier comment about them being on one of the many small Greek islands probably correct.

Although his stomach had clenched when he had first seen the fort, he had also been relieved. Relieved, that at last there was the firm possibility of their survival now. A fort, or whatever it was, *must* have food and water. All he needed to do was convince whoever lived in there that *they* posed no danger to them, and the only way to do that was to go and speak with them.

Turning to Livia, he said, "I want you to stay here. Don't leave this spot until I come back." Then he took off the red cloak and handed it to Livia before unstrapping the sword and passing it over to her.

"Shouldn't…shouldn't you take the sword?" she whispered, "For protection…they might be hostile."

Metellus shook his head. "I don't want to inflame their anger by turning up dressed like a Roman soldier. It might send out the wrong message."

Seeing her mouth open, in what he knew was going to be a protest, he lifted a finger and placed it on her lips, his eyes pleading, "No arguing, Livia. Please."

Livia's mouth snapped shut, and he saw the flare of surprise widen her expressive eyes. She said nothing as she stared up at him, and he nodded his head before turning away from her and walking towards the fort.

"Metellus!"

He turned his head to look back at her, his eyes questioning, as he watched in surprised fascination, colour stain her cheeks as if she had somehow regretted shouting after him. Then, before he could ask her what was wrong, she whispered, "Be careful."

Livia felt her cheeks heat in embarrassment, as Metellus stared at her from unblinking eyes. In an instant she regretted her words, and she stiffened expecting him to say something derogatory.

Instead he said nothing, but he did give a slight nod before he turned and carried on walking towards the fort. Livia dragged in a ragged breath, her stomach quivering as her gaze fixed on the broad expanse of his back as he walked away. Hades, the man made her say, and do things, she never thought capable of.

And all because he had kissed her. Her life in Rome had been so ordered. So boring. She had kept a tight rein on her emotions for years, and did so because it acted as a shield against the struggle

46

of her life. A life dictated by the orders and whims of her father, and her brother, ever since she had been born.

And now? Now it seemed different, as if her struggle for survival, and the feelings she had for Metellus were compelling her to fight for what she wanted. Freedom. Freedom to be the person she really was. And being shipwrecked on this island had finally given her what she had wanted. Here, she was her own person. Able to think, and do, what she pleased, as if she were a bird that had been released from its gilded cage.

But could one kiss *really* mean anything? It had for her, of that there was no doubt. But as for Metellus, she knew he'd regretted it – it was why he'd kept his distance ever since.

Sighing, she shook her fanciful musings away and concentrated on the present.

As she watched Metellus approach the door to the fort, she couldn't help but wonder who would choose to live on such an island and why. The three days they'd spent travelling had revealed nothing spectacular about the island at all. Just endless sand, trees, and now rocks.

Her thoughts were cut short when she saw Metellus stop abruptly as he approached the gate. It was obvious he had been ordered to stop by whoever had spoken out of the small spy-hole which had been opened in the wooden door. She tilted her head, trying to make out the words being exchanged between Metellus, and the unseen person behind the door.

She realised she was too far away to hear anything, but then she saw Metellus nod, before he turned his head and looked towards some hills located to the rear of the fort. Livia looked over to the hills as well, squinting against the bright sunlight reflecting off the rocks, trying to make out what he was looking at. But she couldn't see anything, only the vast expanse of barren rock.

For several more minutes she watched as Metellus communicated with the unseen person, nodding every now and again, until he eventually turned and walked back towards her, his face grim. Livia's stomach dropped when she saw the dark expression on his face. It didn't bode well for them, if the look on his face was anything to go by, and she had to quell the anxiety which assailed her when he approached her once more. "Will they give us shelter in the fort?"

"No—"

"But why?" She exclaimed interrupting him, her voice rising with hysteria, unable to grasp the fact they might die here, right in front of them. She felt tears well up in her eyes at the injustice of it all, "We are no threat to them."

Metellus sighed, rubbing a hand across the back of his neck, the deep lines of fatigue etched on his face making him appear older. "Aye, you are right. *We* are not a threat. But *they* are."

Livia frowned in confusion, but before she could ask what he meant, Metellus continued, his voice calm, collected, "It is a leper colony, Livia. They have set up the colony as a way of trying to live a normal life amongst themselves, and away from a society which shuns them as unclean. One of the lepers is the son of a rich Greek merchant, and he has paid for this colony to be built."

Livia gasped, her eyes snapping back to the fort, as a feeling of compassion came over her. "There are many inside?" She whispered, after a long silence had fallen between them.

Metellus nodded. "Yes, a virtual community. All ages apparently." Like hers, his voice was soft, as he answered her question, as if he too, couldn't quite believe what they were seeing.

"Oh those poor people – to be trapped here for all eternity."

After a few moments of silence she once again turned back to face Metellus. He was staring down at her with a brooding expression in his eyes, and she froze, unable to look away. Her heart skipped a beat when she saw his head lower towards her and her belly clenched with a sudden longing. She wanted him to kiss her, wanted to feel the coolness of his lips against hers once more. And, as if he could read her mind, she saw his grey eyes blaze into life like molten metal as they burned into hers. The air around them felt charged, like it did before a lightning storm and Livia knew he wanted her. Desired her as much as she desired him.

But he also hated her, she knew that the instant he stopped moving closer to her, a hairsbreadth from touching her lips. She watched as he fought the internal battle he waged with himself, and she had to fight the urge to lift her hand and pull him closer so he had no choice but to kiss her.

But she didn't. Because she knew that she, and her family were his enemy, and that was enough to stop him in his tracts. And when she saw the blaze of desire leave his eyes she knew she had lost him. His head jerked back as if she'd slapped him, before he broke eye contact with her and bent down and retrieve one of the sacks holding their supplies.

"They have been kind to us, though," he said, his voice firm, in control once more as he looked back to the leper colony avoiding eye contact with her. "We *are* promised shelter, food and water. There is a cave in the hills behind the fort. It is for the crew of the ship that comes with their supplies. It is kept well stocked in case the ship cannot set sail for some reason. There is a well nearby, and the elder of the colony will provide us with some food. We are to come back later this evening for our supplies."

Livia took in all he was saying, but her brain registered the most important fact, and she asked, her voice full of hope, "A ship? When will it arrive? Will we be able to leave on it?"

"Umm. You are very astute Livia Drusus," Metellus said, a small smile pulling at his lips. "There will indeed be a ship arriving, in about three weeks' time, or even earlier by all accounts. All we need to do is tolerate each other until then, and with luck on our side we will be rescued soon. The leader of the colony will speak to the captain when the ship arrives, telling him we are shipwreck survivors. We need to stay away from the colony so the captain will have no cause to refuse us safe passage."

Three weeks! How on earth was she going to survive being in

such close proximity to Metellus for three whole weeks? *He,* she noticed with a twist of her full mouth, was preparing a fire in a stone fire pit outside the cave entrance without a care in the world, and didn't seem too bothered by the fact they were going to be in each other's company for such a long time.

She, on the other hand, was a mass of seething emotions. She couldn't seem to forget his kiss, the touch of his fingers on her skin, or the way he seemed to look at her as if he could reach inside her very being and touch her innermost emotions. And if *that* wasn't bad enough, she didn't seem to be able to control herself when it came to touching, or wanting him either.

She squeezed her eyes shut. Could she control her desire for him, until the ship arrived? She hoped so, for her own sanity, and she offered a silent prayer to Cupid, the god of desire, that she would be able to. Now was not the time to remember his kisses. She needed to be strong, to focus on their survival, and what the future might bring for her, now she wasn't going to Alexandria. So with a renewed sense of determination, she turned away from Metellus and entered the small cave, to start unpacking their supplies.

As she entered the cave, she gave a small gasp of relief. Metellus was right. The cave had been furnished with all the basics needed for a short stay. There were several wooden cots for sleeping, complete with straw mattresses. With the cloaks they had used for blankets, Livia was sure the sleeping arrangements would be more than adequate, and a lot better than what they had been putting up with in recent days. There was even a small table and some chairs, as well as several pots for cooking. The well, Livia had noticed earlier, was only a short walk away, and she had to control her eagerness to wash away the accumulated grime of the past seven days.

She looked down at the dirty silk of her tattered gown, and smiled ruefully. Her friend, Portia, would faint at the sight of it she was sure, not to mention the state of her hair and broken nails!

Portia had never, as far as Livia knew, ever set foot out of her villa without every curl on her head perfectly coiffured, and every gown clean and wrinkle free. She had often admonished Livia on her carefree attitude to her toilet, but Livia was unconcerned about spending hours getting ready to go to the baths, or the Forum, just so they could impress the men they passed on the way.

But, as she lifted a hand to her scalp, and felt the sand and salt encrusted in her hair, she wondered how Portia would have coped these past days without her much coveted creature comforts. Livia's smiled deepened, as she conceded to herself, that right now even *she* would part with her last *sesterce* to be able to wash her hair!

"Is this all for us?"

"It would appear so. They said they would leave supplies for us – and here they are," Metellus said, picking up one of the wooden crates which had been stacked some distance away from the gate.

Livia looked up at the wooden barricade, and although she couldn't see anyone she was *sure* they were watching them. "Thank you all so much. You are most kind," she said, shouting up the hillside towards the closed gate. She hoped they could hear her; as she wanted to thank them personally for their kindness.

When she looked away from the fort she saw Metellus looking at her with an odd expression on his face, "What is wrong?" she asked.

Metellus shook his head, "Nothing," he said breaking eye contact with her, before walking back to the cave with two large wooden crates loaded in his arms.

As he made his way up the steep hill, Livia watched his broad back in front of her. His refusal to answer her, made her angry. It was obvious he was surprised she had shouted out her thanks to the lepers; but she *was* grateful. She wasn't the spoiled daughter of a rich Senator as he seemed to think; she did have some compassion for the poor people stuck here on this island for their whole lives; and she *was* grateful for all their kindness as it meant their survival.

Metellus entered the cave, a frown of annoyance on his brow. Every time he thought he had Livia Drusus summed up, she did something to confound him! This time was no different. This time it had been her shouting her thanks to the lepers.

Ah, yes. Livia Drusus was a contradiction he hadn't expected. A woman who had gotten under his skin from the first moment he had seen her on board the ship. Metellus shook his head, determined to forget Livia for a few minutes. Concentrating on the task ahead of him, he lowered the crates he'd been carrying onto the floor. A quick look inside revealed bread, flour, olives, dates, fruit, and cheese; and there was enough to last at least a week, maybe even more. He had to concede, the lepers had been very generous indeed.

A slight noise behind him heralded Livia's arrival, and he watched her from the corner of his eye as she lowered the box she carried onto the floor next to his. In silence she unpacked its contents, several wooden plates, some spoons and a terracotta jug of milk.

"Shall I prepare some food while you go and get the other two crates?" She asked a few moments later, breaking the silence between them.

Metellus's eyebrows shot up in surprise once again. Again, she had shocked him with her offer of help, and he was just about to answer when she placed her hands on her hips in a gesture of defiance as he realised he had overstepped the mark and had been caught out.

"You once said not to judge a person by their looks. However, *you* seem to have done *exactly* that where I am concerned! I am not so ignorant of people, or situations, even if I am the daughter of a Senator."

Metellus smiled inwardly at the anger bristling out of her. She reminded him of a small kitten he had once owned that used to spit and fight him. Lifting his hand in surrender he said, "Put your claws away, Livia. I apologise. Yes, some food would be nice.

We will eat like the gods tonight." He bowed, a slight movement from the hips, before he made his way to the cave entrance. But then he stopped, turned and walked back to where she stood. He lifted her chin, taking in the slight widening of her pupils, before his head lowered to hers.

"Do you forgive me?" he whispered, staring at her mouth in fascination. Full and soft he wanted to taste it. Now. The subtle scent of her was like a fever in his blood and it lured him in. He dropped his head, and found her mouth, his kiss a whisper across her lips, as he teased the fullness of hers, absorbing the warmth of her. He felt her shiver in his arms, and it was all the inducement he needed to deepen the kiss. He moulded his lips to hers, his tongue demanding entry to the sweetness of her mouth, and felt a moment of triumph when he heard her gasp, before she opened her mouth and allowed his tongue to plunder the softness within.

He tasted, teased, took what he wanted, what he needed from her, as his hand loosened its hold on her chin, to trail over the pulsing beat at the base of her throat, before it skimmed downwards over the sides of her ribcage, over the soft curves of her waist, until it splayed over her hips allowing him to pull her compliant body into his, so her softness met with the hardness of his arousal.

"Livia. Beautiful, beautiful, Livia," he whispered against the fullness of her mouth once he had finished kissing her and began to trail his mouth downwards. They fit so well together as if they were made for each other—

Reality returned with the force of a tidal wave, and he stopped, as he tried to quell the myriad of sensations he was feeling for her. With obvious reluctance he pulled away from her, putting some much needed distance between them, aware of his chest rising and falling with exertion as if he'd run for miles. He had to supress the urge to pull her back into his arms, when he saw the twinge of disappointment flit across her face. Instead, he turned, and stalked out of the cave as if the fires of Hades were licking at his heels.

Jupiter's blood! He'd done it again. Kissed her, touched her, when for the past day he had expressly told himself to keep his hands off her. She was too much of a temptation, and he wondered how on earth he was going to stay away from her for the duration of their enforced stay on the island. If the past few days were anything to go by, it was going to be an uphill struggle!

She seemed to inflame his senses every time he looked at her. He wanted to take her, to make her his. Slip his hands up beneath the length of her silk gown and caress the smooth skin of her thighs. Higher, until he brushed the dampness of her inner core, until he slipped his finger into the heat of her, and watch as she came apart in his arms.

He cursed. It wasn't supposed to be like this. He'd never felt anything for the women he'd taken before. He only gave of himself physically. He was incapable of feeling anything more. He didn't allow any woman to breach the defences he'd erected so many years ago. It was what he demanded of himself. Because to allow *any* other emotion, apart from revenge to dominate his feelings was anathema to him.

Until now. He felt anger and frustration build up inside him. His feelings for Livia frightened him. She was pushing him beyond his endurance. And he didn't like it. At all.

So what was he going to do about it? For a moment he stopped walking as the question raged through him. If he was honest with himself he didn't know. Staying away from her was going to be hard – considering their cramped living quarters.

But he would just have to, for the sake of his sanity. All he needed to do was remember whose daughter she was. And with that grim thought, he lifted a hand to the left hand side of his face, felt the thin, uneven, raised surface of the scar tissue, and carried on back to the fort to retrieve the last of their supplies.

CHAPTER 7

Considering he had only given himself a stern talking to yesterday evening about his feelings for Livia, they disappeared in an instant at the sight which greeted him when he arrived back at the cave later the next morning.

His body hardened as lust slammed through him. Livia kneeling over a bucket, her head bent over it, her hair falling forward as she scooped water over the long strands. She had slipped her gown off her shoulders so it rested rather precariously, he saw, on the fullness of her breasts. Breasts, that were full and ripe, and quivered with her movements as she lifted her hands and rinsed out her hair.

It was such an intimate act, he felt guilty watching her, like a youth caught up in the first flush of desire, but he couldn't stop himself. It was mesmerising. She was the embodiment of every male fantasy. Beautiful, cultured, a living breathing goddess. And one which was driving him mad with longing.

He swallowed hard, as he stared at her in mute fascination, as he fought the urge to go over to her. She seemed to be taking an awful long time to wash her hair. It was obvious she was enjoying the moment, relishing the act of cleaning her hair, and Metellus couldn't blame her. They hadn't washed in clean water since the night of the storm, and it was obvious she was making up for lost time.

He didn't know how long he stood there watching her, and it was only when she flung her head back, the water spraying into the air like a spring shower, that he started, swallowing a lump of raw emotion when he saw her smile with unbridled joy at doing so. He realised, in amazement, he'd never seen her smile before. And he realised he liked it. It lit up her face, made him want to go over to her and skim his fingers over the fullness of her mouth, to tease the full bottom lip with his teeth and delve his tongue into the sweetness within.

But the illusion was shattered when she opened her eyes and saw him standing there watching her. In an instant her smile disappeared, and he saw her stiffen as she watched him, wariness evident in the hazel depths of her eyes. For some inexplicable reason Metellus mourned the loss of her happiness, and he couldn't help feeling annoyed with himself that he had spoiled her fun. Tension flowed between them, but not before he saw her swallow and turn bright red, trying to readjust her gown. He could see her fingers were trembling and she wasn't doing a very good job at securing it. Perhaps he could—

"I...I thought you had gone hunting, would be away for hours...I didn't—" She said interrupting his wicked thoughts. She stopped speaking, her head nodding at the trap he held in his hand, communicating what she was trying to say to him. The trap had been provided with their supplies, as Metellus had been told there were plenty of rabbits on the island, having been introduced by the lepers to provide a plentiful source of meat.

"I did," he said lifting his other hand which had been hidden behind his back, holding aloft two dead rabbits. "Eukrete, the Elder of the colony was right, there are so many rabbits on this island that we won't go short on meat." Metellus stopped talking, when he realised he was babbling, and an uneasy silence fell between the two of them. He never babbled. Not in all the twenty four years he had lived on this earth. Well not until today...

And why? The answer was in front of him. A woman so

beautiful, she took his breath away, knelt before him, her wet gown clinging to her breasts. Breasts, he could see, which were in immediate danger of popping out of the front of her gown.

"Err. Your gown," he said, swallowing the lump in his throat as he felt colour suffuse his face. It was an experience he hadn't felt for many a year, not since he had been a callow youth.

He saw Livia look down, then back up at him, her mouth forming a small "O" of surprise, before she turned away from him and readjusted her gown.

Realising she needed some privacy, he turned away and walked into the cave. Once inside he exhaled with a heavy breath. By the gods, life was going to be hard in the next few weeks until the ship arrived. He smiled at the irony of his words as he felt the fullness of his hard arousal demanding release. But there was nothing he could do about it, not if he didn't want to lose his sanity. Turning, he went to sit on one of the wooden chairs and started on the unpleasant task of skinning, and gutting, the rabbits. The chore should at least take his mind off Livia's vivid presence.

Well he hoped it would.

"That was delicious. Thank you."

The words were the first to be spoken since the hair washing incident earlier that morning. Metellus looked up to see Livia sucking the residue of the roasted rabbit off her fingers as she smiled her thanks across at him. Once again he felt heat pool in his stomach at her smile. He couldn't help but think it was rather unsettling that with only a smile in his direction, she seemed to have so much power over his emotions.

It seemed everything she did enticed him. The way she looked at him, smiled at him, the way she flicked her hair, the gesture of her hands, the small clicking noises she made with her mouth when she was deep in thought. Everything! Every nuance of her being made him want her so much, and it would be so easy to pick her up and throw her on the bed, seduce her until she begged for him never to stop. He wanted to make love to her until his lust was stated, and he could rid himself of his feelings for her.

Feeling vulnerable, and annoyed, with both himself, and her, he grunted a response to her compliment saying nothing. It was best to keep things neutral between them. There was no way he could become involved with her, no matter how many times his body screamed at him to do so.

Livia looked up into Metellus's closed face, and bit back the words she was going to say in support of his cooking skills.

For some reason he looked to be in a foul mood, and not sure why, she kept quiet. As quiet as she had been, since he had seen her washing her hair earlier.

It wasn't her fault he had returned early. *And,* she was entitled to wash her hair, she thought angrily. Not understanding him at all, she stood up and took her plate outside to where a wooden bucket was being utilised as a makeshift bowl for washing. Scrubbing away at the grime gave her a vent for the frustration she was feeling towards him, and the situation she found herself in.

She just prayed something would happen to take her mind off him, as the constant physical attraction she felt for him was driving her mad.

Mad with desire. Wanting him, needing him. Feelings she had never experienced in her whole life. And never would, if she were to marry Sextus Calpurnius Pullus.

Just thinking about Pullus made her shiver, not with desire like she felt for Metellus, but with revulsion, and dread. The thought of Pullus as her husband, touching her, making love to her, effectively his chattel, filled her with such horror she couldn't help her sob of anguish. And what, if as the result of making love to her she should become pregnant? Her own mother had died giving birth to her. What if she were die too? Who would look after the child—?

"I did not mean to upset you."

The soft words spoken behind her made Livia start, and she

whipped her head around to see him standing behind her, a frown on his face. She watched spellbound as he lifted her chin and stared intensely into her eyes, before his mouth lowered and he kissed her, a sweet kiss, an innocent kiss, a kiss designed to heal and mend her anguish. Then his lips were gone, and Livia blinked, watching as he moved away from her.

She shook her head, her thoughts distracted by the kiss, and without thinking said, "I was thinking of my future – what it holds for me—"

Her words trailed off when she saw his face darken, before he turned and left without a backward glance.

Livia banged her fist on the side of the wooden bucket. *Why in the name of Hades had she said that?* It had just come out. She wanted to call him back to explain what she meant, what was to happen to her. But she didn't. What was the point? Her future was mapped out in front of her. She had to marry Pullus, otherwise there was no telling what Flavius would do.

Hadn't he threatened to send her away if she didn't acquiesce to his demand? Banish her from Rome to some island, just as the Emperor Nero had done to his wife all those years ago. There was nothing she could do about it, such was the anger that seemed to consume Flavius these days. And, if Flavius had his way, she would soon be back on the first ship back to Alexandria.

If only Flavius would confide in her. Tell her what was wrong. But he hadn't, and she had been powerless to stop him. And of course she was unable to speak to her father to find out what was wrong; not that he would have told her anything even if he had been well enough to do so. Livia was, and always had been, nothing to her father, for he had inadvertently blamed her for her mother's death. Livia's mother had died three days after birthing her, and since her death her father had virtually ignored her ever since. She could count on the fingers of one hand the amount of times he had talked to her. And then they had only been for his own personal gain. It was as if she had never existed in his eyes.

And now – here on this remote island – she was in no position to find out anything...

The next few days seemed to pass in agonising slowness.

Livia woke each morning to find Metellus had already left to go hunting. It had become a routine of sorts; a routine which had been played out ever since the hair washing incident. Metellus stayed away from the cave for most of the day, even though Livia knew the task of catching the rabbits was one which didn't take up *that* much of his time! Where he went she had no idea, because he never volunteered anything on his return.

But she did know he went to the gates of the fort on a regular basis, as he returned with provisions provided by the kind people in the colony. But apart from that it was pure conjecture on her part as to what he did all day. And when he did return to the cave, his first task was to skin the rabbits, and set them to roast on the spit outside, in preparation for their daily meal.

He never asked her about how her day had been, not even a thank you for keeping the small cave clean, and tidy, as best she could. But her rebellious mind said she didn't *want* or *need* his thanks. All they had to do was tolerate each other until the ship arrived.

Once again they ate a silent meal, Metellus taking up his usual position by the fire, staring into the white hot embers, as he ate his rabbit and tore off huge hunks of bread from the loaves the lepers provided for them. When he had taken his fill of food, he took his wooden plate and dumped it in the bowl, for her to wash up. When she had finished this chore, she would enter the cave and find he'd already gone to bed, having used several of the red cloaks as makeshift curtains to separate their sleeping quarters from each other. If Livia were not such a patient person she would have screamed in raw frustration by now.

She dumped the piece of rag she used to wash the dishes with unbridled force, and was about to enter the cave but stopped, halted in her tracks, when she saw that instead of retiring to his bed, Metellus was standing in the opening, with several red capes tucked underneath his arm.

"I intend to sleep outside tonight." He said in answer to the unspoken question which must have shown on her face.

"But why? The nights get very cold. What is the point of shivering to death when the cave is warm and dry?"

"You ask too many questions, woman," he bit out, his voice hard, "Just take it that I am. And will be until the ship arrives."

As he strode past her, Livia felt a wave of anger assail her and she placed her hands on her hips in annoyance, before shouting at his retreating back, "You are safe from me you know. I won't attack you in the middle of the night."

At her words he froze, and she saw his shoulders stiffen before he turned to face her, his face in shadow. She swallowed hard, but stood her ground when he came back to stand next to her, ignoring the fluttering of her heart as he stared down at her for a long moment.

One dark brow sketched upwards, and the corner of his mouth curled upwards in a parody of a smile. When he spoke, his tone was low, throaty, "I may be safe, Livia. But *you* most definitely are not."

She huffed her breath in frustration. "Why?" She goaded. "Why am I not safe?"

Metellus dropped the capes and raked a hand through his hair, the gesture one of anger as his eyes bored into hers. "Because I want you in the way a man wants a woman. I want to pull your hips to mine and drive myself deep inside your body until I'm so far inside that we are practically fused together."

His words shocked her into stillness, and she saw his mouth lift once more, as if her response had somehow amused him. Then his face turned serious, "Don't look at me that way, Livia."

"What way?" She whispered, feeling a sense of wonder, of power, wash over her.

"Like you want to be in my arms, and you want me to kiss

61

you and never stop. Like this—" He stepped forward and pulled her into his arms, his mouth finding hers in a heartbeat. His kiss was hungry, but Livia met his passion as an equal. As his hands moved over her hips, pulling her closer into the hardness of his body Livia gasped into his mouth, allowing his tongue to enter.

He moaned, shifting his stance, so he was able to scoop her up into his arms. Without breaking their kiss he walked back into the cave and placed her on his bed, his body following her down until they were both lying side by side.

She could feel his arousal pulsing against her stomach as he pulled her closer. "I want you so much," he growled when he finally broke off their kiss. "But you need to be sure this is what you want, Livia. Very sure, because there is no going back." His eyes bored into hers, hot with desire.

"This attraction between the two of us needs to be assuaged. But nothing will come of it. Nothing."

The hardness in his voice acted like a splash of cold water. Livia pulled away from him, a feeling of dread coursing through her. "Why do you hate my family so much? What did my father do?"

He stared down at her, and she saw a myriad of expressions flit over his face. Anger, frustration, desire all battled against each other. Then he removed his arms from around her and rose from the bed, his body stiff.

For a long moment he stared down at her, and Livia had to fight the urge to beg him to stay. Curling her fingers into the palm of her hands to keep from reaching out to him once more she made herself lay still as she looked up at him.

"I'll see you in the morning." And with that he turned and strode out of the cave, and it was only after he'd left that Livia realised he hadn't answered her questions.

A quiver of awareness coursed through her as she recalled how quickly his passion for her had erupted. Metellus had confessed he'd wanted her, and she felt her stomach curl, as red hot longing flowed through her. She had power over a man in the only way a woman could. And for a small moment it made her feel good. Very good indeed…

But what to do about it? It would be so easy to run after him, beg him to kiss her, make love to her. But dare she? *Could she?* For agonising minutes she lay there, until the coldness of the night air made her shiver, this time in trepidation, rather than longing.

"You are a coward, Livia Drusus. A big coward." She whispered to herself. Somehow, she didn't think she would be able to sleep for many hours to come, not when she kept thinking back to what Metellus had said, and done to her. That, and the thought of his hard muscular body tossing and turning on the hard ground outside, when all the while there was a soft pallet here inside the cave…

CHAPTER 8

The next morning Livia woke with a start, her heart racing for some reason she couldn't fathom, and she glanced around the cave. But there was no one in the cave to have disturbed her, and she shook away the sudden feeling of unease which came over her.

She was alone. Metellus had kept his word and had slept outside; and if she were honest with herself she missed his presence in the cave. There was something about him that demanded her attention, and she wanted him to spend more time in her company.

It was as if she craved something more, something she couldn't quite identify, as if she had transformed overnight from an introverted girl into an attractive woman with the power to lure a man as virile as Metellus. She had been so tempted last night to make love with him. But it was apparent that he was a man in control of his life, and his emotions. She very much doubted he *ever* lost control.

He would have made love with her, but what price would *she* have had to pay for allowing it? She didn't think he would care one iota what her feelings would be.

Yes, he had looked at her as if she were some sort of forbidden fruit, and as their gazes had locked, and her pulse had beat heavy, it was as if he knew all of her secret desires, and was capable of satisfying them.

64

She'd wanted to abandon caution and run into his arms. To beg him to make love to her. To take her to the ends of the world and never come back. But even though she cherished the heated looks he gave her, she knew that all he wanted from her was her body. He didn't care about *her* – Livia – the person. All she would be to him was a convenience. A woman to take pleasure from, rise and then just walk away. But she was far better than that. She was worth more than that…

Getting up, she stretched, feeling the kinks in her muscles protest at the restless night's sleep she'd had. She shook off her dark thoughts and got dressed, before she left the relative security, and peace, of the cave and ventured out.

Squinting against the bright sunlight, she saw that the area outside the cave was deserted. Metellus had long since left to go hunting, so she walked over to the wooden bucket and washed her hands and face relishing the peace and quiet. Once she had finished her ablutions she turned to re-enter the cave. But she stopped short, when she heard a noise, and saw a slight movement out of the corner of her eye. Her eyes widened in shock when she saw a goat, a nanny goat if she wasn't mistaken, tethered to a nearby tree, munching on the long dry grass which grew there.

She walked over to the goat, her steps slow, so as not to frighten it. It must have been left for them by the lepers from the colony, and once again Livia was taken aback by the kindness they had shown her, and Metellus, ever since they had arrived. They would now be able to have fresh milk to supplement their limited diet.

Once she reached the goat, she clicked her tongue, the action designed not to startle the animal; but she saw with some amusement, the goat, far from being scared, ignored her as it carried on eating the grass. It was obvious the animal was used to human contact, and Livia hoped that boded well for making the task of milking it easier.

Not that she had ever milked a goat before. She knew the task of milking would be down to her. It only seemed right. Metellus did the hunting, so she would do the milking. The only thing was how? Turning, she ran back to the cave and picked up two wooden buckets which had been provided for their use. Once she had returned, she placed one bucket upside down so she could sit on it, and placed the other underneath the goat's teats.

She sat down, and was just about to try and milk the goat when a noise – a squeak of sorts – made her jump. Looking over to the nearby copse of trees she heard the noise intensify, and with a sense of shock she realised what the noise was. It was a baby's cry!

Getting up, she walked slowly over to the trees, and soon saw two large straw baskets lying under the shade of one of the larger trees. With a feeling of trepidation she knelt down, and opened out one of the baskets. Her breath hitched when she saw a baby wrapped in a thin cotton blanket. The baby's arms and legs were outstretched, its face mottled red as it cried out in distress. Livia's heart went out at the sight, and with an instinct as old as time, she reached down with both her hands and picked it up. With a gentle action she jigged the baby in her arms, the movements designed to soothe it. After a few moments her actions had the desired effect, as the baby stopped crying, and stared up at her in fascination. Livia smiled, "Aren't you beautiful?" She whispered, "But I think you are hungry too. Am I right?"

The baby let out a gurgle as if to say 'yes' and Livia chuckled. Cradling the child close to her chest, she sat down on a nearby tree trunk, and rocked the baby, crooning baby words and phrases so as not to frighten it. Once the baby had settled somewhat, she removed the thin cotton covering, and was able to see the child was a baby girl. Mercifully, it seemed to be free of the leprosy, having none of the scabs and sores associated with the disease. She realised with a small smile, she hadn't even considered *not* picking her up; as she was convinced that whoever had given birth to the baby wouldn't have compromised Livia's health, if the child had been born with the disease.

Although the baby was well fed, it was still incredibly small for its age and Livia could tell she was not a new born baby either. If she were to hazard a guess, the little girl was about two months old, maybe even three.

She'd had some limited experience with children, as Portia's sister, Attia, had three young children, the youngest only six months old, and Livia and Portia had helped care, and nurse, all three of Attia's children. This baby, compared to Attia's children was a lot smaller, suggesting she may have been born prematurely.

Continuing to rock the baby, Livia leaned over and rummaged in the other straw basket which had obviously been left there for the child's needs. She was relieved to see the mother had left some clothes, and pieces of cloth to be used for the baby's toilet needs.

She also saw the basket contained a thin oval shaped flask made of goat's skin which had some sort of a stoppered end. Lifting it out, she opened it and saw it contained milk, and shifting the baby in her arms she tilted the flask and placed the stopped end into the baby's mouth. With an inborn instinct, the baby latched onto the end, and started suckling. Livia laughed in relief, thankful the baby seemed to know exactly what to do; and for several minutes she watched contentedly as the baby suckled taking in much needed sustenance.

"Her name is Elisha."

Livia gasped aloud as the words, spoken in Latin, but with a strong accent, came from somewhere deep in the copse of trees. She scanned the shaded area but saw nothing. A slight movement caught her eye, and then a young woman stepped from behind a tree some distance away from her and came into view. She was dressed head to toe in dark brown, the perfect camouflage to hide amongst the brown bark of the trees. Her head was also covered with a dark brown shawl, and Livia thought how hot she must be in the heat of the morning sun. Her face was partially hidden, but even so, Livia could see she was young – possibly younger than her.

For a few moments neither of them spoke, until Livia asked, "Are you her mother?"

The woman nodded, "Yes. She is just over three months old."

Livia was right about the baby being small for her age, and as if the woman had read her thoughts she said, "She was born before her time. I...we...weren't sure if she would survive. But as you can see she has."

"She is a beautiful baby."

"Yes." This time Livia heard the catch of emotion in the young girl's voice.

For a few moments neither of them said anything, then the girl spoke, "Will you take her?" The words were rushed, as she continued, "Give her a chance of survival away from here. If she stays here she will have no life. She will catch the disease, and she will die like we all will. She does not have the leprosy, I promise you."

Realising what the young woman was asking, Livia hesitated, her teeth worrying her bottom lip, and the young woman fell to her knees crying, "Please, mistress. I beg you. Please give her a chance. The Elders of the colony are sure the supply ship will arrive soon...maybe in a few days even... You could take her with you. Please, I beg you. Please."

Livia felt tears well up in her eyes at the emotion in the younger woman's voice, and she had to fight the urge to go over to her and take her in her arms. Instead she said, "Please get up. Please. I will look after her, I promise you. But...but I need to persuade Metellus—"

"Your husband looks a decent man," the girl interjected, cutting off Livia's hesitant explanation, "Please mistress. Take her...I...I cannot bear to watch her die here, not if she doesn't have to. Just give her a chance of a normal life that is all I ask."

Livia looked up, hot colour staining her cheeks. "But...but Metellus is not my husband. He...he is..."

Her words trailed off, and both women stared at each other. Livia could see indecision flicker across the young girl's face; and without thinking about the consequences of what she was about to do she blurted out, "I will look after her, I promise you. My father has money, and I come from a good family in Rome. If you will allow me to look after her, then—"

"Oh thank you! Thank you. You are so kind. I knew I was right to trust you. I heard you shout your thanks on the first day you arrived. I…I cannot ask for anyone better to look after her." The girl's voice trembled, and with one last look at her baby nestled in Livia's arms, she turned and started to walk away.

"Wait!" Livia shouted after her retreating back. Relief swamped her when the woman stopped and looked over her shoulder. "What is your name? I would like to tell Elisha who you are when she gets older if I may. Tell her about her brave mother."

Livia saw the flash of white teeth, in the shadow of the girl's hidden face as she smiled. "My name is Ayla," and then she turned, and disappeared into the trees.

For several long minutes Livia stared into the trees willing the girl to come back to talk to her, to tell how to look after her baby. But she didn't, and after a while she looked away and glanced down at the baby. She was surprised to see that she had finished feeding, and was fast asleep, her small hands curled up into fists on either side of her face. She made soft baby noises of contentment, and a bubble of milk seeped out of the corner of her mouth, the teat still in place.

With gentle fingers she wiped away the milky residue. The baby was so helpless, so vulnerable, *so* innocent and she felt her heart swell with some unknown emotion for the child in her arms – pity, love? – She wasn't sure – but whatever it was, it was an overwhelming emotion which suddenly drained her.

For a long time Livia held the child in her arms content to let the stillness of the hot morning soothe her. Could she love this child as her own? Could she really be the mother that the baby needed?

There was no doubt she had missed a female presence when she was a child growing up in the large austere villa in Rome. The indifference shown to her by her father and half-brother had

69

affected her profoundly, she knew that. She had been a lonely child; a child who had cried silent tears for a mother's love. Was this an opportunity to give the love she'd buried deep inside her for years now? A chance to give it to an innocent child? She didn't know, of course, but she would try her hardest to make it so.

"We'll be fine together, Elisha," Livia whispered against the downy hair on the baby's head. "I promise."

Suddenly a vision of her being swollen with child; Metellus's child, impinged on her mind. But she banished those thoughts in an instant, mentally labelling them as total fantasy. Instead she bit the bottom of her lip wondering just how she was going to explain Elisha's presence when Metellus returned later that day.

Whether her anxious thoughts managed to upset the baby she wasn't sure, but at that moment Elisha started stirring. "Quiet little one," Livia crooned. "All will be well." She removed the makeshift teat from Elisha's mouth and replaced the stopper. There was still some milk left, and she was grateful, as she didn't feel like trying to milk the goat right now.

She leaned forward and placed the sleeping baby back into the straw basket before standing up and taking both the baby, and the spare basket, back into the coolness of the cave.

Once she had placed the basket holding Elisha on her bed, she set about tidying up the cave, all the while wishing Metellus would come back soon, although she knew that was unlikely. Unease suddenly filled her, and she stopped folding the blanket, hugging it to her chest in a protective gesture. Once again she wondered how Metellus would react to the arrival of a baby in their camp. Would he be angry? Demand she be returned, just in case she carried the disease?

Livia worried her lip, looking over to where the baby slept in peace in her basket. It's too late now, she thought humourlessly. But one thing she was adamant about, she *couldn't, wouldn't,* take her back now. And if it meant Metellus quarantined himself away from them both for the duration of their stay, then so be it. But she hoped he would show compassion and kindness to the child, just as *they* had been shown kindness from the lepers since their arrival here.

When she had finished her chores, she went and sat on the bed next to the baby, content to watch her sleep. Elisha made her smile, as she gurgled in her sleep. The stillness inside the cave had a calming effect on her, and Livia felt a wave of tiredness come over her. Shifting to the edge of the bed, so she wouldn't crush Elisha, she stretched out and lay next to the baby, her eyes drooping. Within minutes she was asleep, a deep sleep which had eluded her for the past week now.

As Metellus entered the cave he stiffened, a frown creasing his forehead. Even though the cave was in semi-permanent darkness most of the time, he knew something wasn't right, he could feel it in the way his senses went on instant alert. And when his eyes had adjusted to the dimness, he realised what was wrong.

Livia wasn't there.

For a moment his heart thudded in his chest, and a feeling of anger swept over him. Anger at himself for leaving her for so long. His stubborn pride had won out, and he had been absent from the cave for most of the day. But today, he'd left it even later than normal. It was the only way he could trust himself not to touch her, kiss her, make love to her. She had gotten under his skin so much, that even the slightest movement of her body when she walked past him, was enough to cause his body to harden in longing. He found himself inhaling her fragrance, craving it with a desperation. A fragrance so unique to her that it had assailed him for days now.

All he could think of was trailing his lips over her warm skin, kissing all the secret places of her body until…until she was mindless with desire for him – as he was for her…

"Shit!" He turned on his heel, anger evident in every line in his body, as he went outside to look for her. *What if something had*

71

happened to her? What if she had injured herself? Had been lying in pain on the hard ground for hours? Metellus scanned the area around the cave and was just about to shout out her name, when a slight movement in some nearby trees, caught his eyes.

The breath he hadn't even realised he'd been holding, whooshed out of his chest in relief. Livia. He was sure of it, and taking off at a brisk pace he walked towards her.

"Now, this is going to be far worse for me, than it will be for you, I'm sure of it!"

Livia grimaced, as she sat on the wooden bucket, and bent forward to take the goat's teats, pulling a face at the unusual texture of the poor animal's milk glands. But not having much choice in the matter, she pulled at the teat, hoping she was doing it right as Elisha was in need of more milk. Livia had just finished feeding her, and the goat skin flask had been drunk dry. Thankfully, there had been enough for the feed, and the baby was once again fast asleep.

But now she had the unenviable task of getting more milk.

The goat turned around and glared at her, her back legs kicking out, as she expressed her annoyance at Livia. It was obvious she wasn't doing it right, as no milk was forthcoming.

"Sorry," she muttered, relaxing her grip, and this time she didn't yank so hard, "Is this the right way?"

"Are you expecting the goat to answer you?"

Livia gasped, her heart beat accelerating as she glanced up and saw Metellus watching her with a huge smile on his face. He was leaning against a tree, his arms crossed over each other, in what, Livia was coming to recognise, as his preferred way of standing. It was a masculine stance, and Livia was instantly transported back to the time when he watched her on the ship all those endless days ago.

"Now, I can see what you are doing," Metellus drawled, nodding at the animal, "But how in the name of Jupiter did you manage to get hold of a goat?"

Livia couldn't help but smile at the perplexed expression on his face, before she answered, "The goat was left for us – and Elisha. For milk, obviously."

Her words had the desired effect, as the smile which was still hovering on his mouth disappeared, and she saw his eyes narrow.

He moved away from the tree and approached her, his movements slow, his gaze never once breaking from hers. "Who, in the name of Hades, is Elisha?" he asked eventually, when he was within touching distance of her.

His voice was soft, measured, but it didn't fool Livia for one moment, and she stood up to face him. She would need all her wits about her to convince Metellus to let her keep the baby. She could see by the clenching of his jaw, and the darkening of his grey eyes, that he was holding back his anger. Just. Ignoring the shiver of apprehension which went through her, she lifted her chin in an unconscious gesture of defiance, refusing to be cowed by him. She would defend herself, and Elisha, with every inch of her being. "A baby," she said, her tone blunt.

If Livia had said "*the Emperor*" Metellus couldn't have looked more surprised. For a long moment he stared at her until his piercing gaze shifted, roving over the ground behind where Livia stood, until he found what he was looking for – the straw basket, with the baby sleeping inside that Livia had placed under the shade of a tree, and out of harm's way. She watched as he walked over to it, and for several long moments he stared down at the sleeping child.

"One of the leper's?" He finally asked, obviously guessing who the baby belonged to.

"Yes. A young woman called Ayla. She says the child doesn't have leprosy. She just wants her to have a chance of life. To give—"

"But how can you be sure she doesn't have the disease?" Metellus cut in, his voice flat, unyielding, as he turned and pierced her with a hard look, the grey of his eyes icy.

Livia stiffened, prepared to do anything to protect the baby.

"She has no skin lesions or any redness on her body. I…I have examined her. She looks like a normal, healthy baby. Granted she is small for her age, but—"

"But how can you be certain, Livia? Have you miraculously learned a physician's skills overnight, suddenly able to provide a diagnosis?" Metellus interrupted again, anger and frustration evident in his voice.

"No! I…I can't be certain. But…but it's a chance I am willing to take. A chance I have taken. The baby deserves the right to live a normal life. Surely you can see that, Metellus?"

For a long moment he never said anything, and she watched a myriad of emotions cross his face. Then he asked, "What experience do you have for caring for a baby?"

Livia lifted her chin, "I have some experience." She saw an incredulous look pass over his face, and hurried on with her explanation. "I have a friend – Portia – her sister has three young children. I…I have helped take care of them—"

"What?" He said, interrupting her faltering words, his words biting, inflexible, as he cut off her stumbling explanation. "What experience? A few hours here and there, before you hand them back to their wet nurse, before you let the slaves look after them?"

His words held a wealth of irony, and once more he crossed his arms over his chest, this time in a gesture of defiance that spoke volumes, "Hardly a lifetime of experience, Livia. Looking after a baby is a full time commitment, and one I don't think you are equipped—"

"How dare you!" Livia interjected, indignation stamped in every line of her body. She clenched her fists, fighting the urge to go over to him and beat his chest with the rage she was feeling. "I don't care a fig that you think me incapable of looking after Elisha. I *am* going to look after her, whether you like it or not. You don't need to have anything to do with her. I…I will take care of her needs—"

Livia stopped speaking for a moment when she saw that she had managed to pierce the armour of his emotions as he wasn't looking so smug now by her outburst. But she also realised she needed to convince him of her sincerity, so she quietened her voice and pleaded, "Do you *really* want me to take her back to the fort, Metellus? Abandon her on the steps so to speak. Leave her here on this island, to a fate which will mean almost certain death? Because that is what will happen to her. I can't do it Metellus, I made a promise to her mother."

She stopped speaking as emotion clawed at her throat, and swallowed before she carried on, "And...and whatever you think of me, I always keep my promises. I promised Ayla I would do my utmost to look after her, to protect her. I don't want – need – any help from you. I can understand you are scared she might have the disease, but I truly think she is unaffected by the leprosy. Ayla wouldn't have brought her to me if she thought she had it."

Livia walked up to him, and without an unconscious thought laid her hand on his chest looking up into his dark visage, "Please, Metellus," she begged, "Just give her a chance."

Livia saw him swallow, saw the tension leave the hardness of his jawline, and she was suddenly aware of how close they were. She could feel the heat from his body where her hand rested on the fabric of his tunic and she felt her cheeks grow warm. She was so close she could smell the heady aroma of his skin, a scent so unique to him. She knew she should pull away, but somehow her body refused to move. For a long moment her eyes searched his, until she saw the iciness of his gaze melt, to be replaced by a heat which made her whole body quiver.

Once again she watched as conflicting emotions flickered across his face before he lifted his right hand and raked it through the thickness of his dark hair in obvious agitation. Livia prayed her words would strike a chord within him, and that he was not unaffected by the plight of the young mother who had taken the decision to effectively abandon her baby to a stranger.

"I will be able to look after her," Livia said, trying to reassure him. "When I return to Rome. My brother will—"

"But you were headed to Alexandria, Livia. Remember?" Metellus cut in, his eyes narrowing, "Your brother is not there is he? So how will you be able to look after her in a foreign land, *and* explain Elisha's presence to anyone who asks?"

Livia felt the colour drain from her face. Every muscle in her body tensed before she stepped back from him and broke the contact between them. Sweat popped out on her brow, and with shaking fingers she wiped it away. Metellus spoke the truth. She hadn't even thought about Alexandria – or more importantly Pullus – her prospective husband.

"I intend to return to Rome." She said, her tone defiant, as she made up her mind, "I have no intention of going onward to Alexandria. Being ship wrecked put paid to those plans."

"And what do you think your husband-to-be will have to say about your change of plans? Not to mention you turning up in either Rome, or Alexandria, with a young baby in your arms? He's bound to find out one way or another."

Livia gasped. "How...how do you know about my marriage? I never told you—"

"Never underestimate me, Livia. The captain told me all about you remember?"

Her eyes narrowed in suspicion, and she placed her hands on her hips in a gesture of defiance, "That's a lie. The captain didn't know *why* I was going to Alexandria. Only Flavius, Magia and I knew the real reason for my journey."

Her words had the desired effect, when his mouth clamped shut in annoyance. Obviously he had guessed, albeit correctly, why she was on her way to Alexandria. She saw a slight smile flit across his mouth before he shrugged his shoulders, lifting his hands up in mock surrender.

"Call it an educated guess on my part, Livia. Single women, from one of Rome's most prominent families don't go to Alexandria on their own, unless there is someone – a man – a prospective husband – waiting for them. Correct?"

Livia frowned in consternation. Metellus was too quick by half. For a few moments she stared at him in frustration, before she nodded. She met his gaze full on, "But that was then, and this is now and…and as I said earlier, I have no intention of going to Alexandria to marry. I will return to Rome. The storm made that decision for me, and there is nothing Flavius can do about it."

"Strong words, Livia. But I do detect a slight hint of panic in your voice? Are you *sure* Flavius can be persuaded to let you keep the baby?"

Livia looked away from his all too piercing eyes, and walked over to where Elisha still slept in her makeshift cradle. Livia felt the weight of responsibility settle on her shoulders, before she shook her head, "No, I'm not sure. But I'm willing to take a chance. I made a promise to Ayla I would look after her. And I intend to keep it."

"And what if Flavius insists you are to go to Alexandria and fulfil the marriage contract? What about your future husband? Will he not have something to say on the subject?"

The words were spoken next to her, and Livia gasped as she became aware of his presence. She lifted her head, meeting his gaze, keenly aware of the narrowed, watchful way he was looking at her.

"So who is it you are – were – to marry?" Metellus finally asked, when she didn't answer his earlier questions.

"Sextus Calpurnius Pullus, Praetor to the Governor of Alexandria." She said, her voice flat, emotionless.

Metellus's eyebrows shot up. "Pullus! That old coot! Surely not? He's old enough to be your father – grandfather even. Why him?"

"Why indeed? Because it is a good match of course. An excellent political match, worthy of all Rome."

Metellus obviously heard the sarcasm in her voice, because he frowned down at her before he lifted his hand, and trailed his index finger down over the nerve which throbbed at the base of her neck. Livia couldn't stop the shudder of desire that flooded her body when he touched her, the roughness of his work hardened fingers strangely erotic against the smoothness of her skin.

"Do you love him?" he asked, his voice flat, a touch of malice around his mouth, before he lifted his hand and cradled her delicate jawline.

The words were said with a hint of challenge in his voice, as he watched her with hooded eyes. Livia swallowed hard, anger flaring inside her, "Of course I don't love him. I loathe him, he makes my skin crawl," she bit out, feeling hot colour flaring in her cheeks. "But just in case you hadn't realised, *I* didn't have much choice in the matter. Since when do women have any choice in the political arena of the Senate?"

The bitterness of her voice was testimony to her feelings, and she twisted away from him, dropping to her knees to where the baby lay. The baby was awake, and for a long time she stared down at her. Thankfully, Elisha was content to just lie in her basket cooing and smiling up at her. She could still feel Metellus's presence behind her, watching her, evaluating everything she had said. After a long while she turned her head and looked up at him once more.

"Just so you know everything, Ayla said the supply ship should arrive soon, maybe in a few days' time, so you don't have to worry about Elisha, or me, for that matter." And without giving him a chance to reply, she picked up the basket, stood up and walked away, aware of Metellus watching her every step of the way.

Metellus frowned, watching as she walked away from him.

A baby! Hades! He narrowed his eyes, watching as she carried the basket in her arms and entered the cave. He had to acknowledge to himself that she made a striking picture, the epitome of womanhood as she carried the baby in her arms. Unbidden thoughts of her carrying *his* baby assailed him, *their* child suckling at her breast…but as soon as they had arrived he dismissed them, calling himself a fool for even thinking them.

Since when did Livia Drusus feature in his life?

Ever since you rescued her from the sinking ship, his brain mocked, and annoyed with himself once more, he went over to where the goat still ate the coarse grass, oblivious to the recent tension between him and Livia. Sighing, Metellus dropped down onto the upturned bucket and started to milk the goat, his hands sure and steady. As the milk began to flow into the bucket, his mind raced. *Should he let her keep the baby or make her, no demand her, to return the child to its mother?*

His hands stilled for a moment as he admitted the truth to himself. She was right. He couldn't do it. To return the baby to the colony, would be nothing short of inflicting a death sentence on the child. And no matter how much the logical part of his brain demand he do so, the other half won out. He would let her keep the baby. "By the gods I hope I'm doing the right thing," he whispered to himself.

Livia sighed, tossing and turning on the bed, trying to find a comfortable position in order to sleep. She had no idea as to how late it was, but the moon had been high in the sky for what seemed like hours now, and she was still wide awake. She had been unable to sleep, her mind in constant turmoil as she replayed all that had happened between her and Metellus earlier.

His was the voice of reason. She knew that. He had been right. How on earth was she going to persuade her brother – and father if he ever recovered – to let her keep a three month old baby?

But there was no going back now. She had made a promise, and she would stick with it. Turning over onto her side, she looked across the darkness of the cave, able to make out the shadow of the pallet Metellus had used, which was now being used as a makeshift cradle for the baby. Livia had bundled some of the cloaks and blankets together, and had laid the baby in the cocoon of wool and cloth, and she hadn't stirred once since she had put her to bed just before they had been due to have their evening meal.

Smiling wryly to herself in the darkness, she recalled what had happened when she *had* left to cave earlier to go in search of something to eat. Unsurprisingly she had felt nervous, wondering whether to venture out of the cave or plead a headache and stay with the baby. But she hadn't, and taking a deep breath she had exited the cave to see Metellus standing over the cooking spit roasting a rabbit.

Without speaking, she handed him the wooden plates and spoons she'd bought out of the cave with her, and once the rabbit was cooked Metellus had sliced some of the meat off for her and with a murmured word of thanks they had eaten in silence.

But Livia took his silence as being a good sign; a sign that he wasn't going to try and persuade her to take the baby back to the fort. It was only when the meal had finished, and Livia had tidied everything away that she had plucked up the courage to speak to him. "I can move the baby off your pallet if you like. She…she can sleep with me. I know how cold it can be outside."

Metellus had looked up from where he was still sitting by the fire, and with the flames flickering over him she saw his eyes narrow as he stared up at her, his body unnaturally still. Then his mouth had curved in a sensuous smile before he drawled, "I don't think that's a good idea. Do you, Livia?"

They had stared at each other for a long moment, until Livia had let out a breath she didn't know she had been holding. "I…I suppose not," she whispered. And with that she had turned and fled back into the cave, as if Cerberus, the dog of the Underworld, were chasing her.

Now as she lay in the darkness, thinking about what had happened earlier, she couldn't stop the groan that escaped as heat pooled in the lower portion of her belly. *What on earth had she been thinking? She had practically begged him to come back into the cave with her; her words an invitation to make love to her.*

With a sudden restlessness, Livia swung her legs over the side of the wooden pallet and sat on the edge of the bed. Her heart was racing, as if she had run up a steep hill. She could hear Elisha's soft breathing, but it wasn't enough to calm her. She felt a huge wave of frustration wash over her and unwilling to get back into the bed she rose.

Feeling for her cloak, which she had draped over the bottom of the bed earlier, she wrapped it around her shoulders and walked to the entrance of the cave to get some much needed fresh air. There was a chill to the night air, but it was just what she needed to clear away her disturbed thoughts.

"Can't sleep?"

Metellus's words, from the darkness beyond, made Livia start in fright, and she gasped, "You made me jump!"

Metellus came forward, his body silhouetted by the brightness of the full moon, and a light coming from an oil lamp which illuminated the entrance to the cave. "So I see. Sorry."

She could tell by the lightness of his voice he was far from sorry, and Livia walked towards him. "Couldn't you sleep either?"

"No. I was thinking about the baby. I went to the fort after our meal and I spoke to Ayla."

"Oh!" Livia said, surprised, but pleased, he had done so. "How... how was she?"

"Quite philosophical really, considering the enormity of what she has done. She seems convinced you will do your best for her."

"Yes. Yes I will. I made a promise, and I intend to honour it."

"You are not what I expected you know?" Metellus said, after a small silence had fallen between them.

Her breath caught, at the gentle tone she heard in his voice, and her heart skipped a beat in her chest when he came closer to her. She could see a brooding expression on his face as he looked down at her. "Not what I expected at all."

Livia didn't have to ask what he meant. He was referring to her being the spoilt daughter of one of Rome's prominent families. The insult he had hurled at her, when they had first been shipwrecked, and he'd found out who she was.

But now the words he had just spoken caused heat to pool in the pit of her stomach, and she watched mesmerised as his fingers cupped the delicate skin of her jaw, lifting her face up to his. Grey eyes, darkened by the intensity of his emotions, stared down into hers, the harsh lines of his face looked as if they had been carved out by the hard work he'd endured all his life. But even though he lived a hard life, he was also ruggedly handsome. And no more so when his mouth kicked up in a small smile as he looked down at her, before his mouth dipped down towards hers.

"I want you. Do you want me, Livia?" His voice was husky, as she felt the warmth of his breath against her lips.

"Yes," she whispered, unable to control a shiver, when his finger trailed down the delicate line of her neck. It came to rest against the pulse which beat wildly at the base of her throat. Her one word answer was enough, as she heard Metellus hiss, before he removed his hand and stepped forward.

He took both her hands in his, pulling her closer, but not so close that she was touching him. Livia felt a wave of desire come over her, and she heard herself gasp. He was so very, very dangerous, she thought, like a lion stalking its prey, and she watched mesmerised, as he smiled at her reaction. It was as if he knew *exactly* what she was feeling, what she wanted. She felt pure longing come over her as she acknowledged she wanted him with a passion that threatened to overwhelm her.

"The baby? Will she awake do you think?"

Livia shook her head, the movement slight, "No I don't think so…"

"Good."

She saw the brightness of his teeth as he smiled again, the sharp angles and planes of his face illuminated by the moonlight, before he pulled her towards him, his movements slow, deliberate, until she was engulfed in his strong arms, the slimness of her body moulded to his. He released one of his hands, wrapping it around the nape of her neck, and tugged gently, forcing her to do his will as he rubbed his fingers across the base of her skull, before his hand slipped upwards to sift through the silken length of her unbound hair.

"Beautiful. I've longed to do this from the first moment I saw you."

He seemed to glory in the texture of her hair, running his fingers through the long tendrils, time and time again. Livia couldn't stop a sigh of longing, and she felt his hand still for a moment when he heard it. It was her signal that she wanted him, and she lifted her face to his, her eyes wide, her lips parted waiting for him to fuse his mouth with hers. He brought his mouth to within touching distance of hers, so close she could feel his warm breath, see the desire flare deep in his eyes.

"Kiss me, Livia. Show me how much you want me."

His words caused a delicious shiver to slither down her body, prickling her skin, and emboldened by his order she went on tip toes and with an instinctiveness that amazed her, found his mouth. The taste, and scent of him, filled her with longing, musky and warm, and indisputably male, intoxicating her, filling her with a feminine power that was heady, as well as dangerous. And for once in her life she was doing what *she* wanted. And she wanted him – with a desperation which consumed her.

"Yes!" The word was hissed through his teeth, and no sooner had her mouth found his, the tempo of the kiss changed. This time he took control, and he kissed her again, and again, filling her mouth with his taste. His unique taste. She lifted her own hands and cupped the back of his neck, pulling him in closer to her body. This was what she wanted, what she craved. *Was it so wicked to lose oneself in the delights of sharing a body with a man she wanted so much?* She didn't think so. It couldn't be wrong, when it felt so very, very right.

She was vaguely aware of his fingers trailing downwards, until they cupped the fullness of her breasts. Livia arched, felt her nipples harden, and push through the silk of her gown, and she moaned with desire, her breath choppy with excitement. And all the while, he carried on kissing her with total abandonment.

She felt herself being lifted, weightless, carried a short distance from the cave, before he lowered her to the ground, placing her on top of his cloak. The cloak he had been using for his bed.

"Why did you leave me? Leave the cave I mean?" She asked, uncertainty in her voice, as she watched him kneel over her, before he stretched himself alongside her, propping himself up on one elbow as he stared down at her.

"I left the cave because I couldn't trust myself to be anywhere near you." The words were whispered, as he spoke them to himself. "And I still can't," before he leaned forward and kissed her again. His hands skimmed up over her shoulders, pulling her into his body, and by their own volition she felt her own hands push up under their bodies to clasp her arms around his neck. Her hair tumbled down her slim back, and she felt his hand fist in it, exerting pressure so she had no choice but to tilt her head back, exposing her neck to his mouth. His teeth nipped the sensitive skin, and she knew he had left his mark on her.

Her muscles turned languid, like ice melting in a hot sun. Pliant, she moulded to the hardness of his body, and she heard him groan as the softness of her breasts pressed against the hardness of his chest.

His mouth moved downwards, until they reached the hardness of her nipples which thrust impudently through the silk of her gown. He suckled them through the thin fabric, and she arched her back, wanting more, so much more.

"Yes," he whispered, "Yes. I want to make love to you. Now. There's no going back now, Livia. Do you understand?"

CHAPTER 9

Livia swallowed, as his words registered. "Yes. Yes, I understand," she gasped. There was no turning back now, but she knew with a certainty this was what she wanted. Needed.

Metellus needed no second invitation, and once again he drew her into his arms, his mouth fusing with the fullness of hers, his tongue demanding access to the sweet moistness within. His kiss deepened, parting her lips with expert precision to allow his tongue to slide into her mouth, the gesture one of possession; and as the kiss intensified Livia arched upwards, as his hands, no longer idle, stroked and caressed her warm skin through the silk of her gown.

Eventually, Metellus pulled away, and looked at her with such longing it shocked her to the core. Heat blazed from his eyes as she took in the raw emotion stamped on his face. He looked as if he was trying to keep control of his feelings, but was in danger of losing the battle. *What would he see on her face she wondered? Her lips swollen by his kisses? Her cheeks flushed, and her eyes shining as bright as a thousand stars?*

"You are so beautiful. I've never wanted a woman as much as I want you," he whispered.

The words were Livia's undoing, and suddenly she felt emboldened. Lifting her hands, she let them slide through his hair until she came to where his hair grew thick at the base of his neck, her fingers sifting through the silkiness of it. Cupping his head, she tried to bring him closer to her, to communicate her need to him, but his body was stiff, unyielding, as if he were doing his utmost to resist her, as if he were giving her one last chance to stop this passion from flaring between them.

But Livia didn't want one last chance, so she begged, "Please, Metellus. Please."

Her words had the desired effect, and this time, like a starving man who had stumbled on a feast fit for the gods, he let his emotions take over what rational thoughts he still clung onto. He moved away from her and with quick, jerky movements stripped off his tunic, baring his naked body to her eyes. And what a body she thought, as her hands lifted to smooth over the full expanse of his muscular chest, when he once again laid down next to her.

For several long moments she touched him, her fingers skimming over the wonderful texture of hard muscle, overlain with hot, smooth, skin. He seemed content to let her explore him, and with trembling hands she trailed downward, over the hard ridges of muscle at his abdomen, lower until…

"Later," he whispered, his hand trapping hers, halting her movements, bringing them down so they lay flat on his blanket. "Now, it's my turn."

He leaned over her, lifting up the hem of her gown, pushing it upwards until she had no choice but to lift her hips, allowing him, wanting him, to bare her body to his gaze. It was almost too much to bear, and she moaned in longing, watching as heat exploded in his eyes as he took in the pale nakedness of her body.

She swallowed as a wave of shyness came over her and she tried to cover her nakedness with her hands, but Metellus captured them with one of his hands and lifted them over her head.

"You are too lovely to hide," he whispered. "Perfection. Never hide yourself from me again, Livia. Do you understand?"

"Yes." She whispered, amazed by the power of longing sweeping over her at his words.

He used his free hand to trail down over her body. His gentle fingers lingered for a moment, on where the vein in the hollow of her neck pulsed frantically, then slid downwards, to the centre of her breastbone, teasing the slopes of her breasts, stroking her flesh back and forth, with feather light touches. The sensations were too much, and she arched off the woollen cloak, her throat making small mewling noises of need. Her movements somehow communicated her need, and his fingers trailed further down, until they met the tight curls at the juncture of her thighs. She felt him sift through the downy hair and her skin grew taut, so blazing hot, she thought she would explode as his fingers teased and tempted her beyond reason.

"Please, Metellus. Please. I...I can't take any more."

"Hush," he whispered against her neck, his fingers moving back up her body, until they once again rested near her breasts. This time, his fingers found the rigid peak of her nipple and he twisted it with his thumb and forefinger, making it swell, harden, before he leaned forward and took it into his mouth sucking it, laving it with his tongue, driving her insane with longing.

"I want to be inside you," he whispered, his breath warm against her turgid nipple. Livia inhaled, incapable of speech, so instead she communicated her need, her desire, by lifting up her hips.

At her unspoken gesture, she heard him grunt, before he fused his mouth with hers once again, his tongue probing deep inside her mouth, mating with hers in a delicious parody of what was to come.

He still held her hands above her head, and using his free hand, he once again smoothed his hand down her body, feeling the smoothness of her skin, glorying in the texture of her breasts, the silkiness of her flat stomach until he found the warmth of her womanhood, his hand cupping her, as she arched against him.

"Soon," he whispered, as he broke off the kiss lowering his head to the exposed skin of her neck. Eventually he let her hands go, and Livia reached for him, her nails digging into the muscular flesh of his shoulders, wanting to pleasure him with her hands, as he'd pleasured her with his.

His body moved, until it was over hers, and she felt his powerful thighs settle in-between hers, nudging her legs apart so he came to rest against her. He jerked his hips and became primitive man, and she did what his body demanded. With an instinct as old as time she obeyed his silent demand, allowing him entry, relaxing her legs, opening herself for him until he was able to place himself at the apex of her thighs.

Inch, by slow inch, he entered the tight moistness of her body, his teeth pulled back in a grimace as he tried to hold onto his rapidly diminishing restraint. She felt so good, so warm, so tight – so right – it was all he could do to stop himself plunging into her, taking what she offered. But he wanted it to last, he wanted her to experience *exactly* what he was feeling, to make it the best she had ever had.

But then he stilled. Frozen in place at what he was feeling. He frowned down at her, his brain screaming at him that he must be mistaken. But he wasn't – his body had definitely come across the barrier which protected her virginity.

He closed his eyes, his head falling back, as he gritted his teeth, fighting for some semblance of control as what he'd discovered sank into his passion filled mind.

Livia Drusus was still a virgin!

"Please, Metellus. Please. Don't stop."

Livia's hoarsely whispered words brought him back to reality. He lowered his head, his gaze meeting hers as he braced his arms on either side of her body, tension humming through him as he remained rigid, forcing his body not to move. He could see the confusion, and hurt, in her eyes and then her impassioned plea was his undoing. She was begging him, giving him permission to carry on.

"Are you sure, Livia? Absolutely sure? Because I'm not sure if

I can stop this time," he said in a low voice, a whisper away from her ear. His words caused her to shudder, and he felt it go right through her.

"Yes." She gasped out, and taking him by surprise when she lifted her hips, the movement breaking through the barrier of her virginity as she joined her body with his.

He captured her gasp of pain with his mouth whispering, "The pain will go now. And then there will only be pleasure, I promise you."

He inched further into the warmness of her flesh, glorying in the feeling of being inside her, being a part of her, and with slow movements he rocked his hips, his body starting the rhythm that was as old as time. He could hear her small gasps of pleasure, pleasure his body was bringing her, and he bent his head, taking an erect nipple into his mouth, suckling, nipping the swollen flesh as her hands tunnelled into his hair, gripping his head hard in the fever of her arousal.

Once he had finished worshipping her breasts, he lifted his head, and kissed her, his mouth plundering and mating with hers causing them both to pant with pleasure as the intensity of what was happening between them pulsed through them.

His body took over, as he lost control, his hips pumping against hers, and he watched as she arched her back in pleasure, felt her tightness close around him like a vice, milking his body, before she gasped out her pleasure as she came apart in his arms such was the intensity of her orgasm. He could feel her whole body shuddering, as her hot tight warmth clutched him deep within her body, and then his mind went blank, as blackness swamped him, his climax so strong he was unaware of anything else at that moment; only the desire to fill her with his seed, to bury himself so far inside her, that he never wanted to be parted from her.

Metellus fell back onto the makeshift bed, his chest heaving with exertion, before he pulled her into his body, her head coming to rest on the hard expanse of his chest. His hand lifted to smooth her sweat slicked hair away from her face, tracing the slenderness of her neck, down to the still turgid peaks of her breasts. He smiled when he felt her shiver, and secretly he relished the amount of power he held over her. A feeling he very much enjoyed – and wanted to experience – again and again.

His fingers stilled, and he turned his head to look into her face.

"No regrets?" he asked, his tone soft, as his gaze took in the contented look on her face.

He saw a flush of colour stain her cheeks, before she shook her head, a small smile playing around her kiss ravaged lips. "No regrets."

It was all he needed to hear; before he wrapped his arms around her once more. After a few more minutes of companionable silence, Livia looked up at his face, half hidden by the shadows of the night. "I will need to get back to the cave soon. The baby," she explained when he frowned down at her.

"Now?" Metellus asked, his arms tightening around her in a possessive gesture, before they slid around to cup the fullness of her breasts. He smiled when he heard her gasp, her body arching towards him once again.

"No...not now. Later."

Her words were all Metellus wanted to hear, and he pulled her up onto his chest, her legs straddling his body as she leant over him.

"Your turn now. Make love to me, Livia."

"H...how?" she asked, her voice hesitant.

"Don't worry. I'll show you," he said, smiling up at her, his hands spanning the slimness of her waist before he lifted her hips and lowered her down onto his erect body...

Livia felt herself taking him inside – fully. "Oh!" she whispered, as she found the rhythm once more, smiling as she heard Metellus moan her name time and time again.

She lost all sense of time, and place, as she rocked her body in response to his encouragement, his large hands gripping her hips, lifting her up and down with a strength that both frightened and overwhelmed her. She became lost in a maelstrom of sensations. Heat, friction, lust, longing, all merged into one, leaving her glistening with sweat, trembling with passion, as she took both her pleasure, and his, to the peak.

And when she came, she cried out, felt herself convulse around him, her body milking him dry once again, aware in the dim recesses of her brain, of his shout of exaltation, as she felt his body pulse, bucking underneath her, as he once again climaxed deep inside her.

How long she remained lying on top of his chest, listening to his thundering heartbeat she didn't know, but somehow it felt so right to lay there. Contentment overwhelmed her as Metellus stroked his hands through the long length of her hair. His movements were rhythmic, soothing, and so gentle she felt her eyes close, as a feeling of utter exhaustion and contentment came over her in a wave.

Livia woke slowly, the hazy dream she had been having still floating in her mind. She fought to hold onto to it, but it faded to be replaced by the slight noise of someone breathing. Lifting herself up onto one elbow she turned and smiled when she saw that the soft noise was coming from the sleeping baby.

Elisha was still asleep, her fists curled about her temples in what was becoming her preferred way of sleeping, as her tiny chest rose and fell with short shallow breaths. Happy that she was fine, Livia lay back down on the straw mattress, staring with sightless eyes up at the rock hewn roof of the cave, wondering how she had got there. The last thing she remembered was being outside in Metellus's arms—

Metellus! She shot up straight, her hand holding onto the woollen cloak she used as a blanket, making sure it covered her breasts. It was, she thought with a wry smile, a rather inappropriate gesture of modesty considering what had happened last night!

And one that was futile anyway she realised, when she saw she was alone in the cave with only the baby for company.

Falling back onto the pallet with a loud sigh, she brought her hand up to cover her eyes as mortification hit her. *Perhaps it had all been a dream? Perhaps she imagined last night?*

"No," she whispered to herself. Not if the slight soreness between her thighs was anything to go by! Her mouth twisted, and she lifted a finger to her mouth, tracing the fullness of her kiss ravaged lips.

Oh no. She had *definitely* not imagined what had happened last night, and a small smile flitted across her lips. Last night had been magical, never to be forgotten. Nothing could ever wipe out the memory of Metellus's lovemaking.

She had resigned herself to a future which would have involved making love to a husband whom she loathed. It would have been something she would have had to endure. Hated even.

But now? Now it was different. Metellus had shown her that lovemaking *could* be a wonderful, joyful, liberating experience. And one she wanted to enjoy time and time again.

She had loved the way his body had mated with hers. Loved the spontaneous response her body had made when he'd touched her, kissed her, caressed her. Loved every single moment she had spent in his arms. Loved—

She stiffened as she realised what she was thinking. What she was confessing to herself. *Had she fallen in love with Metellus?*

"No!" she moaned. "I can't be." *She couldn't possibly be in love with him. Could she?* Just because she had shared one glorious night in his arms, didn't mean she was in love with him. She closed her eyes in anguish as the truth slammed into her. She *was* in love with him. *You fell in love with him from the moment you saw him aboard the ship*, her mind tormented her. Livia shivered. She *had* been attracted to him, drawn to his sheer masculinity from the first instant she'd seen him. *And you fell more and more in love with him every time he kissed you, looked at you, touched you, caressed you…*

She knew she wasn't the sort of woman who gave herself to a man without feeling something for him. She had morals. Morals that had been drummed into her by her father and Flavius.

And, of course, there had been no denying the attraction which had flowed between them both more or less from the outset. Even with her limited experience with what went on between a man and a woman, she had known with a woman's intuition that he'd wanted her. Hadn't he kissed her, and told her often enough?

But what did it all mean now? Now that they had made love? She very much doubted they had a future together. She was supposed to be marrying Pullus after all. And there was also the huge obstacle of her family. Metellus hated her father, and brother, with a passion bordering on the irrational.

She gasped out loud. Last night! Had she whispered of her love to him? Told him she loved him, just as she fell asleep in his arms?

If she were honest with herself she couldn't remember what she'd said to him, it had all been a blur at the end. A blur of passion, and the delicious aftermath that followed their lovemaking.

Metellus had been both a gentle and forceful lover. Gentle when he'd realised she had been a virgin, but then forceful, demanding her response, taking her higher and higher to the realms of delight she'd never thought she would experience. She couldn't have asked for a more powerful, considerate lover.

A slight noise at the entrance to the cave jolted her out of her reverie. And, just as if she had conjured him up like some sorcerer, Metellus appeared, his tall frame silhouetted in the entrance of the cave. Livia rose from the bed, using the cloak to shield her nakedness. For a long moment they just stared at each other, until he broke the tension by walking up to her, his fingers caressing the smoothness of her cheek, the movements slow, rhythmic, until Livia felt herself relax and swayed towards him.

He leaned down and kissed her. A soft, gentle kiss, which made her want to cry for some reason. His hand cupped the back of her head, cradling her as his lips sought out the sweet nectar of her mouth. But the spell was broken when he ended the kiss, his hand falling away as if he had somehow forced himself to break away from her.

He stared down at her, "How do you fare?" His voice was husky and it stroked her senses like a silken caress.

The words caused Livia's stomach to plummet, and her heart to accelerate, but although he had spoken the words in a soft tone, she saw the hardness in his eyes as he watched her with an intensity that was frightening. She went on the defensive, and lifted her chin, looking him square in the face, "I am fine. Thank you. How do *you* fare?"

Metellus's lips quirked upwards in a slight smile at her question, but he didn't answer her, instead he stated in an abrupt tone, "You were a virgin. I hadn't expected you to be."

"Yes. Yes, I was. But it doesn't matter—"

"Of course it matters, Livia!" he said interrupting her, a frown on his face as he raked a hand through his hair in obvious exasperation. His eyes bored into hers, taking in every expression, every nuance flitting across her face.

Livia said nothing, for in truth there was nothing to say. She heard him sigh, watched as his hands dropped to his sides, and his face become a bland mask as he reigned in his temper.

And then, in a flat hard tone, he asked, "Can you explain to me why you were still a virgin? *Especially*, when all the gossips of Rome crowed about the fact that Faustus Grattus Galvus died a happy man on his wedding night, in the arms of his much younger wife – you!"

CHAPTER 10

An ugly silence fell between them, as Livia assimilated his words, and a lance of betrayal speared right through her. The fact he'd known about her past, and hadn't mentioned it, hurt more than she thought possible.

But she refused to be beaten, and stood her ground, resolute, lifting her chin in a gesture of defiance, and stubborn pride, as she met his watchful gaze.

Over the years she had grown a thick skin. She'd had to. After the disaster of her first marriage, and the ridicule she'd encountered, she'd had no choice but to return to her father's villa. And then, she'd had to spend the next few years having to endure both her father's, and her half-brother's, displeasure at being back there. She had brought shame on her family, and all because her husband – her very much older husband – had had the misfortune of dropping dead on their wedding night!

"It is true as you say" she said, eventually, "My husband *did* die on our wedding night. But not, as you know, because I had sex with him!"

She lifted her head in a gesture of defiance. A gesture which made her feel somewhat better when she saw his eyes widen in surprise, and which gave her the confidence to carry on.

"I was married at fifteen. A marriage of convenience, a joining

95

of the *Drusii* and the *Gratii*, purely for the advancement of my father's standing in the Senate. I was given no choice in the matter, no matter how much I protested at the time, and—" her voice faltered for a moment before she carried on, "And…and when my husband of one day died, instead of being a rich widow, I found myself without one *sesterce* to my name. The powerful union my father had wanted, craved, had been nothing but a sham. Galvus had no money, and I ended up back at my father's villa, to the shame of my family and the amusement of all Rome. As you well know."

She saw him frown at her words, but before he could say anything, she got in first, "Last night I chose to take you to my bed. It was my decision. I wanted it. I wanted you. Just as you wanted me."

A long silence met her words, until Metellus asked, "And what now? What will happen when Pullus realises you are no longer a virgin?"

"It doesn't matter. I've already told you that I intend to return to Rome. I won't marry Pullus. I—"

"Of course it matters, Livia." He interrupted, his words harsh, an indication of the anger he was holding onto.

Livia said nothing, just watched as he once again raked a hand through his hair in frustration.

"It matters a lot. It is obvious you were some sort of prize to be given to Sextus Calpurnius Pullus in marriage. I know of his reputation so to speak. He has debauched tastes. Tastes which run to virgins so I believe. I presume Pullus knew you to be a virgin?"

Heat flared in her face before another long silence fell between them until Livia realised he was still waiting for an answer. She looked him full in the face, and with a dignity she was desperately trying to hold onto, replied, "No, he didn't know."

"He didn't know?" Metellus scoffed, "Somehow I don't quite believe you. I think your brother knew you to be a virgin and "sold" you to Pullus—"

"No!" She burst out, anger making her colour rise, "Flavius

wouldn't—" She stopped speaking, and turned away, her mind whirling. She was a fool. Of course Flavius would do such a thing! He'd done nothing but manoeuvre and manipulate people and situations all of his adult life.

"Knowing of your brother's reputation and how ruthless he is, I think he did," Metellus said, cutting into her troubled thoughts. "What did he do when you returned to your father's villa after Galvus's death? Did he question you about your wedding night?"

Livia flinched at his cutting remark. He was right of course. Flavius *had* been furious to say the least. Not only had he been misled as to Galvus's actual wealth, but he'd had to endure, along with Livia, the snide gossip about how she had effectively rode her husband to death. For days they had been talked and laughed about throughout Rome; until Flavius had had enough and he'd demanded to know *exactly* what had occurred in the bedroom on her wedding night. When Livia had refused to tell him, Flavius has threatened to have her physically examined to ascertain if she still had her virginity.

Livia knew without a single doubt that Flavius would do as he threatened; and not wanting to be put through the indignity of a physical examination she had, in the end, admitted to him that nothing had occurred on her wedding night, and that she still remained a virgin.

Only four people had known the truth. Flavius and her father, and Livia and Portia. Livia had told her friend what had really happened on her wedding night, and Portia being the true friend she was, had sworn she would keep her secret. In truth, all four of them were sensible enough not to reveal the truth to anyone else. The Roman elite had made up their minds as to what they believed had happened between her and her older husband. To try and dissuade them would have been a futile exercise, and Flavius obviously saw the worth in keeping quiet about what had happened until such times as he could tout Livia's virginity and await another "bargain" to be struck with some other influential man of rank.

Realising Metellus was still waiting for an answer, Livia turned and faced him. "Yes," she stated with quiet dignity, "Yes, he did know."

Metellus's eyes narrowed, before he asked, "So why did you give it to me?"

The question was forced out of tight lips, and Livia saw a flash of anger light up his eyes.

Livia stiffened. *What should she say? The truth? Lies?* Truth won out. She lifted her chin in defiance, "You treated me like a woman, not a chattel like my father did, and brother does." She also wanted to say she'd never met a man who had stirred her to passion so much, that she yearned for his touch, his body…but she kept that to herself.

"I'm not so sure," Metellus drawled, after a long heartbeat of silence greeted her words. Then, with a speed which shocked her, his hand snaked out and grabbed her wrist, pulling her towards him, until his face was pressed so close to hers, she felt the warmth of his breath on her face, saw the anger flashing in the dark depths of his icy grey eyes.

"Was it your intention all along to lose your virginity to me? To be *sullied* so Pullus wouldn't want you anymore, because you were no longer a virgin? Is that the real truth, Livia?"

This time his voice held contempt, as well as anger, and Livia's face flushed. Not in embarrassment this time, but in anger. She managed to pull her hand free from his and step backwards, her hands fisting on her hips in indignation, "Sullied! How dare you. In case you have forgotten, *you* seduced *me!*"

She saw his jaw tighten at her words, as a myriad of expressions crossed his face before he bit out, "But you didn't stop me though, did you?"

An ugly silence filled the cave as they stared at each other, his face an inscrutable mask as he waited for a response. When one wasn't forthcoming he narrowed his eyes, and said in a deadly voice, "Oh, and another thing, did you speak false last night when said you loved me?"

Livia gasped. So she *had* whispered the words out loud last night. Hades! She closed her eyes in mortification. How could she have been so stupid? To lay bare her emotions to a man who didn't want, or care, for her.

"Talk of love is foolish, Livia," Metellus said, before she could formulate a response.

His voice was flat, devoid of any emotion whatsoever, and it acted like a splash of icy water. She flinched, as if he had delivered her a body blow, and when she finally opened her eyes she saw him watching her with a cold hard look on his face.

"But—"

Metellus's hand slashed through the air, cutting off whatever she was about to say. "No. *You* listen to me, Livia," he ground out. "Do not call what happened between us last night 'love'. Call it infatuation. Call it lust. Call it sex. But *never* call it 'love'".

The bluntness of his words cut through her like a whip searing flesh, and she turned away from him, not wanting to see the derision on his face anymore.

"Nothing can come of it. Nothing. Do you understand?"

The flatness of his question pierced Livia to the bone. He couldn't have made his intentions clear enough. She meant nothing to him. She had just been convenient, that was all. A body to be used for sex. But even as she tried to acknowledge what he was saying, a part of her refused to believe it.

They had made love because *both* of them had wanted it. It hadn't been one sided. And it had felt right – more than right. They had both been caught up in the intensity of their feelings for each other. And no matter how much he denied it – he had wanted her. Desperately.

Pride made her turn around to face him once more. She wasn't going to just let what they shared last night slip through her hands like grains of sand. She had made love to him because it had felt right at the time. And it still did. She *did* love him. It was just that he didn't want to accept it. "But…but what we shared last-"

"It was just sex, Livia," he said, frustration evident in every line of his body, his brow furrowed as he cut off her halting words. "Emotions getting the better of both of us. The loneliness of being together on an island, miles from anywhere, constantly thrown together. You are beautiful, there is no denying that. It – we – just happened. Accept it."

The words once again ripped through her, and she just looked at him in stunned silence, until a small noise from the bed distracted her. Turning away from him, she saw that Elisha was awake, and she walked over to her, thankful she had something to do to occupy her chaotic emotions. As she lifted the baby out of its basket, she saw Metellus turn and walk out of the cave.

"Metellus," she called out in a calm voice so as not to disturb the baby, "What we shared went deeper than just lust. *You* just refuse to acknowledge it—"

"No!"

The single word froze Livia, and in an unconscious gesture she hugged the baby close to her chest. She watched in stunned fascination as he turned to face her once more. Anger, and frustration, seemed to radiate out of him in shimmering waves of heat, and instinctively she placed the baby back in her basket, thankful when she didn't seem to object too much.

"I bedded you for one reason, and one reason only, Livia Drusus. Revenge." Metellus bit out, when she had turned to face him once more.

Livia swallowed the lump of fear which suddenly formed in her throat, her heart thumping in wild abandon. "Revenge? But…but I don't understand. You—"

"I bedded you for revenge, Livia," he repeated, his words harsh, unyielding, "Because of your father."

"My father? But what has he got to do with all this? *Us*?" Livia lifted a shaking hand to her forehead, as a feeling of dread assailed her. His gaze was penetrating, the grey of his eyes so intense she wanted to look away, but she couldn't.

He frowned, his face a tight mask of frustration before he snapped, "There is no 'us', Livia. The sooner you realise that the better. I took your body for revenge. Revenge against your father, your brother, and the *Drusii* name."

His words were harsh, and they hurt like a physical pain – right to the heart. "But why?" she cried. "What reason do you have?"

He laughed without humour, as his eyes took a leisurely journey from the tips of her toes to the top of her head. "Reason? The reason is simple, Livia. Your father was instrumental in the downfall of my family. And because of that, *you* are the spoils."

"Spoils!" The word was whispered in horror. "What do you mean 'spoils'?"

"I hadn't taken you for a fool, Livia. I'm sure you can work it out. Your father ruined my family; and now I've ruined yours."

"No! I won't believe it," she breathed. How could he be so cold, so harsh and calculating? She thought wildly.

"Believe it," he bit out. "If it wasn't for my uncle, my mother and I would have starved. Nero took everything. *Everything* we had, and all because of the lies spewed from your father's mouth."

Livia felt the colour drain out of her face, as the full impact of his words assaulted her bruised mind. "So what we shared last night meant nothing to you? It was all because of your desire for revenge that you—" Sudden hot anger surged through her, making her unable to finish what she wanted to say, and for several moments a thick silence hummed between them.

Livia was somewhat mollified, when she saw a band of colour darken Metellus's high cheekbones, before he answered in a flat voice, "Yes."

"Is that all you have to say "yes"?"" she spluttered, her eyes flashing as she clenched her fists so hard, her nails dug into the palms of her hands. The pain was welcome, as it reminded her that this was real, and she wasn't caught up in some dark nightmare.

But this time he didn't answer her, and in that instant Livia felt all of her dreams shatter like a rare glass vial. Dreams of a future she had somehow envisaged herself having with Metellus. Once again she was just a pawn in some sort of twisted game of revenge between two warring families. A family feud she knew nothing about – but what did that matter? She had been played for a fool. A total fool.

"Get out," the words were hissed through a tear clogged throat, "Get out!"

She saw Metellus hesitate, indecision flashing across his face, before his whole body stiffened, and he turned once more, and without a backward glance stalked out.

At that moment Elisha started fretting, probably picking up on the stressful atmosphere in the cave, and bending down Livia lifted her out of the basket once again, rocking the baby back and forth to settle her. In a soothing whisper she crooned, "Shh, little one. He's gone. Gone for good. I've been such a fool."

She couldn't stop the tears from falling, and she buried her face in Elisha's blanket as all her dreams disappeared before her very eyes.

Well you made a right mess of that didn't you? Metellus thought in disgust, as he strode out of the cave. *Was she right? Did what he feel for her go deeper than lust and desire?*

There was no escaping the fact he'd wanted her from the first moment he had seen her standing on the deck of the *trireme*. That knowledge brought him no comfort or joy. In fact it made him even more angry and frustrated.

He could offer her nothing. As a mere merchant, he had no social standing among the elite of Roman society. He was effectively an outcast, as was his mother, and they had been, ever since the Emperor Nero had executed his father all those years ago.

And all because of Livia's father. Senator Augustus Drusus. *He* had been the man responsible for his family's downfall, and his father's eventual death.

The so-called Pisonian Conspiracy had been the idea of Senator Gaius Calpurnius Piso to oust Nero and declare himself as Emperor. It had been an elaborate attempt, and co-conspirators had been other Senators, some of Nero's own Praetorian Guards and ordinary merchants. But the conspiracy had been doomed to fail – mainly because there had been so many people involved. Punishment had been swift and just. Many of those found guilty had been told to commit suicide by their own hands. Others, like his father, had been executed.

Gossip had been rife in the upper echelons of Roman power. Gossip, Metellus later found out, having been spread by Livia's father. A few whispers here and there, and even though there had been little evidence to prove his father was involved in the plot, it hadn't stopped Nero from acting with swift justice. Practically overnight Metellus and his mother had become destitute, Nero seizing all his father's assets and money.

Metellus's mother – Antonia - had had to beg his father's brother – Verenus – to help them. Thankfully for them he had, Verenus offering the widowed Antonia and his nephew a home on his farm outside Rome. His uncle was a decent man, and as Verenus had never married, and thus had no children, over the following years Metellus had proved himself very capable of running the farm, turning it from a livestock farm into a very productive vineyard. The wine it produced was for export, as it provided the greatest profit. And it had also been Metellus's idea to import papyrus paper from Alexandria, the paper proving to be very lucrative, as the people of Rome coveted the paper in abundance.

Verenus had been content to allow Metellus free reign with the farm when he'd come of age, for in truth he spent very little time there. Verenus was an architect by trade, a very successful one, who had, and still continued to have, the patronage of the current Emperor, as well as the previous one's before him. Verenus had also been one of the principal architects working for Nero after the Great Fire of Rome, the result of which had made him one of the richest me in Rome.

And Metellus's own hard work over the past five years had also paid off in dividends, as he had amassed a fortune, both for his uncle, and himself. Merchants could earn huge amounts of money, unlike Senators, who were banned from trading.

Even though he was rich beyond measure, he was still not in the same social league of the *Drusii. They* were the elite of Rome – the *patricians.* But money was the key to getting back everything he'd lost, everything he'd been denied. Money could buy power, and the social standing, just like his mother and father had once had.

And like a lion stalking its prey, he'd bided his time, waiting for the moment to strike, to move in for the kill. Livia's revelation that her father was ill, as well as his own knowledge of Flavius's debts at the gaming table, made him more determined than ever to take on the *Drusii,* and implement his long awaited plans for revenge.

And that revenge would be the total capitulation of everything, and anyone, associated with the *Drusii.* Even Livia…

So what if he desired her? Craved her body, and wanted her again and again. He wouldn't allow his desire for her get in the way of all he'd planned. She *had* been the spoils. The spoils of war between him, and her family.

His mood darkened. That was the way of it. And *nothing* was going to change his mind about his chosen course. It was his destiny to succeed, to avenge his father's death. To—

The ringing of a bell down in the leper colony jolted him out of his dark reverie, and he looked down the hillside towards the fort. His heart leapt in response at what he saw – a ship coming into view off the horizon.

The supply ship had arrived! His eyes closed tight in frustration. The gods must truly be laughing at him for his stupidity. If only he had managed to hold onto his lust, his desire for Livia for one more day, then things might not have got so complicated. But she'd invaded his dreams, his thoughts, his mind and there had been nothing he could have done to stop taking her.

"Shit," he ground out through clenched teeth.

For several long minutes he stood there, cursing the fates. Then he opened his eyes, desperate to block Livia out of his jumbled thoughts, as he watched the large ship sail ever closer to the island. Right now he needed to have his wits about him, as he would need all his powers of persuasion to convince the captain to allow them to leave the island; that they were genuine ship wreck survivors and not lepers.

CHAPTER 11

Livia gazed out across the wide expanse of sea, the sunlight glinting off the rippling waves, almost hypnotic in its intensity. Taking deep calming breaths of fresh air, she looked skywards, watching a flock of seagulls float uncaring on the slight breeze.

Oh, how she envied their freedom, wishing with all her heart she could just open her arms and fly away and…escape. Escape from the invisible bonds which held her captive once more aboard this ship. A ship headed, not this time to Alexandria, but one headed back to Rome. Rome, where she knew her family – Flavius – would be waiting for her, disapproval evident in every line of his tall thin body…

Had it only been five days since they had left the leper island, and four since they had boarded the ship heading for Rome? Nine long, endless, days in which she had existed in some kind of stupor, unable to quite believe all that had happened.

Their journey from the leper colony had gone remarkably smoothly considering. They'd journeyed to Crete where it had been a simple matter of getting a ship to Rome from the busy port of Heraklion. Metellus had pleaded their case to the Governor, who it turned out, knew both Livia's father and Metellus's uncle. Within half a day they had been provided with clean clothes and a safe passage back to Rome. And, with evident relief on her part, there had been no awkward questions asked about the baby.

Thrusting a hand through the knotted curls of her hair, she grimaced as the wind whipped through the long tresses. She had been up on deck for far too long, and she needed to get back to her small cabin, where she had left Elisha sleeping.

She also needed to return below deck, to ensure she didn't encounter Metellus. She had managed to avoid him the whole time she had been on board the ship. *Or rather he was avoiding her!* After all, the captain *had* initially given them a cabin to share, assuming, incorrectly they were married and the baby was theirs. But once Metellus had placed her, and Elisha's possessions, in the cabin she hadn't seen him since.

But what did it matter? She was well rid of him. A man eaten up by bitterness, such as he was, would never change. It was ingrained in him, so deeply rooted, that she would become the biggest fool in the Empire, if she thought he would change just for her!

She had tried to unravel *exactly* what had happened between them on the island. But she hadn't succeeded. Metellus as a complex man, revealing layer after layer of contradictions. One minute he was rescuing her, tending to her every need, the next he was cursing her, and her family, to Hades. And then he complicated matters even further by kissing her, making love to her.

Her breath hitched, as she remembered all they had shared. She had given him everything. Laid her heart, her soul open to him. And all he had done was take, giving nothing of himself in return. He'd taken her virginity. Taken her reputation. Taken all of her dreams, and squashed them like an insect underfoot. He'd used her in an abominable way, making love to her just because she was the daughter of his sworn enemy.

But it had been wonderful. Everything she had dreamed of. And no matter how hard she had tried, she couldn't banish him completely from her thoughts.

The way he'd kissed her, caressed her. The feel of his mouth and lips on her face, her neck, her breasts, teasing and tempting her to edge of madness.

Balling her fists in frustration, she refused to believe he had felt indifference to her, refused to believe their lovemaking had been nothing but a desire for revenge. She might have been innocent, but his body's response to her, told her he *had* desired her, *had* wanted her to the exclusion of everything, and everyone.

It was only in the cold light of day he had realised what had happened between them. And then he had lashed out, cursing her, and her family, swearing revenge against her family name.

Shaking her head in resignation, she headed back to her cabin. She had spent too long up on the deck, and it was fast approaching the time when she would need to feed Elisha. But when she opened the cabin door, she froze. Metellus was standing there, his large frame taking up most of the space of her cramped sleeping quarters as he held Elisha in the crook of his arm…

He looked up, and Livia saw dark colour flood his face as if somehow, he had been caught red handed holding the baby.

"She was crying, fretting," he said by way of explanation.

Livia felt a surge of guilt assail her at having left the baby for so long. But she had been desperate for some fresh air. "I wasn't gone for that long," she bristled, not wanting him to think that she hadn't been looking after the baby properly.

She heard him sigh, before he said, "I know that, Livia. I'm not judging you. If anything, you have been a virtual recluse ever since we have set sail." His lips twisted in wry humour, "If I didn't know better I would think that you were avoiding me."

Livia raised her eyebrows in disbelief. The retort she was about to snap out was interrupted by Elisha's sharp wail. The baby was hungry and she needed to be fed. Not having much choice, Livia walked up to Metellus and lifted her arms, the gesture obvious, and Metellus handed the baby over.

Livia had to fight the urge to close her eyes when she came close to him. She could smell the masculine scent coming off the heat of his body, and she was once again transported back to the time they had made love in the cave.

Stepping back from him, she went and sat on the edge of her bed. Taking the goatskin from the basket by the bed she placed the teat in the baby's mouth and fed her, managing to ignore Metellus the whole time.

But once Elisha had finished her feed, and Livia had placed her in her makeshift crib, a wooden box which had been provided by the captain, she faced Metellus once again. He was watching her, leaning against the wooden door of her cabin, his arms crossed over his chest. Meeting his enigmatic gaze she asked, "What do you want, Metellus?"

For a moment he didn't answer her, just stared down at her, the heat in his eyes causing her heart to thump in an erratic way, and her blood to pulse hot, and heavy through her body. She hadn't seen him in the four days since they had boarded this ship bound for Rome. He was right. She *had* been deliberately avoiding him, staying in her cabin with Elisha and asking for her meals to be served there, using the excuse of her needing to care for the baby as the reason for not joining the captain for the evening meal.

"What do you want, Metellus?" she repeated, when he hadn't answered her earlier question, "I thought you'd said all you wanted to say to me on the island."

"Are you pregnant?" Metellus asked, his voice flat, but his eyes piercing as they bored into hers.

"No!" Livia gasped, taken aback by his terse question, her self-control slipping, as embarrassment pulsed through her. She shot up from where she had been sitting, desperate to run out of the cabin, but frustrated from doing so because his large frame blocked her exit. Pride held her still and taking a deep breath she held onto her anger – just…

"How do you know? I took no precautions."

His words were devoid of emotion, as if he were delivering a statement of fact. His face was unreadable, and somehow, his voice made her blood pulse faster throughout her body.

Once again Livia marvelled at the way he affected her. Her fingers, she noted, shook with emotion, and not wanting him to see how vulnerable she felt in his presence, she hid them in the folds of her *stola*. Affecting a nonchalance she was far from feeling, she met his hooded gaze head on. "Because I'm not, that's why."

"Have you had your monthly flow?"

Livia blushed to the roots of her hair. No man had *ever* asked her that before, and she was consumed by another bolt of red hot anger, mingled with equal measures of embarrassment. She turned away, refusing to meet his piercing gaze. After a long silence had fallen between them she answered his question. "Yes. I...I started the other day."

"You are not lying to me are you, Livia?" His voice came from just behind her, and it had a husky deepness to it, stirring passions within her that had her thinking of the night they had shared outside the cave. She could feel his breath on the back of her neck, and an instant wave of longing coursed through her body.

"No!" Her voice was little more than a squeak, as it passed out of her parched throat, as she felt his fingers stroke the nape of her neck, the caress so soft, so gentle she shivered in response to his touch. His hand reached around to cup her jaw, gripping it with enough force that so she had no option but to turn into his body, to look up at him. She felt her eyes widen in shock when she saw his mouth move towards hers.

Sweet Jupiter, he was going to kiss her, and there was nothing she could do to stop him! It was as if she had turned to stone, unable to move if she wanted to, and her eyes fluttered closed as she felt his mouth fuse with hers. The moan of pleasure that escaped from her throat seemed to echo around the small cabin, as she lifted her hands to cup the back of his neck bringing him closer to her body.

His kiss was gentle, yet firm, brooking no resistance, demanding a response from her she was more than happy to give. Her mouth parted, and this time it was *he* who grunted with pleasure, as his tongue explored the softness of her warm mouth.

Livia lost all sense of time, and place, as she met kiss, for long hot, searing kiss, felt his work roughed fingers graze and skim over the rapid pulse at the base of her neck. A pulse he must have been able to feel…

Shame slammed into her, as reality crashed through her like a wave smashing onto rocks. *He was using her again*! Her eyes flew open in shock, and she pulled away, stumbling, as the swell of the ship caused her to miss her step. Her mouth felt full, throbbing, kiss ravaged, and she had to fight the urge to touch it with her fingers. How could she be so stupid? To allow him access to her mouth, eager for his touch and kisses…

"Is this some kind of sick jest, Metellus?" The words were whispered, as a sudden rush of nausea hit her. All the tension she had been holding onto for days now exploded out of her, and she whispered, "Why are you doing this to me?"

The tears that had threatened were quashed in an instant. She needed to be strong. *Had* to be strong, and hardening her voice she bit out, "I've told you I'm not pregnant. Now go. There is nothing more to say on this matter. *You* have made your opinion of me, and my family, more than clear."

She saw his jaw clench, his eyes as cold as the deepest sea, but she refused to back down, and kept her expression blank, when in reality, deep inside, her heart was breaking. For a long moment he just stared at her, saying nothing. Then, as if somehow she had felt the crackling tension in the room, Elisha woke and started to cry. It was all that was needed, as Metellus stepped away from her, both physically and mentally. She could see it in the closed expression on his face, the stiffness of his body, before he turned and left her cabin.

For several long minutes Metellus paced up and down in his own cabin, uncontrollable fury surging inside him until he couldn't bare it any longer. His fist launched out as he slammed it into the wooden hull, the force of which caused him to wince in pain.

But the pain felt good. So very good. It was just what he needed to purge Livia from his mind one way or another. He felt like a callow youth caught up in the throes of his first passion. Never in all of his life had he been affected so much by a woman.

Granted she was beautiful, but he had known beautiful women before, and he wasn't in the habit of denying his sexual needs. But the women he had taken to his bed in the past had never affected him as much as Livia had, and continued, to do. In truth he was known to be cold. Hard. Women came to his bed knowing that the relationship was only about the physical. He couldn't give anymore of himself, it was only his body he could give, nothing more. He always, *always* kept his emotions under strict control. Until now…

This infatuation, if it could be called that, had to stop. She was his enemy by the gods! She deserved to suffer for what her father had done. And hadn't he made a promise to his dead father on the day of his burial, that he would extract revenge for his death even if it took him a lifetime to do so?

But then reality hit him hard. One night simply wasn't enough to purge her from his memory. Revenge now tasted bitter, after experiencing the nectar of her body, her sweet lips. He couldn't get enough of her, he realised. The gasps she made when he had kissed her breasts, the arching of her back when he'd trailed hot wet kisses down over her stomach, lower until…

She enticed him beyond endurance. He wanted more. More of her in his arms, in his bed. He wanted to please her, taste her, strip her naked and gorge on her flesh, like a man starved of food as she cried out in pleasure when he slid into the wet, enveloping heat of her body, until they were both sated.

There was no denying it. Sex with Livia had been the best he'd ever had.

"No!" He bit out, cursing himself for wanting her so much.

This was about revenge. It *had* to be about revenge – and nothing more. Striding over to a small wooden sideboard, he took

112

a flask of wine, and poured a hefty measure into a wooden goblet, drowning the contents in one long swallow, welcoming the burn of alcohol as it slid down his gullet. He refilled his goblet once more, and this time before he drank from it, he lifted it in a toast. "To you, father. I won't let you down. I promise."

Livia's head throbbed with tension, as she listened to the shouts of the sailors above deck as they prepared to bring the ship into dock.

For another three days she had stayed in her cabin like the recluse Metellus had accused her of being. But it had been worth it, as she'd managed to avoid Metellus once more. And now, in a matter of minutes, they would soon be docking at Ostia, and thank the gods, this odious journey would be over.

Elisha's cry tore her out of her stupor, and she got up from the bed, lifting the baby out of her wooden crib. As soon as she had her in her arms, the baby stopped crying and Livia smiled. Reaching across to the basket, which sat next to the wooden crib, she took out the goatskin and started to feed the baby. Elisha was a joy, no trouble at all, considering all the disruption she had endured, and still had to endure, in her small life. Elisha was about to find herself once more on dry land, and in a strange city - Rome. Somehow, Livia thought darkly, as she looked down at the suckling baby, she knew Elisha was going to fair far better than she would in the next few hours!

She, on the other hand, had the unenviable task of explaining everything that had happened in the past few weeks to Flavius. And she very much doubted her half-brother would offer a sympathetic ear when he heard of her plight. To him, it would be nothing but an inconvenience that she hadn't managed to reach Alexandria, and marry Pullus. *And,* worst of all, she would also have to beg, and plead with him, to let her keep Elisha.

She had already planned what she was going to tell him about the baby. Elisha was going to be an orphan, the child of one of the women who had been on board the ship, and who, tragically had drowned when the ship had sunk. She couldn't tell him the truth about Elisha. Flavius, unlike Metellus, would *never* allow the child of a leper to live with them at the villa.

Livia closed her eyes. Metellus. How in the name of Hades was she going to forget him, to try and convince herself he'd never existed? Even though she hadn't seen him for days now, ever since he'd kissed her in her cabin, she still ached for him.

Loving someone was not an easy emotion to admit to, and an even harder one to forget. But she was determined to remain strong, she couldn't let Metellus's rejection get to her. The next few days, weeks even, were going to be very difficult. She wasn't a fool. Shipwrecked or not, arriving back in Rome with a small baby in her arms was going to bring the gossips out in force. And no matter how much she protested her innocence it would fall on deaf ears. She could hear the questions and snide remarks already. *A baby? So that's why she left Rome in such a hurry! How did she manage to keep it a secret? Who is the father?*

As Livia held Elisha in her arms she was conscious of being watched. A pricking sensation at the back of her neck made her turn and scan the quayside below her, as she slowly made her way down the gangway.

Her steps faltered, as her gaze found, and collided, with Metellus's. He was leaning against the wall of a massive stone warehouse, his arms crossed over his chest in a casual way which belied the intensity of his eyes boring into hers. He looked scruffy, several days growth of beard were evident, and his hair was longer, as it was ruffled by the slight breeze which blew in off the sea. Standing there, he looked like one of the many workers who toiled day in and day out on the dockside.

His gaze was inscrutable, no emotion whatsoever flickered across his face. He looked dangerous, fierce even, and she couldn't control the tremble that slithered down her spine.

Then, in what was meant to be a calculated move, he turned his back on her and spoke to a man who had been standing next to him. His dismissal cut through her like a knife. He couldn't have made his intentions clearer. She was history. Elisha was history. All she had ever been was a diversion, a warm willing body to use as he saw fit, in his desire for revenge against her family.

"Move along, woman." The gruff voice behind her startled her, as she realised she'd stopped walking, and was blocking the gangway. Glancing behind her she murmured an apology to the sailor who stood behind her, before moving forward once more.

Forced to concentrate on the uneven steps of the wooden gangway, it was a few minutes before she made the safety of the quayside, and unable to resist, she glanced once more to where Metellus had been standing. But he had gone, swallowed up amongst the swarms of people who crowded the busy dock-side area.

And then the finality of it slammed through her like a physical blow. She meant nothing to him, and she very much doubted she would ever see him again…

CHAPTER 12

Two weeks later…

"What you are offering is most unusual. Most unusual indeed, and I'm intrigued to know why?"

"Personal reasons."

"Personal! Is that all you have to say on the matter?"

"Yes."

"Umm. You are indeed a man of few words!" Publius Asicus leaned back in his chair, his hands adorned with gold rings, steepled in front of him as he surveyed the man in front of him, a wry grin on his face. Considering he was surrounded by five of his body-guards the man showed no fear, of him, or the situation he found himself in. And that was something which rarely happened when strangers approached him; for his reputation came before him – and quite rightly. Publius Asicus was the most powerful man in the all the gambling dens of Rome. And the most dangerous one…

Metellus watched the man who sat contemplating him, his gaze unwavering as he stood his ground. Publius Asicus was right. What he was offering was unusual, but he did have his reasons.

"One hundred thousand *denarii*. Take it or leave it." Publius Asicus said, interrupting Metellus's thoughts.

"Done." Metellus said immediately, biting back a smile at the surprised look that flashed across the older man's face. It was obvious Publius Asicus hadn't expected him to agree to his terms so quickly; and his highly inflated terms at that. But before Publius Asicus could change his mind and ask for more money, Metellus held out his hand, and with obvious reluctance Publius Asicus leaned forward and shook Metellus's hand sealing the deal, the older man's many gold rings winking in the lamplight.

"I'll have the money delivered tomorrow," Metellus said, as he stood up, ending what had been a very short meeting. "Have the markers ready." And with a slight nod of his head he left Publius Asicus sitting at his table, a bemused look on his face as he watched him walk away. Metellus smiled as he walked out of the dark room, sure in the knowledge he had somehow managed to get the better of Publius Asicus. A feat not many men had achieved in many a year, of that he was certain…

"You have brought shame on this family once more. Have you seen the drawings on the wall outside?"

"There is no need to shout, Flavius."

If possible, Flavius's face flushed even more, his fists clenching in anger as he glared at his half-sister.

"There is *every* need, trust me, Livia. You are ruined. This family is ruined."

Livia didn't reply, instead she stared at him unflinching, refusing to let Flavius's tirade break her. She could see he was near to breaking point, and she was in serious danger of being beaten within an inch of her life. But for Elisha's sake, she had to remain calm and strong, *and* keep her wits about her.

Flavius raked his hand through his thinning hair, a clear sign of his agitation, as he didn't normally touch his perfectly groomed hair for fear of losing more of it.

"The baby has to go. You will get rid of it. Send it to our villa in Brundisium. She will be looked after there adequately. "

"No!" Livia said, defiance in her tone, as she met his angry gaze,

"I will do anything you ask, Flavius but I will *not* get rid of Elisha. What is the point of abandoning her? The harm has already been done. Everyone in Rome has made their own mind up about me, even though I have tried to explain—"

"Explain! Explain what, Livia?" Flavius burst out. "You leave on a ship, and barely one month later you return with a child in your arms? You were pregnant before you left. Just how did you manage to fool me, *and* the rest of Rome, I'll never know?"

"I was not pregnant, I'm telling the truth," Livia said in a placating tone, "The child belonged to one of the women aboard the-"

"Enough!" Flavius slashed his hand through the air, cutting off her words. "I have heard of women who gave birth without anyone even knowing they were pregnant. What is to say that this didn't happen to you? Who is the father? Who did you spread your legs for?" Flavius barked out before he stepped forward and grabbed Livia's forearm.

"Let me go, Flavius," Livia demanded, as pain shot up her arm as she tried to pull her arm free. But his strength was too much and he shook her like a dog shook a bone.

"You open your legs for any man, and now I pay the price is that it?"

"No!" Livia exclaimed. "It isn't like that. I'm not pregnant. It's the truth I tell you."

Flavius's eyes narrowed, as he stared at her. "So are you still a virgin then? Is that the truth, or do you lie?"

Livia stilled, her heart thumping in fear as they both stared at each other like combatants in the arena sizing each other up before the fight began. Livia used the element of surprise and managed to pull her arm out of Flavius's grip, her stomach churning with anxiety, as she stared at her half-brother. Thankfully he didn't grab her again and Livia was able to step back from him. "My virginity is no concern of yours. I am a woman grown. You should respect my right to privacy. Father should be the only one I answer to.

Not you, my half-brother."

Flavius, if possible, went even redder as her words hit him. Leaning in so his face was level with hers he hissed, "How dare you talk to me like that? I am in charge of this household now. You will obey me, as you would our father. Now answer my question woman, or by the gods I will beat it out of you. I'll not be taken for a fool again."

Livia knew she had pushed her half-brother to the limit. And although he'd never beaten her before, she wasn't about to chance it. Livia took a deep breath, trying to keep her poise and dignity as Flavius glared at her. "I'm not a virgin anymore that is the truth. But I've also never been pregnant. The baby is not mine."

"Who is the man who took your virginity?"

Although she was expecting the question, Livia still blanched. "Does it matter, Flavius?" She said with false bravado. "The deed is done is it not? No-one would have believed you anyway if you told them that I was still a virgin after my marriage to Galvus."

Silence descended in the room at her words, as Flavius assimilated what she was saying. Livia held her breath wondering whether Flavius would beat her anyway, regardless that she had told him the truth. Thankfully he didn't. Instead he moved away from her and started pacing. It was obvious he was thinking rapidly, trying to make up his mind about whether to believe her or not. Although she didn't get on with her acerbic half-brother, she did have a twinge of sympathy for him. The gossip about her had been ferocious to say the least ever since she had walked down the gangplank of the ship holding a baby in her arms.

Within the day, crude drawings had appeared on the walls outside their villa, showing a pregnant Livia on a ship. The gossips were relishing the story of how the *Drusii* had planned to send her to Alexandria to have her baby in secret, but had been thwarted by her being shipwrecked and having no choice but to return to Rome. There was also scepticism as to her "arranged" marriage to Sextus Calpurnius Pullus as well; and no matter how hard Flavius had tried to quell the rumours, he had failed miserably. And if *that* were not bad enough, it had been unfortunate for her that Flavius seemed to believe the baby was hers as well.

"You are still betrothed to Pullus. Do you think he will want to marry you now, now you have whored yourself?"

Livia blushed at the crudity of his words, but answered recklessly, "I have no intention of marrying Pullus. Not now. Not ever."

The words hung in the air, and Flavius's eyes narrowed in anger once more. Her words added to the already tense atmosphere, and Flavius leaned forward to grab her. Livia, realising his intention, managed to move away, stepping backwards in an involuntary movement. But instead of gaining the freedom she'd hoped for, her back slammed into an immoveable force. She turned her head to see what was amiss, and her heart stuttered when she saw Metellus standing grim faced, his gaze locked onto Flavius's face.

"Have I come at an awkward time?"

"Who in the name of Hades are you? And how did you gain access to my villa?" Flavius barked, his face flushed in anger.

Metellus! What on earth was he doing here? Livia's heart started a rapid beat against her rib cage as she tried to assimilate what was going on, but an innate sense of self-preservation kept her from saying his name out loud, as she stepped away from both men.

Metellus stood there, his face inscrutable, as he watched Flavius, weighing him up, judging him…and if the mocking smile which appeared on his face was anything to go by, finding him wanting.

"My name is Metellus."

"Metellus? Metellus who? I do not have time for games, man. State your business and go." Flavius's voice was full of scorn as he looked Metellus up and down. It was obvious he found him lacking in social graces and *definitely* not up to Flavius's social standing. Metellus was wearing a tunic of dark blue, the colour complimenting the silver grey of his eyes, but the tunic, although clean and tidy was made of plain cloth, not the silks her half-brother was used to wearing. To Flavius's self-important ego the stranger was no-one of consequence, and was to be treated as such.

"I am here because we have a mutual acquaintance," Metellus finally answered, "Publius Asicus. I gather you know him?" His voice held a mocking edge, even though he speared Flavius with a hard look.

At Metellus's words Flavius's face paled, and he immediately became flustered. Livia watched in stunned fascination as he raised a hand to wipe away the sweat beading his forehead. She had never seen him react so, as his normal demeanour was one of sarcasm, anger, or distain no matter what the provocation.

Instead of answering Metellus, Flavius turned his ire onto Livia, his eyes flashing in anger as he ordered, "Get out. I'll deal with you later."

Livia bristled at his tone, and the manner of his order, but knew she had no choice in the matter. She stepped forward, her gaze lifting to meet Metellus's. It was only then, she realised belatedly, that her exit was blocked by his presence as he still stood in the open doorway. Her stomach plummeted when she saw the intensity of his gaze as it travelled over her.

His eyes missed nothing, from her expertly coiffured hair, down over the slimness of her body, clothed in a peach coloured *stola* made of the finest silk, until they came to rest at her expensively shod feet before returning once more to her face. His mouth twisted, a touch of malice around his lips, before he stood to the side to let her pass.

She endured his gaze, because she had no choice, but as soon as she moved past him she avoided any eye contact with him. She thought she had escaped him, but then he commanded, "Wait."

Livia froze, staring ahead. *Was he going to expose her? Tell Flavius all that had happened between them on the island?* She angled her head, schooled her features into what she hoped was a neutral look and looked up at him.

Why are you here Metellus? And what games do you play? Her eyes communicated the unspoken questions at him as he continued to stare at her for endless seconds. Then she firmed her chin, and her eyes *dared* him to tell Flavius everything. *Do your worst,* they said, *for I no longer care anymore.*

The tension in the room was palpable, until he finally broke eye contact with her, and looked over to where Flavius stood. "Introduce me," he demanded, and Flavius, picking up on the *minutiae* of the situation, for once in his life obeyed a direct order made to him.

"She is Livia Drusus. My half-sister."

Metellus stepped forward and reached down to take her hand in his. His gesture surprised her, and she stood there in shock as she became aware of his thumb stroking the underside of her hand, the small movement causing a hot warm flush to suffuse her body. She shuddered in response to his touch, as feelings she'd suppressed for weeks now, burst forth. She looked down, her fingers seemed so small, as he closed his large hand around hers, and she felt the rough callouses on his fingers rasp against the softness of her skin before he lifted her hand and kissed it, his eyes flashing with mocking humour as they met hers.

Heat flooded into her face. Anger, vied with desire, as she fought her traitorous emotions, felt the heat of his lips on her skin. Her whole body seemed to be on fire, as his mouth lingered for far too long on the back of her hand, before he moved his lips from her skin but still held onto her hand. The feel of his lips brought back long supressed memories of a hot night on a Greek island, when he had made love to her.

Needing to supress the memories of that night, she tried to snatch her hand away, but Metellus's grip tightened, the movement imperceptible, refusing to let go. She stood there feeling helpless, berating herself for still wanting him, for falling in love with him. He was nothing but a mocking stranger. A man who had thrown her declaration of love firmly back in her face.

But now he was back, and kissing her hand with such audacity it took her breath away. Kissing her without any trace of remorse for his previous actions, as if he had only left her on the quayside yesterday, promising to return, when instead he had left her without a backward glance. And remembering the way he'd left her caused her to stiffen, as her eyes flashed their displeasure at him. *Exactly what games are you playing Metellus?*

"Ah. Of course," Metellus finally drawled, "Livia Drusus. I have heard a lot about you."

This time the sarcastic tone to his words made her angry, and gave her the strength she needed to snatch her hand away. Stepping back from him she was able to put some much needed distance between them.

"Lies! All lies!" Flavius blustered, and this time his voice brooked no resistance as he snapped out, "Leave us, Livia. Now!"

Livia needed no second invitation, and fled the room as fast as possible, running down the long corridor of the villa, her sandals click clacking on the marble tiles, as she made for the sanctuary of her bedroom.

It was only when she closed her bedroom door, leaning her full body weight against it, her heart pounding so hard she thought she might faint, that the reality of what had just happened in the *tablinum* hit her. And hit her hard.

Metellus was here! In the family villa. Demanding to see her brother and pretending not to know her.

But why? What reason did he have for being here? But more importantly, why the pretence of not knowing her? Feeling a headache gathering in the front of her temples, she went over to her window and pushed open the wooden shutters, just enough so it enabled her to see out into the *atrium*. The *atrium,* Metellus would have to pass through, in order to exit the villa once he had finished his business with Flavius.

Livia didn't have to wait long, only a matter of minutes in actual fact, before she saw him stride down the path which bisected the *atrium,* and make his way out of their large villa that sat in majestic splendour on the Palatine Hill. His stride was purposeful, as confident as ever, and she even heard him whistle as he walked past her window.

Whatever he'd discussed with Flavius hadn't taken long, and by his confident demeanour it had was obvious it had gone in his favour. Not many men got the better of her half-brother, but he seemed to have. *But what business could he possibly want with Flavius? And who in the name of Hades was Publius Asicus?* As she watched the huge gates close behind him, she couldn't help but wonder how on earth he had managed to gain entry in the villa in the first place.

Deciding she needed answers, Livia made the decision to confront Flavius, and she left her bedroom in search of him. She would ask, even beg if she had to, and make him tell her *precisely* what was going on between him and Metellus.

But when she entered her brother's office she stopped short. The *tablinum* was empty apart from a slave who was tidying the room. The slave also informed her that Flavius had just left the villa, and hadn't said where he was going.

Frustration ate at her as she realised she was going to have to wait for an explanation. Providing, of course, Flavius would give her one in the first place...

CHAPTER 13

"Psst! Livia! Over here!"

Livia turned towards the voice hissing her name, and she watched bemused, as silk curtains that covered the litter parted, and a slim arm adorned with distinctive bracelets poked out, beckoning her over.

Livia hastened across the street from where she had been buying some fresh fruit. It had been the first time she had ventured out of the villa since her return to Rome *and* Metellus's visit to the villa several days ago. Several days, in which she'd hadn't been able to get any sensible answers from Flavius as to *why* Metellus had visited with her brother in the first place. Frustration had clawed at her, and in a fit of rebellion, she had ventured out of the villa, pointedly ignoring the whispers and stares which followed her.

Now, for the first time in weeks, a genuine smile broke across her face as she peered into the litter to see her friend Portia reclining on silk cushions.

Portia's face was flushed, her prostrate body stiff with tension. "Quick, get in, before anyone sees us."

Doing as her friend bid, Livia climbed into the litter, making sure the curtains concealed them both, giving them the privacy they needed.

"What—"

"Quiet. Not now," Portia interrupted, cupping her hand to her ears as if to warn Livia that whatever was said could be overheard.

Livia nodded, and sat back against one of the silk cushions saying nothing more. Eventually, the litter stopped, and Portia peeped through the curtains and nodded, before she flung them back and stepped out, gesturing with her hand for Livia to follow.

"Why have you brought me to your family's burial ground? Has someone died recently?" Livia asked, when she realised where they were.

Portia shook her head, "No. It was the only place I could think of where we could be afforded some sort of privacy."

Livia mentally applauded her friend's ingenuity, but as she looked around the mausoleum, she couldn't stop a shiver of apprehension.

"My father thinks I am being a dutiful daughter this afternoon by honouring the dead of our family" she said derisively, "It is a good thing he has no inclination as to the *real* reason why I am here." Portia stopped talking, and with a small cry of anguish, pulled Livia forward into a tight embrace, "Oh Livia! How I've missed you! How do you fare?"

Livia relaxed when she heard the earnest tone in her friend's voice. Oh, how good it felt to finally be cared for. To be believed. Livia broke the embrace, stepping back so she could face her friend. Taking both her hands she smiled at her, "I am well. Lucky to be alive, and so very thankful to be back in one piece," before her mouth twisted and she said, "Even if I am the talk of all Rome."

Her voice faltered for a moment as she watched a myriad of expressions chase across her closest friend's face, before saying, "But you shouldn't have compromised yourself, Portia. Being seen with me could ruin your reputation."

Portia's face suffused with anger, "My father can be a pompous oaf sometimes. Always the first to believe the gossips. Always the first to believe the worst. I tried to tell him the baby was not yours – but he refused to listen."

Livia felt tears spring into her eyes at her friends heated, and heartfelt words. "You are a true friend, Portia. You are the only person amongst my friends, and family to believe in me!" Livia shrugged, "I swear even *I* was beginning to doubt myself!"

Portia giggled, and took hold of Livia's hand once again, "I'm so sorry it has taken me so long to see you, but my father forbid me to go anywhere near you. I've not spoken to him since of course, *and* I've made my displeasure known by spending a large amount of his money!"

Livia laughed out loud, "Portia you are incorrigible. Trust you to shop on the basis of my misfortune!"

Portia pouted, her face breaking out into a smile, "Livia you wound me! But you also know me too well!" She flapped her other hand in the air, "But enough of all this. What of the baby? Do you still have her?"

"Yes, for now at least," Livia replied, her laughter dying, "I've got a wet nurse for her. But I'm not sure for how long. Flavius is still undecided as to what to do with her – or me – for that matter." Livia's back stiffened, "But I am fighting him all the way."

"And your father?"

Livia shook her head, "He has improved slightly since I have been away. He awakens sometimes and mumbles words, but it is difficult to make out what he is saying as the left hand side of his face is still paralysed. But at least he has regained consciousness. But he is still too ill to do anything, and unfortunately, that means Flavius is still in charge of the villa, and all of our affairs – more's the pity."

"Would it do any good if I had a word with him?"

"Speak with Flavius?" Livia asked incredulously, "You are friendly with my half-brother?"

"No. But I am a woman am I not? And unless Flavius's tendencies go the other way, if you know what I mean, what harm could it do?"

Both women looked at each other for a split second before

they dissolved into helpless giggles, tears of mirth rolling down their faces.

Once they had calmed down, they sat talking for several minutes catching up on gossip – gossip which was mostly about Livia! Livia listened as Portia told her how she was trying to convince some of their acquaintances that the baby couldn't possibly be Livia's.

"And as I said to Octavia – she's such a cat by the way – hadn't we seen you in the Baths not two days before you had set sail, naked as the day you were born?" Portia paused and leaned forward, excitement evident on her face, "And when Octavia had nodded, I went in for the kill, asking her whether there had been any hint of a baby when your stomach had been as flat as it always had been."

"Do you think they believed you?" Livia asked, when Portia paused for a breath.

Portia shrugged, a small frown marring the perfection of her immaculately made up face. "I'm not sure, but some are beginning to question the facts I'm sure of it. They have even asked me who the baby's real mother is, and why she had been aboard the ship."

For a moment Livia hesitated, wondering if she should tell Portia the whole truth. She had obviously heard the tale Flavius had put about, about how Livia had taken the baby and cared for her. Indecision assailed her. Would Portia be shocked if she told her that Elisha was the child of a leper?

And as much as she loved, and trusted her friend, she decided it would be in hers, and Elisha's, best interest not to tell Portia. For now at least.

It was a secret only known to her and Metellus.

Thinking about Metellus caused a sharp pain in the region of her heart, and she rapidly dismissed him from her mind. Coming back to the present she smiled across to her friend. "Portia you are a true friend. But to be honest I think the damage has already been done. It will be nigh on impossible to reverse what has happened. We both know what the gossip is like in Rome. Once the seed has been sown there is no turning back."

Portia's shoulders slumped in defeat as she acknowledged the truth of what Livia said. "But it is not fair! You have done nothing wrong."

A long silence filled the quietness of the burial ground, until Livia broke it by saying, "I think we should go. I do not want you to get into trouble on my account."

"I don't care if I do," Portia said, defiance in her tone, before she sighed, her shoulders slumping even further as she realised Livia was right, and as if by mutual consent they both made their way back to the litter, and the four slaves who waited patiently beside it.

"Oh, I forgot to mention," Portia said, a short while later, "I was at Senator Crito's gathering last night, and Sextus Calpurnius Pullus was asking me all manner of questions about you once he realised I was acquainted with you."

"Pullus is back in Rome! But how? Why?" Livia exclaimed.

Portia lifted her shoulders in a slight shrug, "He's been summoned back from Alexandria by the Emperor. Something to do with grain prices apparently."

Livia had to hold back the urge to laugh hysterically. The Fates were truly laughing at her misfortune, as she mentally calculated that Pullus must have left Alexandria *before* Livia had been due to arrive there! How ironic. She would have arrived in Alexandria, only to find her betrothed had gone back to Rome! How typical, that once again women meant nothing to men like Pullus and Flavius. Women were nothing more than goods and chattels to be used and bartered to gain ever more wealth and prestige-

"He arrived yesterday morning I understand," Portia said breaking into Livia's dark musings. She shuddered dramatically, "He's the most odious man I've ever met. His hands were every-where, and as for his eyes—"

"What did you tell him about me?" Livia asked, interrupting Portia's heated words.

Portia frowned when she heard the alarm in her voice.

"Nothing! I love you too much to resort to idle gossip about you with men like Pullus."

Livia was immediately contrite, when she saw the hurt look on her friends face.

"What does Pullus mean to you?" Portia asked, before Livia could apologise. "I'd assumed he was only asking about you because of the gossip he'd heard," Portia tilted her head questionably, "But I gather that's not the full story is it?"

Livia said nothing for a moment, before she replied, "He was the reason I had to leave for Alexandria. I was to be married to him."

Portia gasped, "Oh, no! How horrible!" Her hand flew to her mouth in shock, the gold bangles on her wrist jangling nosily in the darkened interior of the litter.

"Horrible, indeed," Livia said slowly, "And I have a nasty feeling that now he is back in Rome, he wants me to go back to Alexandria with him."

"You wanted to see me?" Livia said, tempted to add "again" but didn't, when she saw the hard expression on Flavius's face.

"Yes, come in and close the door," he snapped.

Livia did as he bid, but no sooner had she stepped into the *tablinum,* Flavius launched a ferocious attack on her once more.

"The frenzy about you shows no sign of abating. This family is being ridiculed throughout Rome."

Livia once again braced herself as Flavius launched into his usual tirade of verbal abuse as to how she'd brought disgrace on the family, until finally he barked, "It must end, and it will end. Which is why you leave me with no choice."

Livia's heart lurched. *Was he finally going to take Elisha off her, as he'd been threatening to do ever since she'd arrived back in Rome? She would have to be raised by strangers, but at least Flavius wasn't going to kill her. She knew of families who had done such things to unwanted children. Girls mostly, or those born with some illness or malady.* Her breath hitched in her throat. *How would she bear it? The baby had come to mean so much to her—*

130

"...married tomorrow. Be ready at the Sixth hour."

Flavius's words came out of nowhere, and hit her with such force she felt the earth shift under her feet. "What...what did you say?"

Hot colour suffused her half-brothers face, causing it to mottle in an unbecoming way. "H...have you not listened to anything I've been saying, woman?" he stuttered, apoplectic with rage, "You are to be married in the morning. Make sure you are ready. At least you will be off my hands. The fool is prepared to marry you."

Bile roiled in her throat. All her nightmares had come true. Pullus still wanted to marry her. And even though she knew it would be futile, for Flavius had no heart, she still begged, "Please Flavius. Don't allow this. What purpose would it serve?"

Flavius stiffened, his face hard, immobile, "Serve? It serves *my* purpose, that's what. Your hand in marriage in exchange for a large amount of money—"

"But...but we don't need money. Father is rich—"

"*Was* rich Livia. Was." Flavius said, interrupting her halting words. "This family is burdened by debts you know nothing about, and I need money quickly, or we will be ruined. Your marriage will enable me to pay those debts, *and* keep my standing here in Rome."

"But I don't understand? Why—"

"There is nothing for you to understand," he shouted, cutting off her question, "You will do as I command. You will be married tomorrow. *I* will get much needed money, and *you* will be off my hands. It is that simple."

Livia felt her nerves scream out in protest, defeat overwhelming her with its intensity. She wanted to shout and scream at him at the injustice of it all. But what was the point? Her brother had never changed his mind about *anything* once he had decided upon a course of action.

She dared to ask, "And Elisha? She can come with me?" Her words were neutral, giving nothing away of the inner turmoil she was experiencing about the possibility of having to give up the baby.

"Yes. Although I don't know why."

At his words Livia's shoulders sagged. *Thank the gods!* Relief surged through her. Even if she had to endure Pullus touching her – and she recoiled at the thought of him making love to her – at least she could keep the baby.

"Now leave. I have work to do."

At Flavius's clipped words Livia said nothing more. She was just about to leave the *tablinum* when Flavius's words stopped her in her tracks. "Oh, one more thing, Livia. Once you leave this villa tomorrow you will *never* be welcome back here. You will make your bed and lie in it once you are married. You've made fools of us once too often. Firstly, with your sham of a marriage to Galvus, and now the trouble you've caused with the child. Father, and I, want nothing more to do with you. Do you understand?"

"Oh, I understand fully, Flavius," Livia said, her voice full of scorn, refusing to succumb to his hateful words. She stared at him in defiance, "But, tell me one thing before I leave this villa for good. Do you know if I'm to go back to Alexandria?"

Flavius shrugged indifference in every line of his body, "I have no idea where you are going, Livia. And frankly I do not care."

It was the final humiliation. Flavius couldn't have made his feelings any plainer. Both she, and Elisha, meant nothing to him.

The next morning seemed to pass in agonising slowness. Livia had arisen early, bone tired from having spent a sleepless night thinking of her impending marriage to Pullus, and how she would endure his touch, his kisses, his body covering hers when all she could think of was the passion, the pleasure, she had felt, and shared, with Metellus when they had made love.

And now, with little over an hour before the wedding ceremony was due to begin, she was trying to quell the nerves that assailed her.

Maude, her new *tire-woman*, was brushing her hair, the movement of the comb through her long hair rhythmic, and the silence in the bedroom going some way to soothing her frayed nerves.

Portia's revelation yesterday about Pullus questioning her at Senator Crito's gathering was now painfully obvious. He still wanted to marry her; and had lost no time in getting her brother to arrange the betrothal.

She frowned in confusion. Nothing made sense. Surely he was aware of the gossip about her, and the fact she had returned with a baby? What on earth was Pullus playing at? What reason did he have for wanting to marry her? Especially now, when she was the current laughing stock of all Rome!

Well you'll have a lifetime to find out why won't you? She thought humourlessly.

Once Maude had finished styling her hair, she passed her a mirror of polished copper to view the finished result. The face that stared back at her looked every inch the daughter of a rich Senator. Her hair had been pulled back off her face, secured by tortoise shell combs, before it cascaded down her back in a riot of curls.

Her face had been made up, mainly at Maude's insistence rather than Livia wanting it done, to emphasise the fullness of her lips and bring out the hazel of her eyes. Her cheekbones had been tinted a dusty pink, and as she stared at her reflection, she couldn't help noticing that they had become more pronounced since her return to Rome.

The weight loss was partly due to the anxiety about having to give up Elisha, and if she were truthful, partly due to Metellus. Because, no matter how hard she'd tried, she had been unable to get him out of her head ever since he'd turned up at the villa. His presence had robbed her of what little appetite she'd had.

"It's time, Mistress."

Maude's words jolted her out of her dark musings, and she stood up, lifting her arms so the young girl could slip the silk stola over her head.

She didn't have a wedding gown of course, there hadn't been enough time to purchase one. Instead, she had picked out her best gown, a silk *stola* in the palest shade of jade green, the silk shot through with silver thread, so when she moved the dress shimmered in the summer sunlight.

Although she didn't want to marry Pullus, she knew without a shadow of doubt that if she didn't dress well for this marriage, Flavius would be furious with her. And right now she didn't have the energy, or the inclination, to rile him, for if she did he might change his mind about letting her keep Elisha.

Once Maude had finished dressing her, she made her way out into the *atrium* to gather her thoughts. She had sent a message to Portia earlier, begging her to come this morning, as she desperately needed her friend here for moral support. If nothing else, Portia's displeasure at the wedding would be known to all, as her friend very much let her emotions rule her head! Thinking of her friend, she felt a small twinge of guilt. Should she have told her about Metellus? Somehow, telling Portia about what had happened on the leper island, and the feelings she still felt for Metellus was one step too far. Her feelings were too raw, too special, to even share with her best friend at this time.

And Livia thought, with a wry twist of her lips, she was also a realist. She knew Portia wouldn't have been able to keep it secret. Her friend loved gossip – whether it was hearing it – or sharing it!

A slight movement caught her eye as she saw her *tire-woman* coming towards her. "I will be but a few moments," Livia said, before she walked over to a small stone statute which stood in the corner of the *atrium*.

Closing her eyes she dedicated a prayer to her mother, wishing with all her heart she could have been here today. "Wish Elisha, and I well, mother," she said, fighting back the tears that threatened, before she turned and followed Maude back into the villa to where Flavius stood waiting for her, his face expressionless. Without a word he turned, and Livia followed him into the *tablinum*.

As she entered the small room she saw that it was empty, with no sign of her husband-to-be and a small dart of annoyance shot through her. She was obviously not worth the effort of rushing for. But knowing Pullus, it didn't surprise her. Portia had been right in what she had said about him. He *was* the most odious of men, and keeping her waiting was just another attempt to assert his dominance over her.

She had the sudden urge to flee. But deep down she knew the futility of doing so. Flavius would just drag her back – but more importantly – it could compromise Elisha's safety. He had made it clear he didn't want her, or Elisha, anywhere near this villa ever again.

So she tempered her emotions, and sat down in the wooden *curule* chair and waited, facing forward, refusing to glance behind her. After what seemed like an eternity, but could only have been a few minutes, a noise from outside the *tablinum* broke the silence in the room. Tension slammed through her, and she clasped her hands together, trying to calm her nerves.

"Stand up and turn to face your betrothed," Flavius hissed, grabbing her arm and pulling her roughly out of the chair.

With reluctance she did as he ordered, turning to face the open doorway. She saw the tall, thin figure of the priest dressed in his distinctive white robes come through first, followed by a taller figure who walked directly behind him. Confusion caused her to frown. Pullus was short and fat, and before she could assimilate anything further she saw who it was. The room tilted on its axis as she swayed, a feeling of faintness coming over her. She felt Flavius's grip tighten on her arm and was thankful for it as she would otherwise have fallen to the floor.

"Metellus!" she breathed, her heart beating so fast she thought it would leap out of her chest.

Metellus was here. On her wedding day! Was this some sort of foul trick both Flavius, and Metellus, had agreed to when he had visited with her half-brother the other day? Did Metellus know Pullus, and he had asked him if he could attend the wedding? But it couldn't be that! She remembered his scorn when she had mentioned who she was marrying on the island. By the gods, none of this made any sense. No sense whatsoever.

Her eyes widened as they clashed with Metellus's expression-less ones. Deliberately, she broke eye contact with him, her gaze taking in his silk tunic, the colour of rich claret. It clung and emphasised the width of his shoulders, and the outfit he wore today was in marked contrast to the rough woollen tunic he had worn on the ship.

She closed her eyes for a moment, wondering if she were dreaming, and when she opened her eyes she would discover it had been her mind playing tricks on her all along. But she picked up the scent of sandalwood on his skin as he came to stand next to her. It was so distinctively him that she knew without a doubt that Metellus wasn't a figment of her imagination.

With reluctance she opened her eyes. Metellus was definitely no apparition. He was a full blooded male who seemed to dominate the room. Not just his physical presence, but also the aura of power which seemed to ooze out of him.

Even Flavius, in his silk robes paled into insignificance.

Some sort of unseen force made her eyes rise to meet his once more. This time his grey eyes held hers, and she felt hot, sweet pleasure pierce her. Just one look made her insides quiver, turning them to hot molten lava.

Still holding his gaze, she leaned closer to Flavius and whispered, "Where is Pullus?"

Flavius frowned down at her, "What are you talking about woman?" he hissed out of clenched teeth, "You are marrying *him*. Now be quiet and do as you are bid."

Livia was thankful Flavius was still holding her, as she seriously doubted whether her legs would have been able to hold her upright as the realisation of what he'd said hit her.

In the deafening silence following his words, a shrill voice broke the tension within the room, "Have I missed it? Tell me I'm not too late."

Portia! At last a voice of reason, in what was rapidly becoming a farce worthy of any a comedy performed in the playhouses of Rome.

"Who invited you?" Flavius burst out, frowning in annoyance as Portia pushed forward and came to stand next to Livia, her customary bracelets jangling in the sudden silence which pulsed through the room.

"Livia did," Portia said haughtily, "Do you have a problem with that, Flavius?"

Flavius glared at both women before snapping out, "Jupiter's cock, this past week is turning into a nightmare. Now let's get this marriage ceremony over with. I have important business to attend to later this afternoon."

CHAPTER 14

"I thought you were marrying Pullus?"

Livia looked across to her friend, and shrugged, "So did I."

Portia's "O" of surprise, would have been amusing in other circumstances, if only for the fact it hadn't been so traumatic a day.

"He's very handsome."

"Yes."

"Yes? Is that all you have to say about your new husband?"

Livia noticed her friend's demeanour was one of annoyance, and concern for Livia, in equal measures.

"How did you meet?" Portia asked, pushing on with her questioning.

"On the ship to Alexandria."

This time Portia's "O" made Livia smile, and she elaborated. "He was the one who rescued me."

Portia's expression changed from concern to happiness in an instant, and she clapped her hands in glee. "So it is a love match! How lovely. I'm so pleased—"

"No." Livia interrupted, cutting off her friend's exuberance, "No, it isn't a love match, Portia. Far from it."

"But I don't understand?"

Livia sighed, glancing away from Portia, to where Metellus stood talking to her half-brother. By the grim expressions on both their faces, it didn't appear to be the most cordial of conversations.

Realising Portia deserved an explanation, she glanced back at her friend, meeting the concern evident in her eyes. "I have kept many things back from you, Portia, and for that I am sorry. But suffice to say, Metellus isn't marrying me because he loves me. He is marrying me to avenge the death of his father. He hates my family, and I can only assume our marriage is based solely on his desire for revenge."

For a long time Portia said nothing, before she took Livia's hand in hers. "Oh, Livia, I'm so sorry. I can't profess to understand all that has happened, but he doesn't look like a man who will harm you." She bit her bottom lip in consternation, staring across the room at Metellus, "But you never know…"

Livia smiled at her friend's words. Typical Portia, she spoke before thinking. "I don't think he will harm me. He hasn't up until now."

"Well that's good isn't it? A start of sorts, if you like." After a small silence fell between them, Portia asked. "Do you know what will happen to you? Where will you go, where you will live?"

"She will live at my farm, and here in Rome once my – our – new villa is built."

Both women jumped at the words, neither of them having heard Metellus approach, where they sat in the coolness of the *atrium*.

"I would like a word with you if I may be permitted. In private," Portia said flatly, before she stood up and placed herself in front of Metellus.

Livia looked up at Portia in surprise. *What on earth was her friend up to?* But before she could stop her, Portia walked away, and Metellus, not having much choice, followed her.

Livia looked from under her eyelashes to where they stood at the other end of the *atrium*, Portia talking to him earnestly, her hands lifting and falling in equal measure as she gesticulated whatever she was trying to convey to Metellus. As she watched them both, she noticed Metellus's face and body language gave nothing away as he listened to what Portia was telling him.

Once Portia had finished what she wanted to convey, Livia watched in fascination, as instead of appearing angry at Portia's words, he threw back his head and laughed.

Portia obviously wasn't expecting *that* response from Metellus, because she stiffened and her face turned grim, before she turned and flounced back to where Livia still sat on a marble bench watching them. She saw with some amusement that Portia's face was flushed a brilliant red, either in embarrassment or vexation – or a combination of both.

"Well, are you going to tell me what you said to him, or are you going to sulk here all night," Livia teased, when after a full five minutes of fuming Portia still hadn't said anything.

"That man is the most obnoxious man I have ever met! Without manners or deportment, and I—" Portia stopped her tirade, when she realised she was in actual fact insulting Livia's new husband. She took a deep breath, and in a calmer voice said, "I merely asked that he be gentle with you, told him you are still untouched—"

"Portia! You didn't!" Livia gasped, her eyes flying to where Metellus stood watching them both, a goblet of wine in his hand. Her eyes met his, and she saw the dark humour shining in them, before he lifted the goblet up in a mocking salute to her. Hot colour suffused her whole body as she met the humour in his eyes before she turned away. *Could the day get any worse?*

"Well someone had to tell him the truth," Portia finally said, "I didn't want him hurting you. Although you were married previously, *we* both know your dead husband didn't do anything, that you remain untouched—"

"He wouldn't have hurt me," Livia said quietly, interrupting Portia's impassioned speech.

"Wouldn't have hurt you? What are you talking about? You are still a—" Portia stopped talking, her hand slapping over her mouth, her eyes wide, as Livia's words sunk in. Finally.

"When?"

Livia lifted her shoulders, knowing her friend deserved an explanation. Even so hot colour flood her face once more. "On the island."

"Oh!" Portia squeaked, her eyes darting back to Metellus. Livia's gaze followed hers and she noticed that he still leaned against the marble column watching them both. Although this time there was no humour on his face, instead it was blank, devoid of emotion offering no inclination as to what he was thinking.

"I had better get ready." Livia finally said, breaking eye contact with Metellus before she stood up when it became clear her friend had nothing more to say. "We are to travel to Metellus's farm this afternoon, and I'm not sure how far from Rome it is—"

"Oh, Livia!" Portia cried, interrupting her hesitant explanation, and her friend, always prone to tears when distressed, grabbed Livia's hand halting her. "I will pray every day to the gods for you. Please send me a message when you get to…to wherever it is you are going. Tell me everything, for if you don't, I swear I will never be able to sleep again."

Livia smiled down at Portia. "I promise. I will send word as soon as I can. Now dry your tears and come help me pack."

"Before you leave I want to know one thing."

Livia looked up as Flavius strode into her bedroom. She was in the process of packing a wooden crate with her belongings, and had insisted on packing her own things, much to her *tire-woman's* amazement. But she needed something to occupy her whirling thoughts before the time arrived for her to leave the villa for good.

As usual, her half-brother's tone was sharp, and she bristled. Livia turned and faced him, crossing her arms, in an unconscious gesture of defiance.

"What?" she asked, her tone brisk, resenting the fact he had interrupted her relative peace, now that Portia had left the villa unable to stay for as long as she'd liked, as her father was still prohibiting her meeting with Livia.

"Are you, and Metellus lovers?"

Livia gasped, hot colour surging into her face at the abruptness of his question, "No!" she burst out, before she turned away, and with shaking hands carried on folding a silk *stola*, her eyes unseeing. She was unprepared when Flavius grabbed her arm and roughly spun her around.

His face was flushed with anger, and his eyes flashed, "You lie, girl. He was – is – your lover, isn't he?"

Not bothering to answer him, Livia snapped back her own question, "What difference does it make now, Flavius? I am his wife. He can do what he wants with me. And what do *you* care anyway?"

"So that's the way it is. I should have known. You *did* know him before, I had my suspicions. After all, why would he marry you – you have no dowry. Where did you meet? How long has this affair been going on? By the gods you had me fooled girl."

He finally stopped his tirade of questions and Livia realised that there was no way out, so she said, "You are wrong, Flavius. There has been no affair. Metellus was on the ship to Alexandria, it was *he* who saved me from drowning, *he* was the one who rescued me."

Flavius's grip on her arm tightened, "Don't take me for a fool girl," he snapped, "Did he take your virginity?"

Livia looked away, refusing to answer him, but her unspoken gesture was proof enough of her guilt in Flavius's eyes.

"So it was him you rutted with, and now I reap the consequences, is that it?"

Livia gasped at the crudeness of his words, and anger surged through her, "*You* reap the consequences, Flavius? How ironic. Haven't you ever thought how *I* might be feeling? How all this has affected *me*? Everything you've ever done has been for your own ends. For the glorification of the *Drusii* name—"

"How dare you talk to me like that?" Flavius interrupted, his face flushing an unbecoming shade of red, "I am in charge of this household now. You will obey me, as you would our father, as if he were still in charge of this family – remember that."

"Really? But I don't belong here anymore, do I Flavius? You've already made it abundantly clear, I am no longer welcome in this house, remember? I've been forced to marry Metellus...*and* I would wager you made sure enough money changed hands as a result of it. Just how much I wonder?"

"Three hundred thousand *denarii* give or take." A voice drawled from behind them.

Both Livia and Flavius turned to where Metellus watched them both. He was leaning nonchalantly against the wooden doorframe, a look of bored indifference on his face, and Livia wondered how long he'd been standing there listening.

"Lost for words, Flavius?" Metellus eventually asked. "Were you about to tell Livia how you've managed to gamble away the family coffers? Tell her about the debts you've racked up over the past year?"

Flavius's silence spoke volumes, and Metellus straightened, walking into the room, never once taking his eyes off the older man. "I thought not."

He looked at Livia, his eyes unreadable, "You should thank me for saving the family name. It wouldn't have been too long before all of Rome found out how Flavius had managed to single-handedly bring down one of Rome's leading families." He tutted before he shook his head from side to side in a mocking gesture, "Your brother isn't a very good gambler I'm afraid."

For a moment indecision warred across Flavius's face before he retaliated. He shrugged his shoulders as if he didn't have a care in the world. "So I am a poor gambler, and I took your money in exchange for her. What does it matter? She was your whore anyway. I'm surprised you bothered to marry her. You should have just taken her as your mistress. I wouldn't have cared one bit."

Livia gasped at the vitriolic hatred evident in Flavius's voice. She saw Metellus's eyes narrow, before he bit out, "What did you say?"

"You heard. Now I understand fully what this is all about. You bedded Livia. The baby you are trying to pass off as an orphan is yours, *and* you have taken me for an idiot. What I want to know is how long you have been bedding her behind my back?"

With lightning reflexes, Metellus shot forward and grabbed Flavius by the throat; his strong fingers squeezing the life out of him. Flavius, she saw, was powerless to fight against Metellus's superior strength, as he desperately grabbed at Metellus's muscular forearms, trying to loosen the deadly grip from around his neck.

If Livia hadn't been so traumatised by what had happened today, she would have smiled at the sheer horror she saw reflected on Flavius's face as he struggled against the hands fastened around his throat.

"You have a sick mind, Flavius. The baby is not ours. You will do well to remember that. As for the reason for my marrying her. I thought *you* would have some semblance of intelligence, but obviously I am mistaken. I will give you a hint. Go back to the history lessons you had as a young boy. Not too far though. Recall all that you learned about the Pisonian conspiracy, and then you may make a connection."

And with those words, Metellus's lips curled in disgust, before he loosened his hold on Flavius's throat and pushed him away as if he were an annoying insect. Flavius staggered backwards, his arms flailing wildly in an effort to stop himself from falling flat on his backside. While he'd managed to keep upright, he was gasping for breath, his face flushed as he coughed and spluttered.

Flavius, like the coward he was, stepped back out of Metellus's reach, and Livia watched as he rubbed his throat. She could already see the beginnings of a bruise where Metellus had grabbed him.

"The Pisonian Conspiracy," Flavius finally said, after he had managed to compose himself somewhat. "I do recall it, I even remember the furore it created. I was around thirteen years old I think; but what has it to do with either of our father's?"

Metellus' face hardened, his eyes icy before he bit out, "My father was Lucius Quadratus Aurelius. He was implicated in the conspiracy, and arrested for treason and all because Nero believed the lies spread by your father. And on the back of it all your father became a very rich and powerful man."

Silence greeting Metellus's words, until Flavius snorted, "What nonsense. This is just pure fabrication. Lies—"

Metellus's face hardened and he stepped forward once again. Flavius gave an unmanly squeak, and Livia saw the colour drain from his face as he hastily lifted a hand in surrender. Metellus stopped, his fists bunching by his side as he reigned in his anger.

"Believe it, Flavius," Metellus bit out, "For it is the truth. My father was innocent of all charges. He had no interest in politics – unlike your father – who stood to gain everything by winning Nero's favour and trust. Lies and false evidence spread by your father lead to his execution."

Livia watched as her half-brother took in all Metellus had to say. But the stubborn look on his face still remained. It was obvious he did not believe what Metellus was saying. Finally, into the silence that had fallen between the three of them, Flavius snapped, "You are not welcome in this villa ever again. Both of you. I suggest you leave. Now!"

Metellus laughed dryly, and in a mocking gesture, placed his hand on his chest, "My heart is broken, Flavius. But don't speak too soon. Don't forget who has paid all the debts you accrued recently. I own this villa. It is *I* who chooses – nay *allows* – you to stay here. Never forget that."

Flavius said nothing, his jaw working as he bit back his fury. He glared at Metellus, before he barged past them both and left the room.

"Do you really own this…our villa?" Livia finally asked in the silence which precipitated Flavius's departure.

"Yes," Metellus said flatly, "My family used to live here. This was my father's villa before all his assets were seized by Nero." His mouth twisted, "Nero gave it to *your* father after mine was executed."

Livia stared at his harsh profile, her thoughts racing, "Will you want to live in it soon? Take it away from my father and Flavius?"

Metellus barked, no humour in his voice at all, "No. I *never* want to live here again. It ceased to be my home the night my father was arrested. *Your* family villa is safe for now, providing Flavius – and your father – do nothing to rile me of course." His lips sneered in obvious derision, "And I would bet my last *sesterce* Flavius is going through all the paperwork right at this very moment wondering if I actually really do own it."

Livia bit her bottom lip, before she asked the one question which plagued her, "But why marry me? Why not just humiliate me – my family? You could have so easily crushed us all. As Flavius said, you didn't have to marry me to extract your desire for revenge."

"Power."

Livia frowned. "Power, but I—"

"Your family has connections," Metellus interrupted, "Connections in places where *I* as a mere merchant have no access to. Yes, I have money, more money than your family will ever have. But *I* have no connections. By marrying you, I gain access to the higher echelons of Roman Society. You, as my wife, will give me access to that society, and my money will pave the way."

"All this is because you want power?"

"Of course. Power and revenge. Why else would I have married you, Livia? But don't get me wrong. You suit my purposes very well indeed. It wouldn't do to marry an ugly wife would it?"

Livia gasped in outraged shock, her heart breaking open at his words. *Where had the passionate lover on the island gone? The man who had rescued her from certain death and who had accepted Elisha without a qualm?*

"You are despicable. Hateful," she whispered.

At her words hot colour surged along Metellus's cheekbones, before he grabbed her arm and pulled her forward so she was a mere breath away from his mouth. Anger pulsed in every line of his hard body, before he whispered savagely, his hot breath on her face, "And why am I like this? Because your family *made* me like this, that's why.

You will be a dutiful wife, or you will rue the day you cross me. If you don't obey me I will crush your family. Obey me and no-one will be the wiser, your family's dirty secret is safe with me – for now. The *Drusii* will be as they were before debt nearly brought them to the edge of ruin. Your father – if he is able –will resume his seat in the Senate, and one day your brother will be there too because *I* have the necessary money to make it so. And by marrying you I will one day gain status too. Marriages such as ours are what makes Rome great. Don't ever forget that Livia. Not for one minute. Do you understand?"

Livia tried to tug free, but his grip was too tight. Then she saw the anger in his eyes disappear to be replaced by desire as his intentions became clear as he leaned in closer. Livia gasped, "No! I don't—"

The touch of his mouth on hers silenced her protest, as his lips plundered hers. She held herself rigid, but couldn't stop the tidal wave of emotion that suffused every part of her body. Passion replaced anger as his mouth demanded a response from hers. A response she couldn't stop even if she wanted to. The kiss was a bittersweet reminder of all they had shared on the island. And no matter how much she protested to herself, she had longed for the touch of his mouth on hers for weeks now.

Metellus's mouth softened, and his punishing kiss changed. Now his lips tasted, teased hers and took what they both wanted, eliciting from her a deep groan of desire.

"Yes," he whispered against her mouth, "Open your mouth for me."

Livia did as he commanded, relishing the feel of his tongue mating with hers. The hand holding her arm loosened, and moved upwards to cup the back of her neck, tilting her head so he could capture the fullness of her lips.

Now it was he who groaned, as the kiss deepened, intensified. She felt his other hand cup the underside of her breast, his fingers trailing upwards until he found the evidence of her desire, her response to him, as her nipple hardened and pushed through the silk of her gown.

Livia didn't know how long the kiss lasted, but eventually he broke it off, stepping away from her. He stared down at her, his eyes once again unreadable, shuttered, as if he'd put on a cloak of indifference to protect himself.

"You are a sad man, Metellus," Livia finally said, her voice cracking with strain, as she stared up at him, "If you are only driven by revenge, and power, when you could have so much more."

Metellus's jaw clamped shut at her words, and she saw his eyes turn frigid. His stance was that of a man who knew his position in the world. Confident. Sure. Strong. "I don't deal in anything else, Livia. Revenge has sustained me for fourteen long years. It's the code I live by. The *only* code I live by. You had best remember that for your own sanity."

"You are ready? Everything you need is packed?"

"Yes."

"Good. It is time to leave. We have an hour's ride out of Rome, and I don't want to travel when it is dark."

"Fine," Livia said, unable to think of anything else to add. She realised she wasn't exactly full of sparkling conversation this afternoon. *But then why should she be, after hearing Metellus's declaration earlier? It hardly boded well for a harmonious future, did it?*

Following Metellus out of the villa, she glanced over her shoulder as the large brass and wooden gate slammed shut behind them. The finality of it caused a pang of regret to pierce her, and she knew this would probably be the last time she ever saw her family home. Granted, it hadn't been much of a home for practically all of her life, but still, it was the only home she'd ever known.

She had even managed to go to her father's room to bid him farewell, but it had been a futile exercise as he'd been asleep. And even though this would probably be the last time she would ever see him, she was reluctant to wake him. He still looked so ill, and she knew it would be many months before he would recover. If he ever did.

She had hoped he would be awake, as she'd wanted to ask him whether he would have made her go to Alexandria to marry Pullus. And whether he would have made her marry Metellus, too. Twice now, in the space of a few short months, her life had changed beyond her wildest imagination. The first time had been when she'd found herself on the way to Alexandria. The second, today, when she'd found herself married to Metellus. And both these life changing events had occurred when her father had been unaware of what was going on around him.

Livia's mouth flattened in anger. Flavius had a lot to answer for!

CHAPTER 15

The farm was immense, as was the villa which stood proud in it.

That was the first thing Livia saw, as she sat atop the carriage looking down into the verdant valley below, staring at what would be her new home. The late evening sunlight glinted off the marble walls, and terracotta tiles of the villa, and the scene laid out before her was one of tranquillity as horses lazily ate grass in a nearby paddock.

She was taken aback by the size of the farm. For some reason, she had envisioned Metellus living on a small family farm, not this vast villa which wouldn't have looked out of place on the Palatine Hill. She smiled to herself as she had to acknowledge that Metellus had once again taken her by surprise.

And, as if he had read her mind – yet again – he said, "The estate and villa used to belong to my uncle. He designed, and built the villa, and farmed the land for many years. But I recently bought it off him. He said he was getting too old for farming, and has now retired to his villa in Rome."

Livia turned to where Metellus sat next to her, "Was this where you came after—" Her words trailed off, as she realised her mistake in raking up the past.

Thankfully her words didn't seem to upset him too much this time for he just nodded, his eyes faraway as he gazed down at the land below him. "Aye. This is where my mother and I came to live. My uncle was extremely generous in opening up his home to us at the time, especially when we were considered enemies of Rome." His mouth pursed, "It was kept a secret of course. My uncle was one of Nero's chief architects. It wouldn't do to upset Nero too much. He was, as we now know, completely mad by that time."

"Your uncle's wife didn't mind?" Livia asked, thinking out loud, and wondering how *she* would have coped with relatives – relatives who were in effect—*persona non grata.*

"My uncle has never married."

"So you've lived here all alone since your uncle sold you the farm?"

"No, not alone. My mother still lives here."

"Your mother?" Livia squeaked.

"Yes, my mother," Metellus replied, a hint of humour in his voice, "I do have one. They are considered essential for the creation of life I believe."

Livia ignored his dry humour, "Well I know that. It's just…I thought…well I thought she was dead," seeing his dark frown she elaborated, "You have never mentioned her, that is all," before she asked tentatively, "Does she know about me? About…about us?"

"No."

Once she had uttered the questions she realised the stupidity of them and turned her head away. Of course she wouldn't know about her! What he had been plotting, and planning, wouldn't have involved his mother, she was sure of it. A knot of tension pooled in her stomach at the thought of meeting his mother, and she couldn't help but wonder what kind of a reception she would have. Friendly? Hostile?

"I'm sure my mother will love you," Metellus said, his tone dry, as if he had read her mind, "I'm not sure what she will say to *me* though."

Livia's head swivelled to look at him. Again, he seemed to be able to read her thoughts as there was a hint of wariness in his

151

eyes. He broke eye contact with her, clicked his tongue, and the horses started pulling the wagon towards the villa.

The ten minutes or so it took to get to the farm were the longest of Livia's life, as a thousand different scenarios flitted into her head. But all too soon they arrived, and as they pulled up into the courtyard, slaves appeared from everywhere to help unload the carriage and lead away the horses. The journey had been relatively easy; and as Metellus had predicted, no more than an hour's ride south of Rome. But as she sat atop the wagon taking in the opulence of the villa, she somehow felt as if she were a million miles from Rome, and a world away from what she was used to.

Realising she couldn't sit there all day, Livia stood up, and swung herself around, ready to climb down from the carriage. She was unprepared for the large hands that circled her waist, as they helped her down off the carriage. The heat of his hands seemed to burn through the silk of her gown, and she stiffened when Metellus pulled her closer into the hard strength of his body; a body she remembered all too well as it moulded against her.

Swallowing, she bit back the thought of how well they seemed to fit each other, and she supressed the memories of what they had once shared on the island. There was no point in thinking anything could come of this union. Metellus had made his intentions more than clear. She knew *exactly* why she was here, and what was expected of her.

And with that thought at the forefront of her mind, she pulled out of his grip, and walked to the back of the carriage to check on Elisha. Thankfully, the baby was asleep, and for a moment she envied her as she stared down at her lying in her basket. Oh, how she longed to be as content! It had been a long, tiring day. And it wasn't even over yet…

"Your wife! You have a wife? Oh, Metellus, how could you marry and not let me know?"

Sending a scolding look towards her son, the older woman

152

turned to where Livia stood next to Metellus. Livia's stomach clenched with trepidation and nerves, wondering how she would be received by the older woman.

But she needn't have worried, as Metellus's mother reached forward, and took Livia's hands in hers, pulling her forward and embracing her in a tight hug. There was warmth in her grey eyes when she stepped back, and Livia noticed her eyes were the same grey colour as her son's.

But, in truth, that was the only similarity between mother and son Livia could see. Where Metellus was tall, his mother was a tiny, petite woman, a woman who still held onto her youthful figure. She had light coloured hair, streaked with a few strands of grey, in complete contrast to Metellus's dark hair. Her face was delicate, and oval shaped, full of grace and beauty and again nothing in her face resembled the hard planes and angles of her son's.

"My dear. It is so good to meet you. Metellus has always been prone to impulsiveness; but on this occasion I can see why he married you so quickly, *and* without telling me. You are very beautiful."

Livia swallowed the lump of emotion which seemed to be lodged at the back of her throat as she relished the motherly contact, and her kind words. Thankfully, Metellus was right, his mother was kindness itself, and didn't seem too concerned about the hastiness of their marriage.

"I...I am pleased to make you acquaintance, madam. And you, too, are beautiful," Livia finally said.

"Madam! Oh please do not call me that. My name is Antonia. I would be honoured if you would call me by my given name, and I will call you Livia. Such a pretty name." Then she laughed, "And I am not beautiful. I am far too old to be beautiful. But never mind." She looked at them both, and clapped her hands before shooing them both towards the open doorway of the villa. "Come. Come. You must both be tired and hungry. I will have the slaves prepare a bath for you, and once you have refreshed yourselves we can eat."

Taking Livia by the hand she started to lead her into the villa, but Livia stiffened, as panic assailed her when she realised Antonia didn't know about Elisha. She threw a pleading look over her shoulder to where Metellus stood impassively watching them both, his arms crossed over his impressive chest.

"Mother!"

Relief surged through her as Metellus's voice halted the older woman in her tracks.

"Before you take Livia away, you had better come over and meet another new member of our family."

Frowning at her son, Antonia did as he asked, following Metellus as he walked to the back of the wagon. Livia trailed behind, her steps hesitant, but when she heard Antonia squeal in surprise she couldn't stop her smile of delight.

"A baby?" Turning she glanced back to Livia, and then to Metellus, "Yours?"

"No!" Both of them spoke in unison, and Livia felt her face flame with colour.

"No." Livia said more calmly this time, when she realised Metellus wasn't going to speak, "Elisha is an orphan…of sorts. I…I know Metellus hasn't had time to tell you, but I was rescued by him when our ship was shipwrecked," she hesitated for a moment, unsure how to explain Elisha's presence, but she chose caution, "The…the babe was also on the island."

Livia glanced to Metellus for reassurance. His slight nod told her she had said the right thing. Seeing the concern on Antonia's face, she could tell Metellus's mother was a compassionate woman; but she didn't want to scare her – or the others who lived on the farm – by saying Elisha was the child of a leper.

"What is her name?"

"Elisha."

This time it was Metellus who spoke, as Livia watched Metellus's mother reach down and lift the baby from her basket. As she looked down at the baby, swaddled in a blanket, a soft tender look came

154

over her face. "It is many a year since I held a young child in my arms. Not since you were a babe, Metellus," she said, turning to look at her son, and Livia had to hide her smile when she saw colour stain his high cheekbones.

"It will be a pleasure to help look after you, Elisha." Antonia whispered to the sleeping baby, and Livia felt a ball of warmth curl in her stomach. There was no doubting Metellus's mother was a kind woman.

The only thing that troubled her, as they walked into the villa, was whether Antonia would still be as kind to *her* when she found out who her father was, and the real reason why Metellus had married her. She prayed she would be, for she was in desperate need of an ally…

"Where do you think you are going, Livia?"

At the softly spoken words, Livia closed her eyes and bit back a groan of frustration. She halted in her tracks and turned to face Metellus. He was standing next to a marble column watching her, his face in shadow, the only light coming from a solitary wall sconce which cast its flickering light down the darkened corridor.

She knew what he was referring to of course. A slave had told her earlier where Metellus's *cubica* was, assuming that she would be sharing his sleeping quarters.

But she had other plans. She *had* intended to sleep with Elisha, as her room was at the other end of the corridor from where Metellus slept. And she'd nearly succeeded too, for she hadn't seen Metellus for hours, ever since he'd left the *triclinium* straight after the evening meal, announcing he had a lot of farming matters to catch up on.

"Well?"

This time his one word question was abrupt, and Livia had to quell the nerves pooling in the pit of her stomach. Squaring her chin she replied, "I think it would be best if I stay with Elisha tonight. She may be fretful. A…a new home…" Her words trailed

155

off, and the excuse sounded hollow, even to her ears.

"Indeed? A baby, no more than a few months old, who has travelled across an ocean to reach Rome, is unlikely to be fretful just because she has travelled no more than an hour in the back of a wagon." Metellus's voice was dry, and his mouth flattened before he continued, "And, I might add, a journey she slept the whole way through, if I'm not mistaken." He tilted his head, as if listening for a noise, "I can hear no baby's cry. No fretful moaning. No wet nurse wailing in despair. So..?"

Livia bristled. He was right, she knew. But still... Lifting her head in defiance, she retaliated, "What kind of a guardian would I be if I didn't check on her?"

He nodded in acknowledgement at her words, "By all means check on her. But remember the bedroom – *our* bedroom – is down there," his words were clipped, precise, followed by a jerk of his head as he indicated the closed door of his bedchamber down the other end of the corridor. "I'll be waiting for you."

Livia felt the colour drain from her face. Saying nothing, she headed for Elisha's room, noticing that her hands shook as she pushed open the door. Once she was inside she sat in a chair next to a wooden crib, her mind working furiously as she watched the sleeping child.

Metellus was adamant she was to share his bed. *But why?* On the island he'd said their lovemaking had been a mistake, never to be repeated. Hadn't he only taken her body in his twisted desire for revenge? She had meant nothing to him. And up until a few days ago, she had firmly believed she would never see him again.

Yes, he had married her, but only to get access to her family's name and the status it brought in Roman society. And also, she was convinced, to extract the revenge he had planned for years now. To crush her family once and for all.

And what of her feelings for him? He had thrown her declaration of love firmly back in her face and it had hurt—hurt so much. She had tried to forget him, but the moment she had seen him standing in the doorway of Flavius's office she realised she had been only fooling herself. She still wanted him, she still desired him, *and* if she were to acknowledge her true feelings, she still loved him. She was in love with him, and she wanted him to love her back. But it was impossible. She knew that.

And now she was to share his bed again. Livia shook her head as mixed emotions assailed her. The truth was plain enough—she wasn't sure what she wanted. She craved his touch, but at the same time apprehension about the future played heavy on her mind.

Deliberately blocking him from her thoughts for a moment she went over to the basket and saw Elisha was awake. She picked the baby up and carried her over to a large table and changed the swaddling before putting a clean gown on her. Then she fed her, using the same leather goat pouch Elisha's mother had given her, before she placed the baby back into the basket, waiting for her to fall back to sleep. She was such a contented child. She rarely cried, only when she was hungry, and even then it wasn't a shrill piercing cry, more a small cry of disapproval.

As she watched the sleeping baby, Livia realised she couldn't postpone the inevitable. Bending over she tucked the light blanket around the child before she closed the door behind her and walked down the long corridor towards Metellus's – *no their* – bedroom.

For a long moment she stood outside the door, undecided. But mindful of his earlier words, she eventually pushed open the door and stepped inside the darkened bedchamber. But once her eyes had adjusted to the darkness, she couldn't contain her gasp of anger.

Metellus wasn't there! The room was empty. He had played her false, the lying toad! Demanding she return to his bedchamber had just been a ploy to see if she *would* obey his command. "*I'll be waiting for you,*" she growled, mimicking his earlier order. "We'll *I'll* not be waiting for you!"

And with that, she stomped over to her wooden chest which had been placed at the foot of the bed, and flung open the lid taking out a thin cotton gown. With jerky movements she stripped off her *stola*, uncaring if she ripped the delicate silk or not, before donning the night gown. Once she had finished, she walked over to the door. Her hand was even on the handle but then the futility of what she was doing hit her.

Where would she go? Where would she sleep? She didn't even know what other rooms had been given over to sleeping. *Hades*, she didn't even know where Antonia slept! The only realistic option was to sleep with Elisha, but Metellus had already warned her of doing that hadn't he?

A feeling of helplessness hit her, and she lifted her hands and placed them flat against the wooden door. Even though the door wasn't locked she was still in effect a prisoner here in this room. There was no hiding from him. She was his. *He* was the one in total control of this situation. His to take. Anytime. Anywhere.

The thought of him stripping off her shift, his hands skimming over her naked flesh made her blood heat. She was catapulted back to the island, to the night he'd made love to her, his mouth and body seeking, and taking everything from her.

"Stop!" She shook her head, dispelling the erotic memories of all they had shared. "Stop now." She *had* to suppress these feelings, because if she didn't, there was no accounting what he would do to the tattered remnants of her mind, and her heart.

She had to be strong. She would refuse to be a willing bed mate. Whatever his reason for marrying her, it wasn't out of love or respect for her was it?

Tiredness stole over her in a tidal wave of exhaustion, and she leaned her forehead against the rough planks of wood. Suddenly she went beyond caring what Metellus would do when he came into the bedchamber. It had been such a long day, and she was in desperate need of sleep. With reluctance she moved away from the door and climbed into the bed and within minutes she was asleep.

Metellus gazed down at Livia's sleeping form. She was curled on her side, her knees almost reaching her chin, in what was almost a childlike pose.

He'd watched, and waited for her earlier, hiding himself in the shadows behind one of the marble columns which lined the long corridor. Watched as she'd exited Elisha's bedroom and walked with slow steps towards his bedchamber. She'd hesitated for so long outside his door before going in, that Metellus had been tempted to make his presence known.

But he hadn't. And then, when she had finally opened the door and stepped into his bedchamber, he'd let out a rush of air he hadn't even known he'd been holding in.

A slight noise interrupted his thoughts, as Livia moaned something in her sleep before she straightened her legs and turned over onto her back.

Lust slammed into him like a vicious blow to the stomach when he saw that the thin material of her gown did nothing to hide the lushness of her body. He could see the hardness of her nipples pushing impudently at the material, the thin cotton clinging to her long slim legs making him hard with longing. More than anything he wanted to go over to her, wrap his arms around her, press his body – his fully aroused body – against hers and make love to her all night long until both his mind and body were sated once and for all.

He inhaled, taking in the subtle aroma of her body, fighting the temptation to crawl into his bed and make love to her. He lifted one hand and raked it through his hair, rubbing the tension which pooled at the back of his neck. He realised with a start, that he'd never watched a woman sleep before. He had always left after having sex. It was his way of ensuring no woman ever got under his skin.

He grimaced. Hah! Who was he trying to fool? One night wouldn't be enough. He knew with a certainty he would want her again. And again. There was no denying Livia – his wife – had *definitely* burrowed deep under his skin.

Sighing, he turned and left the bedroom, making his way to the *tablinum*. Once inside the room he walked over to a sideboard and poured himself a goblet of wine, frowning in annoyance at the way his hands shook. He swallowed the wine in one go, before he poured himself another. This time he sipped it, savoured it, hoping the alcohol would ease the tension inside him.

But it didn't, and his mouth twisted in derision. Never in all of his adult life had one woman affected him as much as Livia did.

He'd had other women, of course he had. The men who worked for him, constantly teased him about his good looks which brought women flocking to the docks just to get a glimpse of him. Women of all ages watched him, smiled at him, encouraged him, offered themselves to him. And sometimes, when the need for sex had eaten away at him, he'd taken what they offered, satisfying them both.

But he was also blunt, to the point of rudeness, with the women who came into his life. He offered only his body, nothing else. And as long as they knew where they stood with him, then, and only then, did he take them to his bed.

He had been without a woman for nearly a year until he'd made love to Livia on the island. His work commitments had driven him hard this past year, to the exclusion of everything. Ever since he'd heard rumours of the *Drusii* fortune being whittled away, he'd been more determined than ever to make as much money as possible in order to buy what he needed, and implement his plans for revenge.

A noise behind him distracted him, and he turned round, thinking for a moment it might be Livia. But when he saw his mother standing there his shoulders slumped, and he called himself all kinds of a fool for even contemplating that Livia would come to him. *She* had no reason to seek him out, no reason whatsoever.

"What ails you mother?" he finally asked, seeing the frown of concern on her face.

"Nothing. Well—" She stopped, lifting her hands up in a gesture of frustration.

"Mother," Metellus said calmly, seeing the concern darken the grey of her eyes. "Tell me what is wrong."

His mother wrung her hands, indecision flashing across her expressive face, before she blurted out. "I...I want to know why you married Livia?"

His jaw tightened, and he turned away to pour himself another goblet of wine, but not before he saw sadness, and disappointment cross her face.

Inwardly he fumed with anger. Not with his mother, but with himself. He realised he shouldn't have brought Livia here. He should have taken her to his apartments in Rome instead, and just sent his mother a message informing her he had married. Yes, it was the coward's way, but maybe it would have been for the best. Sighing, he turned to face her. "My marriage has nothing to do with you—"

"Oh Metellus, of course it has!" He saw the hurt on his mother's face as she looked up at him. "I knew what you were planning the moment I saw her. I remember Livia's mother from when we were children growing up in Rome, and Livia is the spitting image of her."

In her distress she laid her hand on Metellus's arm, the gesture one of pleading, "This is all about your desire for revenge isn't it?" And not giving him a chance to respond she pressed on, "But why, Metellus? This has nothing to do with Livia. It is not Livia's fault who her father is. Metellus, you need to forget the past, for the sake of your marriage. If you don't, the hatred you feel inside will drive her away. Is that what you want?"

For a long while Metellus didn't answer her. Instead he walked over to the window and stared with sightless eyes out into the darkness beyond. He heard the soft silk of his mother's gown as she came up beside him. Once again she placed her hand on his forearm.

"Please stop with this madness, Metellus," her tone was soft, pleading as she tried to get through to her son. "Will your desire for revenge bring your father back? No it won't. Livia is the innocent party here. She has nothing to do with the past. A past which has festered within you for too long now. Beware of revenge, Metellus. It can sometimes twist around and bite you when you least suspect it. And bite hard."

Metellus said nothing as he listened to his mother speak. She had been saying more or less the same thing to him for the past ten years, ever since he had told her he intended to atone for his father's death. His mother wanted him to forget the past, to put it behind him. But he couldn't. The day of his father's arrest and subsequent execution was indelibly branded on his brain, buried so deep inside him that it could never be dislodged. Never.

It was something he would never forget, and he'd promised to avenge his father's death – even if it took him a lifetime to do so.

"Livia doesn't deserve this," Antonia repeated, breaking the silence between the two of them, "She is an innocent—"

"Enough, mother. This does not concern you." His words were harsh, and guilt made him lash out. Even though he knew she spoke the truth, he refused to be distracted from his life's chosen course. Yes, Livia was the innocent party, but nonetheless she was a *Drusii*.

He heard his mother's sharp intake of breath at the abruptness of his voice; and this time he moderated his tone. He didn't want to argue with her, but she needed to know in no uncertain terms that he was not going to back down. "My marriage to Livia is my business, and mine alone. I would be grateful if you could respect that."

And, before she could say anything more, he walked out of the room without a backward glance.

CHAPTER 16

The dream was one of the best she had ever had.

Feather light kisses trailed slowly over her face, came to rest for a brief moment on her closed eyelids, before they once more made their way over the smoothness of her face, down until they reached the throbbing pulse in her neck.

Livia arched in response to the silent demand of that mouth… and the silent demand of it was everything she had waited for.

For an eternity it seemed.

She felt as if she were floating in warm water, as warm lips soothed and caressed her skin. The sensations were wonderful, sublime, and she never wanted them to end. Every nerve ending she possessed fired into life when the mouth finished its exploration of her neck and moved downwards, with infinite slowness, to the deep valley of her collarbone. She could taste and smell the heady scent of warm male skin, and her hands lifted upwards without conscious thought.

A smile stole over her face, and with a feather light touch she let her fingertips roam over male shoulders, feeling every sinew and muscle bunching and flexing beneath her hands. She felt strong hands slide around, and under her back, lifting her, making her back arch off the bed so her body moulded against warm, male flesh.

Her nipples hardened, pushed against the silk of her gown as they made contact, and a small moan of pleasure escaped when the wet heat of his mouth found one of them. She grew hot and feverish as he suckled her, and her hands lifted to the back of his head, pulling him even closer to her if that were possible. His mouth moved to the other breast, suckling, biting, nipping, demanding a response from her, and heat pooled into her lower belly, pulsed right through her, bringing her body to life.

Time became suspended. Oh, he was good. So very good this dream lover of hers. His mouth knew *exactly* what to do to bring her to the precipice, and when his mouth left her breasts and descended lower, she became nothing more than a molten mass of hot seething emotions.

His mouth came to rest at the top of her thighs where the silk of her night gown had bunched. His hands slipped underneath, pushing the fabric ever upwards allowing him access to her body, the callouses on his fingers scraping across her sensitised skin, as the coolness of the night air caused her to shiver in delicious anticipation. She groaned as his mouth found the bare skin of her stomach, kissing and nipping at the sensitive skin, her body arching and writhing, desperate to communicate her desire for him without words. She never wanted this dream to end. She wanted it to last forever. This was like nothing she had ever experienced before. Well, not since the time on the island when—

The island! Reality returned and crashed around her, and her eyes flew open. This wasn't a dream. This was now, and she stiffened, unsure what was happening.

"Quiet now, there is no need to be afraid."

Metellus's words reverberated in the stillness of the darkened bed chamber. It took a moment for her eyes to adjust to shadowed darkness, and when they did she swallowed hard. Metellus was leaning over her, his arms braced on either side of her hips, so close she could feel the heat of his body. She tried to sit up, but she couldn't. Instead she placed a hand on the hard expanse of

164

muscle on his chest and pushed him away.

Or tried too. But the hard muscular wall refused to move, and Livia's eyes met his as he loomed over her, unyielding, unmoving.

"It's too late, Livia. Far too late."

She heard the huskiness in his voice, the passion, the intensity, and she watched mesmerised as he inched upwards before his mouth descended towards hers.

"No. No I don't want this." She heard the desperation in her voice, but knew it was futile.

"I think you do, Livia. I think you do."

And then his lips met hers, the coolness of them re-affirming those feelings she'd experienced a few minutes ago. And of their own free will her eyes closed and her mouth opened, and as if by tacit agreement he kissed her hard, stamping his authority, his lips firm, demanding against hers. His tongue plundered the softness of her mouth time and time again and there was nothing her traitorous body, and mind, could do about it.

And as he kissed her with an intensity which was frightening, as well as exciting, she realised he was right. She *did* want this. She did want him, and a pang of longing assailed her.

She heard the silk of her night gown rip, as Metellus, impatient for her, tore it away from her body, revealing all of her nakedness to his eyes.

"Yes," he hissed, "Open yourself for me. Give yourself to me,"

Livia, no longer able to resist him, did as he bid. She arched her back to give him full access, gloried in the feel of his mouth as it trailed down her neck to find the aching fullness of her breasts once more. He suckled, laved, worshipped them, until she was no longer able to deny him anything, and when, with a firm but gentle movement of his knees, nudged her thighs apart, and slid into her wet warmth, she couldn't help the small cry of pleasure which escaped from her mouth.

"Let yourself go, Livia," Metellus whispered against the softness of her neck, his teeth nipping and biting the delicate skin. The sensations were such that they were part pleasure, part pain. She was vaguely aware he would leave his mark on her neck, visible for all to see, like some brand of possession, but she was too far gone to care, too caught up in the sheer hedonistic pleasure his mouth and body were inflicting on her.

His hips started to move, pushing him further, deeper inside her; the motion demanding a response from her, and with an uninhibited movement she lifted her legs, wrapping them around him, the movement pulling him deeper into her body, giving him the pleasure he sought as well. She heard him groan, and the rocking of his body grew intense.

The powerful thrusting brought her to the edge of sanity, and she tried to hold onto the wonderful feelings coursing through her body – greedy for it all – greedy for more – But then she fell apart in his arms, unable to hold back as wave after wave of ecstasy slammed into her, carrying her away with the intensity of her orgasm. Her body pulsed around his erection, milking him and she watched in stunned fascination as Metellus, too, lost control.

Watched as he flung his head backwards, his teeth bared, the corded muscles of his throat straining as his body convulsed deep inside her, as he too found the ultimate release his body craved. He was, at that exact moment, man at his most primitive, and it made her feel powerful that she had made him so.

It was only when her heart had returned to some sort of normality, that she finally met his eyes. He was staring at her with an intensity that went bone deep, causing Livia to shiver. He felt it, and she watched in fascination as his eyes narrowed. His body was still intimately joined with hers, his weight heavy as he lay fully on top of her. For a long moment he didn't move but then he lifted himself up with his arms, the muscles bunching as he did so, and started to withdraw from the warmth of her body, slow by slow inch, watching her all the while as he did so. It was such a personal moment, designed to show her it was his right to be here in their bed.

Livia licked her lips, unable to look away, as he moved off her. She thought he might leave her now, leave the bedroom, now he'd had her body, but he didn't. Instead he levered himself away from her, and lay down next to her, propping himself up on one elbow to watch her.

Neither of them said anything for a long time, and it wasn't until he broke eye contact with her, and swept his gaze over her naked body that she realised what he wanted. *Surely he didn't want her body again? So soon after… But the heat and hunger in his eyes gave him away.*

Unsure what he wanted from her, she lifted the thin silk sheet, her movements jerky, as she covered her breasts to hide herself from him. But as the silk grazed her erect nipples, she was reminded that her breasts were still sensitised after the recent onslaught of his mouth.

"What do you want of me?" she finally managed to whisper.

He didn't answer for a long time, before he drawled, "You. I want you. You are my wife, and it is my right."

His voice was measured, controlled, without emotion and Livia bristled at the tone. Gone was the passionate man who'd shared himself with her only minutes ago, now replaced by a cold hard stranger. And once again she felt her heart shatter into a million pieces.

"Right? I don't—"

"I want a son, Livia. You will give me a son," he said, interrupting her faltering words.

"No." The word was forced past the tightness of her suddenly dry throat, and her eyes widened when she saw the hard resolve on his face. "You married me for revenge. Only for revenge. You never said anything about children—"

"I want a son, Livia," he repeated, "And you will give me one."

She closed her eyes, pain lancing through her. *Was this the way it was going to be between them? A marriage which was nothing but a battleground?*

Her eyes snapped open, meeting his watchful gaze. "I am not a brood mare, Metellus…to…to be serviced by you so you can fulfil your sick desire for revenge." And with that, she jumped out of the bed, swept the thin silk cover off the bed, and wrapped it around her naked body. Without a backward glance and purposeful strides she walked over to the door with the intention of leaving the room and sleeping with Elisha if she had to.

But she wasn't quick enough. She had only made it halfway across the room when she felt his hand grip her upper arm, spinning her around so she faced him. With his other hand he held onto her waist, pulling her into the hardness of his naked, and aroused body.

"You will stay in this room with me, Livia," the words were brisk, commanding, and not to be disobeyed. "You will sleep in *this* bed, with *me*, every night until I tell you otherwise. Do you understand?"

Livia didn't answer him, instead she tried to pull away from him, but it was futile, his grip didn't loosen on her arm, or her waist, and she didn't have the strength to pull away. Righteous anger surged through her, but she refused to be dominated. Looking up into his closed face she spat, "Oh I understand all too well, Metellus. I just hope you know what you are doing."

At her words he stepped back, releasing both her arm and her waist before walking without a backward glance back to the bed.

By letting her go, he was asserting his authority over her. She recognised the power games being played out between them, her eyes unable to look away from the perfection of his muscular back, his taut buttocks and long firm legs before he leapt back onto the bed. With a mocking smile, he sat up against the ornate headboard, uncaring that he was still naked, before he patted the empty space next to him.

The action was deliberate, designed to set the ground rules between them. For several long moments she stood there, wondering if she should refuse him, thwart him. But she knew the reality of disobeying him, antagonising him. He would only come and get her from wherever she ran. So, with a shrug of indifference she was far from feeling, she walked back to the bed and climbed in beside him. For several minutes she lay there flat on her back, staring up at the bronze rafters high in the ceiling, her body stiff and unyielding, wondering what Metellus would do next.

But after a few minutes of silence, she heard his deep and even breathing. Her head whipped around, and her eyes took in what her ears had not quite believed. Metellus was fast asleep!

Should she defy him? Leave the room and sleep with Elisha? But she had the strange feeling, that even though he was fast asleep, if she left the room he would somehow know and wake up. So, instead of bolting from the room, she turned away from his sleeping form, unwrapped the silk sheet from around her body and pulled it up to her chin willing herself to fall sleep. Surprisingly, the deepness of Metellus's breathing seemed to act as a soothing balm to her sensitised nerves, and she felt her eyelids close, as fatigue, caused by the excesses of a long day and night finally caught up with her. Within minutes she was asleep.

Livia opened her eyes, watching as the sunlight filtered in through the open window, casting shadow and light in equal measure. For a moment confusion addled her brain. Surely the sun didn't shine so brightly in her bedchamber at this time in the morning? Then reality dawned, and she sat bolt upright in bed. Of course! She wasn't in her father's villa anymore, she was at Metellus's farm *and* she was in his bed!

With a quick jerk of her head she glanced to her left, and saw with a small measure of relief, that Metellus wasn't there. Her hand reached out, her fingers tracing the indentation of where his head had rested on the silk pillow beside her, and she had to fight the urge to lift it to her face and smell the unique scent of him.

Groaning, she flopped back down on the bed staring sightlessly up at the ceiling, as her mind relived the events of last night. There was no denying they had given each other pleasure, immense pleasure, and a sudden flush of heat covered her whole body.

Well, it very much looked like she would have to remain in this bed every night if Metellus had meant what he'd said last night. His orders has been clear enough. She was to provide him with a son.

And then what? Would she be free to leave? Surplus to requirements? "It's not right," she said out loud in the stillness of the room, "Not right at all." *But what could she do about it?* "Nothing," she whispered, "Nothing at all…"

Her mind whirled in confusion as she remembered all they had shared last night. Their lovemaking was every bit as good as it had been on the island. More so, if the truth be told, as a soft bed was a lot more comfortable for making love on, than a thin cloak on the hard ground outside their cave! But it wasn't just the comfort of a soft bed either. Their lovemaking last night had been more intense, more emotional, more *everything*, than what they had shared that first time.

So why give her passion, when he could just as easily take? Surely, if he wanted revenge against her, and more specifically her family, he could just take her, use her, and not care one bit if she found pleasure in his arms or not? She blew out a puff of air in vexation as she realised she didn't have any answers or explanations for *any* of the questions she had just posed to herself.

Metellus was, she realised, a man of many contradictions, and a man of many complex layers. She'd heard horror stories of women marrying their husbands, only to find themselves treated abominably by them. Beaten, half starved to death, and some had even been killed at the hands of their husbands. The Emperor Nero had murdered his wife hadn't he? And if *that* wasn't bad enough, some husbands had even killed their new born babies. Livia was well aware of the tradition which allowed men to either reject, or accept, a new-born child, literally having the power of life or death over them. But Metellus had shown nothing but kindness when it came to Elisha. He could easily have got rid of the baby – exiled her somewhere – as Flavius had threatened to do.

Elisha had been lucky. Metellus had accepted her without a qualm, and she knew she should be grateful for that. Not many men would have been as forgiving as he had been.

Thinking of the baby, or more specifically, *their* baby, Livia couldn't stop a shiver of apprehension. Metellus wanted a son - and soon by all accounts. But she hadn't told him of her fears about becoming pregnant – or rather the actual act of childbirth itself.

Should she tell him, her mother had died in childbirth giving birth to her, and her father, eaten up with grief at the time, had refused to accept her? Would he offer her any sympathy if she told him, that for virtually all of her life she'd had no contact with him, having been raised by slaves, as if both her father, and her step-brother, had forgotten her very existence?

It was only when she had become a commodity of sorts, to be bartered on the marriage stakes to the highest bidder, that they had become aware of her worth to them. And at the time it had been a bitter potion to swallow. She had been heartbroken when her father had told her she was to marry the elderly Senator Galvus, and no amount of begging, or pleading, had altered her father's course of action at the time. She was expendable. To be used for his political gain and nothing more.

And what if history were to repeat itself? What if she did get pregnant – and being a healthy specimen of womanhood – there was no reason to suspect she wouldn't – and what if like her mother, she died in childbirth? Would he look after the baby – girl or boy – and Elisha as well?

Livia curled both her fists and thumped them down on the feather filled mattress. *Was she being selfish to think such thoughts?* She realised with a jolt that she could already be pregnant. Metellus had used no protection – protection she knew existed - if the whispers of the women at the Baths were to be believed.

The thought of Metellus's child growing inside her right now caused a warm glow to flow through her. There was no denying she had wanted Metellus last night with a primal longing, a need so intense she hadn't been able to stop herself coming apart in his arms just as she had the first time they had made love.

Livia sighed, swallowing the lump of emotion which seemed to have lodged itself deep inside her throat. There was no getting away from it, *and* she was only denying it to herself anyway, but she was still in love with Metellus. Deeply, irrevocably in love with her handsome husband. A husband who wanted her for only two reasons. Revenge, and the necessity of providing him with a son.

The knock on the door distracted her out of her dark musings. She stiffened, thinking for a moment it was Metellus, but she realised *he* wouldn't have knocked, *he* would have barged in without hesitation.

"Enter," she called out, relaxing somewhat when she saw the wet nurse enter the bedchamber. She held a crying Elisha in her arms, and getting out of bed, Livia wrapped the silk sheet around herself, and padded over to the older woman, "What ails her? Is she ill?"

"I do not know, mistress, she has had some milk but still she cries."

Livia held out her arms and the wet nurse – Addie – handed her over. Immediately the baby stopped crying, and the tension inside Livia disappeared as she looked down at her. Elisha was looking up at her with wide brown eyes, and Livia smiled, before she looked over at Addie once more.

"I think Elisha knows more than we give her credit for, don't you little one?" she crooned. "She realises she's in another strange place, and that I didn't spend much time with her last evening. She needs time to settle into her new home, that's all." And as she rocked the baby, soothing her, she whispered, "Just like us all."

CHAPTER 17

"Livia! Come, come, the food is ready. Sit down, join me, and keep an old woman company on such a glorious morning."

Livia smiled at Metellus's mother, buoyed by her warm greeting. At least someone in this household didn't seem to hold a grudge against her, or her family!

"I'm sorry I am late. Elisha was fretting. I had to calm her down."

"Yes, yes, of course you must. I am so glad to have her here. It is so lovely to once again hold a babe in my arms."

"Has Metellus told—" Livia broke off, unsure what to say, just in case Metellus's mother didn't know all of the facts about Elisha.

"Everything." The whispered word was full of meaning and understanding, and Livia instantly relaxed.

"I think it was so very brave of you to take her in, and look after her. It couldn't have been easy."

Livia smiled, and laughed gently, "The word "brave" does not come into it, Antonia. I promised Elisha's mother I would look after her as best I could." Livia sighed, her shoulders slumping before she continued, "But you are right though. It wasn't easy. There are those in Rome who believed the worst when I arrived back with a small child in my arms."

"Your father?"

Livia shook her head, "No, not my father," and she went on to tell Antonia about her father's illness.

"Oh," Antonia said, once Livia had finished, "I did not realise he was ill. So if not him, then who?"

Livia's lips twisted in derision, "My half-brother, Flavius. It is he who has believed the worst. He, and all the gossips in Rome, think the child is mine."

Antonia laughed, a somewhat hollow sound as her eyes took on a faraway look. "Aye, I know too well the price which has to be paid if you fall foul of the gossips. It happened to me many years ago. It did not bother me so much, but Metellus…"

As Antonia's words trailed off, Livia went hot all over. How stupid of her to rake up the past, "I'm so sorry. I did not mean to offend—"

"My dear Livia, you have not offended me, rest assured. I know of this revenge Metellus insists on pursuing. I do not agree with it, I never have, and I told him so in no uncertain terms last night. "

Antonia smiled, probably at the surprised look which must have appeared on Livia's face, before she leaned across and patted her hand. "Eat now. You must be hungry. I'll wager you had little food yesterday."

Livia didn't see Metellus for the next two days.

It was only when Antonia mentioned in passing, during the evening meal on the second day that Metellus was in Rome meeting with his uncle that she realised where he had gone.

"Verenus needs to be watched you see," Antonia elaborated, a smile on her face. "If he had his way, the villa would be twice the size Metellus wants. Verenus has such ostentatious ways. As one of the principal architects in Rome he likes to build big. But Metellus does not want too grand a villa."

It was obvious from the tone of Antonia's conversation, that she thought Livia knew where Metellus was. Pride kept her quiet. She couldn't bear to tell his mother that Metellus had left without telling her *anything* of his plans, or his whereabouts.

174

But then why should he? He has told you quite clearly what your role is to be. You are to give him a son and nothing more.

"Are you ill, Livia? You have gone quite pale."

Antonia's words brought her back to the present. Smiling across at the older woman, noticing the frown of concern on her kind face, she shook her head, "No. No I am fine. I…I was just wondering when the villa will be completed, that is all." The small lie tripped off her tongue as she tried to placate Antonia.

"I believe we will find out soon enough. Didn't Metellus tell you?" At Livia's frown she continued, "We are to leave for Rome tomorrow morning to meet up with him and Verenus."

Livia blushed in mortification, "Oh. Oh, yes of course. How stupid of me. I am such a goose these days, I…I forgot all about it."

"You are not a goose, my dear. You have had a lot on your mind recently."

Livia looked away, picking up some fruit to occupy her whirling thoughts. *She was to return to Rome? But she had only just left the city. Why did he want her to return to Rome so soon? Didn't he realise she would be an easy target once more for the gossips?* Shock held her still as her mind raced frantically. *Was this part of his revenge, to parade her like some trophy? The ultimate prize in the downfall of her family? Surely he couldn't be so cruel?*

Inwardly she seethed, as the questions she was asking of herself remained unanswered. Livia looked up to see Antonia watching her, a concerned look on her face. If Livia was petty enough to tell her what she suspected Metellus was up to, she knew his mother would be very annoyed with him. But even though it was nice to have an ally in Antonia, she was old enough to fight her own battles. So she kept her own council for now and said nothing.

The next day Livia couldn't control her nerves as she sat atop the wagon once more as it trundled its way back into the city. She hadn't realised how anxious she was about the thought of returning to Rome, *and* having to live in Metellus's new villa. It hadn't helped either, when she had found out Metellus was building his new home in one of the most sought after areas of Rome. The Palatine Hill. And it was going to be a sumptuous villa by all accounts, if Antonia's description of it was anything to go by.

But she knew from experience he was taking a gamble. His desired place in Roman society could all come crashing down – metaphorically speaking – if the people – the *patricians* – in particular, deemed him – them – unsuitable. *Wasn't her own situation enough to warn him?* Livia's rapid descent into ruin, because they had thought she had given birth to a child, was testimony as to fickle nature of Rome's elite.

Sighing, she blocked all thoughts of what had happened to her out of her mind, and concentrated on soothing Elisha who was fretting.

"Shall I take her?"

Livia turned to where Antonia sat next to her, and smiled her thanks as she handed the baby over.

Eventually, they pulled up outside a half-finished villa, and as Livia dismounted, her eyes widening as she took in the sheer size of the building. Antonia had not exaggerated the size of the place.

"I never realised it would be so large. I thought—"

"You thought I was just a poor humble merchant."

Livia gasped, turning to see Metellus standing behind them. *Where on earth had he come from?* Annoyed with him for sneaking up on them, and still cross with him for leaving her without saying where he was going, Livia firmed her chin and said, "That is not what I was going to say, Metellus. You seem to misjudge me all the time."

"Do I?" And before she could react to his words, he leaned forward, cupped her chin, and kissed her. The heat from his lips seared through her like a burning flame and Livia gasped into his mouth. But the kiss ended as quickly as it begun as Metellus stepped away from her. A brief smile played over his mouth before he murmured, "Welcome, wife. Welcome to your new home."

Livia bit down hard on her bottom lip, unsure what to say or do next, as an awkward silence fell between them. She felt hot colour flood her face as his eyes roamed over her, undressing her, as if he wanted nothing more than to take her in his arms and carry her to the nearest bed.

Thankfully, the tension was broken, when Antonia asked, "Is Verenus here yet?"

Metellus reluctantly pulled his eyes away from Livia's, and answered his mother, "Yes, he is inside. Doing what he does best. Organising people."

Livia raised an eyebrow at the dry tone she heard in Metellus's voice, and Antonia laughed, "Yes, that sounds like Verenus. I will go and find him. You show Livia around the villa, and we will all meet up later." And with that, Antonia walked away from them both, still carrying Elisha, seemingly content to carry on looking after the baby.

"Would you like to see the villa?"

Livia looked away from Antonia's retreating back, to find Metellus watching her, a closed look on his face. She felt her heart jerk, before it started to beat a rapid tattoo against her breastbone as she remembered the last time he watched her...the night they had made love. And, as if he could read her mind, he smiled down at her and lifted his hand, stroking his finger over her still flushed cheeks. The caress was soft, gentle, and it awakened a multitude of emotions within her.

"I like it when you blush, it makes me feel wanted."

Livia looked away, unsure why he was teasing her. This light hearted banter was alien to her, and she didn't quite know how to deal with it – or him – for that matter. But she had to acknowledge, it made a change from his normal acerbic nature.

"The...the villa," she stuttered, trying to focus on the matter in hand, "I would love to have a look around."

Metellus gave one of his enigmatic smiles, and after giving her a slight bow he said, "Of course, follow me. The majority of the building work is finished, apart from the kitchens and slave quarters. Then all that is needed is to paint both the inside and outside and furnish it."

As Metellus walked her through the impressive villa, she was amazed at the size and opulence of it; although, she was pleased to see, it didn't appear as ostentatious as her own family villa.

The rooms that had been finished were all tastefully done, and she was thankful for that, as she didn't really see Metellus as the sort of man who demanded excess when it came to outdoing all the other wealthy families of Rome.

Which was in complete contrast to how her father and Flavius were, she thought. Everything in the *Drusii* family villa had been about out-doing their friends and rivals, buying the latest statues, commissioning the most sought after artist to do a mural on a wall, all designed for maximum exposure so when anyone came to the villa they would see in an instant that the *Drusii* were one on the most affluent families in all of Rome, and a family to be reckoned with.

"Do you like it?" he asked when they had entered the *triclinium*.

Striving for neutrality she replied, in what she hoped was a normal tone, "What is there not to like. It is a magnificent villa, your uncle has done you proud. He is a very good architect."

"Do I detect a hint of reproach in your voice, Livia?"

Livia looked at him from under her lashes, once again torn by her feelings for him. The twinkle in his eyes belied the dryness of his voice, and she felt a tug of emotion deep in the pit of her stomach.

Trying for a cool tone, in case he guessed her feelings towards him, she shrugged, a mere lift of her shoulders, "I may disappoint you with my response, but I have never been drawn into the subtleties of grandeur and wealth. To me a villa is a home, to be filled with love and laughter. A place where I would want to come home to every day. Not just a decorative shell to be paraded about in the pursuit of wealth and power."

She took a deep breath, before continuing, "That was the type of place I lived in before. Our villa was never a home. Never somewhere where I wanted to live. All it was to me was a place to eat and sleep in. Nothing more."

She stopped speaking when she saw a closed look come over his face. Perhaps she'd said too much? Been too honest. But her resolve hardened her. *He had asked her what she thought hadn't he? And if he didn't like it, then so be it. She wasn't going to lie.* So she took another deep breath and ploughed on. "Is this to be *our* home Metellus, or is all this," she waved her hand expansively to include the whole villa, "Just another piece of ammunition to aid in your overall plan for revenge against my family?" Her question did not sit well with him, if the angry flush of colour staining his sharp cheekbones was anything to go by.

"You go too far, Livia," he bit out finally. "Like I said to you the other night. As your husband, you will obey me, and do as I say. Do you understand? We were married *in manu* – you belong to me. Your family has no control over you anymore."

"I know, Metellus. *That* was not what I was implying. I merely asked if you intend to make this our *home*?"

She saw him rake a hand through the crisp darkness of his thick hair, ruffling it, and Livia had to fight the uncontrollable urge to walk over to him and smooth it down. She resisted. Just.

"Yes, it will be our home, Livia. Have no doubt on that score. As I said earlier, there is still some building works to be done to the rear of the villa, but I am confident we will be in residence in about a month or so. And until then, we are to be the guests at my uncle's villa here in Rome."

"But I thought we would return to your farm?" she asked anxiously, not sure if she was ready to remain in Rome right now.

He shook his head, "No, it is too far away. I have too much work to do here. Supervising the building of the villa, not to mention my business holdings at Ostia harbour makes it impossible to return to the farm any time soon. Besides, I only took you to the farm so you could meet my mother."

"And this will be our room," Metellus said a short while later once they had continued on with their tour.

Livia couldn't stop the ripple of awareness at the softness of his words. As she gazed around the empty room, she knew he was testing her, baiting her, as if he knew *exactly* the effect he was having on her already heightened senses. The *cubica* was massive, the largest of the sleeping rooms and intended to be the master bedroom.

"Yes. So I see." Her words were stilted, and she saw Metellus smile, as if she had amused him for some reason. Turning, she made to leave the room, but Metellus's hand snaked out, grabbing hers, halting her movements. Desire pulsed inside her as she felt the heat, and strength, of his fingers as they meshed with hers.

His eyes bored into her, demanding, and with a woman's instinct she knew what he wanted.

"No."

But her denial was futile. He was the hunter and she the hunted. He wanted her, she could see it in darkened depths of his eyes.

"Yes," he whispered, drawing her further into the room, his eyes never leaving hers as he led her over to the window at the rear of the room.

Livia wasn't quite sure what he was intending to do, so she was unprepared when he lifted her up, his large hands spanning the slimness of her waist, before he sat her on top of the wide window ledge. With his hands still wrapped around her waist, he pulled her forward until their mouths were in touching distance. She could smell his minty breath as his mouth hovered near hers.

"Kiss me," he breathed. "I've missed the pleasure of your mouth these past few days."

Livia's heart accelerated at his husky command, and unable to resist she leaned forward, and this time of her own inclination, she placed her mouth on his.

It was as if he were testing her, waiting to see if she would make the first move and initiate the kiss. And when she did, his tongue snaked out and demanded entrance to the sweetness of her mouth. As one they groaned, as sensation after sensation flowed between them, both of them caught up in the heat of the moment. The kiss seemed to last an eternity as they both took, and gave, of each other.

Metellus's hands lifted, coming to rest on the underside of her breasts, and Livia felt frustration claw at her. Oh, how she wanted to feel the touch of his hand on her breasts. Then, as if her silent communication had somehow reached him, his hands moved upwards and he cupped them both.

"Oh," she breathed, leaning in closer as his long fingers touched the sensitised nipples, causing her to moan into his mouth as Metellus pinched the hard buds, rolling them in his oh, so, malleable fingers. Pleasure, and pain, in equal measure shot through her, as his fingers drew out so many different responses from her she lost all sense of time, and place, as his fingers worked their magic.

Eventually he stopped, his hands moving away from the heated swollen flesh, trailing lower until they reached the soft roundness of her hips.

"I want you, all of you."

"Yes," she whispered, blinded by passion. She felt Metellus lift the hem of her gown, pushing it up over her legs until it pooled around her hips. The slight breeze from the window caused a delicious shiver to run over her as the coolness caressed the sensitised skin of her now bared legs and thighs.

"Lift yourself."

She obeyed his husky command, raising herself up on one hand so he could push the silk fabric of her gown further up so it now bunched around her waist.

The coldness of the marble against the nakedness of her buttocks and thighs had to be one of the most erotic things she had ever experienced, and she shifted slightly to heighten the pleasure now made even more intense when she once again felt Metellus's fingers stroke up and down the long expanse of her thighs. Her wantonness grew with each delicious stroke and touch, his fingers eliciting feelings and sensations she had never experienced before. She heard her breath catch, as if she were on the precipice of something totally new and exciting, and she leaned forward, gripping the hard muscles of Metellus's shoulders, unaware of her nails digging into his flesh.

"Yes!" He groaned against the softness of her neck. "I want you so much."

The words were nearly Livia's undoing, and she let him have what he wanted, spreading her legs, giving Metellus the access he needed as they melted together, his erection pressed against the softness of her belly.

"I...I..." The words she wanted to say froze in her throat, when she saw him remove his tunic in one fluid motion, revealing his naked body to her fascinated gaze. She realised with a sudden sense of awareness, this was the first time she had actually seen him naked in the full light of day, and her glazed eyes took in the bronze smoothness of his chest, so temptingly close to her fingers that she reached out and touched the smooth expanse of hardened muscle. She felt him shiver at the lightness of her touch, and she glanced up, taking in the darkness of his eyes as desire and need flared in them.

"Lower."

The one word, spoken with an intensity that was empowering, caused her hand to still for a moment. She could feel the rapid hammering of his heart under her splayed fingers where they rested on his chest. She knew what he wanted, what he was asking, and without breaking eye contact, she lowered her hand, down over the corded muscles of his abdomen which rippled under her fingers, lower until they encountered the crisp hairs at the top of his thighs. She saw his pupils dilate, daring her, wanting her to go lower.

And she did. She skimmed her fingers over the fullness of his

182

erection, saw his mouth flatten before he hissed his pleasure at what her fingers were doing to him. Feeling emboldened, she trailed her fingers downwards, teasing him, bypassing the thick root of his erection, until she rested her hands on the muscles of his thighs. Thighs which bunched and tightened where her fingers touched and stroked.

She leaned in closer, pressing her lips to where a vein pulsed in the corded muscle of his neck. "Say it," she whispered, "Say 'please'." She felt him stiffen. He obviously didn't like the fact that she was trying to dominate him. Smiling against his skin, she closed her eyes and inhaled the musky scent of him. Then without a thought about how her actions might be perceived, she trailed her tongue down the column of his neck.

The saltiness of his skin was like a powerful aphrodisiac and she felt her insides melt as liquid fire pooled low down in her belly. He felt, and tasted so good, and she wanted to feast on him for eternity. Was it like this for him? Did he want her as much as she wanted him, longed to feel his hands upon her body? She hoped so, for if the feelings were only one way and he didn't reciprocate them, then she was lost.

"Please."

Livia smiled once more, when she heard the growled response to her demand, heard the huskiness of his voice as he voiced his needs. Emboldened once more she moved her hand until she once again wrapped her fingers around the fullness of his erection, amazed at how it felt, strong, yet silken to the touch. Instinctively she tightened her grip, creating a friction which made Metellus moan deep in his throat, amazed to see a dark flush suffuse his face. A rush of feminine power came over her, she literally held him in the palm of her hand and he was totally at her mercy. It was a heady feeling to have such control, such mastery over him.

But her power only lasted a few more moments because Metellus grabbed her hand, stilling her movements. She could feel him throbbing in the palm of her hand, knew he was on the verge of losing control.

"Keep that up and I won't be responsible for my actions," he growled.

With a swiftness she wasn't expecting, he once again took control, pulling her forward, lifting her, the palms of his hands holding the softness of her buttocks, giving him the angle he needed to slide the hardness of his erection into the pulsating soft warmth of her flesh.

Both of them groaned in unison as flesh met flesh, and Metellus pumped his hips, burying himself, seating himself fully within her hot and willing body as she wrapped her legs around his hips, the movement bringing them even closer together.

She felt her body tense, as he rocked against her time and time again, propelling her towards a climax so strong, so intense, she couldn't believe it was happening so fast. A moan of pure pleasure came from deep within her as her orgasm slammed through her, her body squeezing him as she climaxed on a tidal wave of emotion. It was as if her body had started some sort of chain reaction, because she felt Metellus stiffen, and she watched in stunned fascination when his head fell back, the muscles and sinews of his neck standing out in response, as he pumped his body, and his seed, deep inside her.

Emotionally, and physically spent, Livia rested her head on the wide expanse of his shoulder, slowly coming back to reality, aware of the sweat coating his skin, the unique manly scent of him invading her senses…and the even more heady aroma of their combined lovemaking. The silence of the bedchamber broken only by the harsh rasping of their combined breaths. Their bodies were still joined together, the position so intimate she could feel his heart beating against the softness of her breasts.

A loud bang, and a curse from outside the villa, jolted them both out of their passion induced lethargy. Livia stiffened as the ramification of what had just happened, or more pressingly, *where* it had happened impinged on her dazed mind.

184

What if someone had come into the room?

"I have to go. Elisha. She needs me." Livia could hear the panic in her voice, and she stiffened in his arms, gripping the hardness of his upper arms, communicating her need to get away.

For several long seconds he didn't move, but then she felt him pull away, breaking the sexual contact between them, and Livia shivered as the coolness of the room hit her exposed skin. The coldness, a marked contrast to the heat and passion they had just shared.

Refusing to meet his gaze, she jumped off the window sill and hastily rearranged her gown, pushing the silk down, covering her nakedness, aware he was watching her every movement.

Heat flooded her body. *How could she have been so wanton? Let herself go without thinking of the consequences? What if Antonia had come looking for them?!*

Shame coursed through her, as she bent down to pick up one of her sandals which had fallen off during their lovemaking. Unable, and unwilling, to look at Metellus, she ran from the room without a backwards glance.

CHAPTER 18

As soon as Livia walked into the *peristylium* she spotted Antonia sitting on a chair holding Elisha and talking to two older men at the same time. Making the most of the older woman's distraction she halted, took a deep calming breath, patted her hair to ensure it was still in place and stole a quick glance down at her gown. She was relieved to see that it had somehow managed to survive intact during their heated lovemaking, neither ripped nor creased.

Feeling somewhat calmer she walked towards Antonia. As she got closer she noticed Antonia looked a little perplexed, a frown marring the elder woman's brow, and when she saw Livia coming towards her, a smile of relief came over her face.

"Ahh, Livia. Thank the gods you are here. These men have come with the fabrics needed to furnish the villa. I was originally going to do it on Metellus's behalf, but I thought you might like to choose them instead."

As she spoke, Antonia handed Elisha over to Livia, responding to Livia's open arm gesture. Thankfully, Antonia didn't seem to notice anything amiss, and Livia was relieved at the chance to take her mind off what had just happened with Metellus. *Had she really just made love with her husband in an empty bedchamber in the middle of the day?*

"Yes. Yes of course," she finally replied, "But perhaps you could assist, as I don't really know what furnishings need fabric, or how much is needed."

Her response seemed to please Antonia, and if her words seemed a little stilted, Metellus's mother didn't seem to notice. And so, for the rest of the day, both women worked side by side, choosing and picking out the fabrics needed for the villa. Once they had finished, they made the short walk to Verenus's villa.

"I understand Verenus has invited several acquaintances to dine with us tonight – a sort of wedding celebration for you and Metellus," Antonia said, as they arrived at the gates of Verenus's villa.

Taken aback, Livia stammered, "Metellus never said anything to me about this."

Antonia smiled, "That is because he does not know about it. It was to be a surprise for you both, but I thought you would like some advance warning so you can prepare yourself. I know if it had been me, I would have wanted to know. You don't object to me telling you do you?"

Livia saw a worried look steal over Antonia's face, and held out her hand, taking the older woman's hand in hers. "No. No not at all. You are very kind to tell me. Is it to be a large gathering?"

"Oh no! Nothing too grand at all. No more than fifteen people I would imagine."

As they walked through the villa – a very sumptuous villa – as would befit an architect of Verenus's standing, Livia was approached by a slave who had been instructed to show Livia the *cubica* Elisha was to sleep in. As she entered the room she found Addie the wet nurse in attendance, and smiling her thanks, she handed Elisha over to her. As she left the baby in the woman's capable hands, the slave then showed her the bedchamber allocated to her and Metellus.

Once the slave had left her alone in the room, she leaned back against the closed door, taking in the opulence of the room. Like her father's villa, no expense had been spared in the lavish decorations adorning the room. But the one thing that captivated her the most was the bed. Raised on a dais, the huge bed dominated the room. Silk covers, and matching cushions, the colour of peaches adorned the bed, whilst suspended above it was a swathe of silk drapes. There was no doubt this bed was made for loving…for sharing the intimacies between a man and a woman.

She prised herself away from the door and walked towards the bed, almost trance like, as if commanded to do so by some unknown force. Trailing her hands over the silk covers, she was tempted to climb up and see if it was as comfortable as it looked.

But she didn't. It was far too tempting, and she was afraid that if she did, sleep would claim her. So instead, she made her way over to where several of her, and Metellus's, trunks sat along the back wall. Opening one of them, she took out a silk gown the colour of emeralds and started to prepare herself for the meal which was to be given in their honour.

Once she had finished bathing, and had donned her gown before rearranging her hair with the help of a slave, she left the bedroom and made her way to the *peristylium* where Antonia had told her to go once she was ready. Of Metellus there had been no sign, and pride prevented her asking any of the slaves if he'd arrived at the villa yet.

Her stomach knotted at the thought of seeing him again. How, in the name of Hades, would she be able to look at him without remembering what had happened between them at their villa this afternoon?

Deep in thought about what had transpired earlier that afternoon, Livia was unprepared for the sudden silence which greeted her when she entered the *peristylium*. It seemed as if everybody stopped talking at once and turned to stare at her. Hot colour surged through her, and her stomach dropped, as she encountered the many gazes of the people assembled there. With a sinking feeling, she realised she knew some of the people present, and if their mocking smiles were anything to go by, *she* was very much the object of their speculation and gossip.

She was saved from further embarrassment when Antonia came to her rescue, taking her hand before leading her over to where an older man stood watching her with a neutral expression on his face.

Verenus. It had to be, Livia thought, as she took in the similarities between him and Metellus. Although not as tall as Metellus, he was still taller than a lot of the men present in the room. Again, he wasn't as broad in the shoulder as her husband, but he still had a commanding presence; a presence accentuated by his greying hair, and piercing blue eyes. Dark blue, the colour of the deepest ocean she noticed, not the silvery grey of Metellus's, and they were trained on hers with an intensity which caused her stomach to knot in tension. For some reason she felt nervous about meeting the man who had effectively raised Metellus; and provided him, and Antonia, with a home.

"Verenus. This is Livia. Metellus's wife. She is a delight, and we are firm friends already," Antonia said, her tone light, as they approached.

Livia saw the older man's eyes narrow as he looked her over, before he masked it by bowing from the waist and taking her hand, pressing a brief kiss on it. As she felt the coldness of his fingers envelop hers, she had to fight the urge to pull her hand away from his. With an intuition she was certain of, she could sense, that for some reason, Verenus did not like her. Instinctively she knew this was one man she wouldn't want to cross, and one she would have to be on her guard around.

"I'll leave you two to get to know each other. I need to speak to Senator Critto," Antonia said once the introductions had been completed, and then she left them alone, unaware of the tension flowing between them.

For a few moments an uncomfortable silence fell until Verenus said, "I have to confess, I was slightly taken aback when I was told of your marriage to Metellus."

"I thought as much." At her words, she saw his eyes narrow,

but before he could say anything she continued, "But I didn't have much choice in the matter. It was decided without any input from myself. As a man of Rome, you should know that."

"Indeed. But it was still a shock." He stared at her for a long moment, before he bit out, "How is your father these days?"

Livia looked at him in askance, wondering at the sudden change in conversation. *Was he probing to find out more about her father's illness, when in reality he knew all about her father's condition?*

Keeping her tone measured and precise she replied, "He has been very ill. For months now." When she saw him frown it became clear that he was taken aback by her words, and Livia had to acknowledge that maybe Verenus *hadn't* known of her father's illness.

Again, it would seem Flavius had done a good job of keeping news of her father's illness quiet to all but his closest allies – quite an achievement in the cut throat arena of the Senate – *and* the gossip filled gatherings of Rome's elite.

"What ails him?"

For a moment she hesitated in telling him, but then she decided that if she didn't tell him, he would only find out from Metellus, so she gave him the brief details of her father's illness.

Verenus listened intently, and when she had finished he stared at her for a long while before he murmured, "I see."

Those two words held a wealth of meaning, and once again Livia wondered what was racing through his brain. She saw his face harden, and his eyes became shards of ice as he glared at her before he murmured in an ominous tone, "I am very fond of my nephew, and my sister-in-law, and I would not want them to come to any harm. You—"

"Harm? Livia spluttered, taken aback by this unprovoked attack on her character, "And how, *sir*, do you think *I* could harm either Metellus or Antonia?"

"I do not trust your father, even if he is as ill as you say. I do not trust your half-brother, and I certainly do not trust you." His words were forced out through gritted teeth, anger flashing in the blue depths of his eyes.

At his words Livia felt tears spring into her eyes, but she forced them back finding an inner resolve. "I would never hurt Antonia. She has been very kind to me," she said passionately. She firmed her chin, and looked him in the eyes, "And as for Metellus. May I suggest *you* ask *him* why he married me, because it is as much a mystery to me, as it is clearly to you? He—"

"Is there a problem, Livia? Uncle?"

Metellus! Her head whipped around, and she saw him standing behind her, his face impassive as he watched them both. Both she, and Verenus, had been so caught up in their argument, neither of them had seen Metellus approach. *How much had he heard?*

"There is nothing wrong, Metellus," Verenus replied cordially, before Livia could say anything. "We were having a healthy discussion on politics. My outdated views, are not Livia's I fear. Your wife is quite charming."

Livia just managed to contain her gasp of astonishment. Verenus had become the perfect gentleman within a heartbeat, and she realised that as well as being a liar, he was a consummate actor. Her intuition had been proved right. She needed to be wary of Verenus. Very wary indeed…

"Now, I will leave you two young people to your own devices. I need to speak to a few people before we eat. I intend to leave Rome in the morning, as I am overseeing the building of a new villa outside Herculaneum. My villa is yours for as long as you need it," then he bowed to them both, before walking away.

As Livia stared after the older man, she couldn't help but be pleased that he was not going to be staying at his villa whilst they were in occupation. She didn't think she could bare his anger, and suspicions, about her family—

"I don't think it was politics' you were discussing with Verenus was it?"

Livia stiffened at the mocking tone of his voice, but not wanting to inflame the tension any further, she shrugged slightly, "It was nothing of any major concern."

She was spared any further questions when the doors to the *triclinium* opened, heralding the commencement of the evening meal, and before Metellus could question her further she asked, "Shall we follow the others in?"

Thankfully, Metellus didn't probe any further, and he offered his arm for her to take as they made their way into the dining room. But when they reached the couches they were to lie on, Metellus leaned in and whispered, "This conversation is not finished, Livia."

It was only when they were lying on the couches, after the evening meal had finished, that Livia was able to relax. Verenus had laid on some entertainment, jugglers and dancers, but in order to accommodate them in the room, the couches had been moved so they were now up against the walls of the room. It also meant Verenus and Antonia were on the other side of the room, seated together, and for the first time that evening she wasn't subject to his hooded stare. It was also during the show that Livia made one startling discovery...

Verenus seemed to be totally besotted with Antonia.

As she watched him from under her long lashes, she saw he couldn't take his eyes off her. He seemed to hold onto every word Antonia said, seemed to drink in the beauty of the older woman as she conversed with him, and several other people around her.

The longer she observed them she realised that Antonia seemed oblivious of Verenus's infatuation with her, and as she looked around the room she wondered if she was the only one to see it. Again, call it a woman's intuition, but Livia was convinced Verenus was in love with his sister-in-law—

"You left very quickly this afternoon. I trust you had no ill effects?"

Livia snapped out of her reverie, glancing sideways to see Metellus propped up on one elbow watching her, a goblet of wine in his hand. Livia blushed, as she was once again reminded of the wanton way she'd behaved earlier.

Striving for calm, and trying to control the sudden thudding of her heart, she smiled up at him and said flippantly, "No ill effects. And you?"

Metellus threw back his head and laughed, and Livia saw several people turn to watch them. It was obvious they were the couple of the moment, and Livia knew that everything they said, and did tonight, would be recalled in minute detail, and talked about on the morrow.

"No, Livia. No ill effects whatsoever. Quite the opposite in fact. It was the best sex I've ever had."

"Metellus!" Livia gasped, unable to stop the flush of colour staining her cheeks, and again Metellus laughed at the shocked expression on her face.

"I like to tease you, Livia. You are so easy to tease." He leaned forward and whispered, "And I like it when you laugh and smile. But best of all, I like the little noises you make in the back of your throat when we make love," he lifted a shoulder, "It was such a shame I had important business to attend to this afternoon, otherwise..."

The huskiness of his voice, and the way he was looking at her with undisguised longing, was nearly Livia's undoing. She had to resist the urge to lean forward and kiss him. But she didn't of course. This was hardly the place to do so – not with so many prying eyes watching them – Verenus included – if the dark looks he was shooting over at them was anything to go by. Instead, she leaned forward and picked up her wine goblet, looking at Metellus from under her lashes.

He looked very handsome this evening, and she would have had to be blind not to notice the covert looks the other women were giving him, as he lounged on the couch next to her. Dressed in a dark blue tunic of the finest silk, the fabric moulded his strong muscular physique, and she had to stop herself from reaching out and running her hands over his chest—

"If you keep looking at me like that, I won't be responsible for my actions, Livia. And, I think *your* embarrassment will be far greater than mine, if I were to carry you away right now, and take up where we left off this afternoon."

His words were whispered close to her ear. Unconsciously, her tongue wet her suddenly parched lips at the thought of him carrying out his threat. She watched, as his eyes lowered to her mouth and for a moment a long, heavy silence hung between the two of them.

It was Livia who looked away first, to stare across the room to where the dancers were performing, forcing her mind away from the thrill of his words. It was only when the dancers had finished, and had left the room that Livia risked glancing around the room watching the assorted guest's converse with each other. There was definitely a relaxed atmosphere in the room, everyone seeming to have enjoyed the food, and entertainment, which had been laid on.

All except the host, she realised with a start, when she met Verenus's dark brooding gaze once more.

Her eyes widened when she saw the hostile look he shot at her. Why did he hate her so? It didn't make sense. Surely, he must know she wasn't a threat to him – or to Metellus and Antonia? The only logical reason must be that he hated her family, as much as Metellus did. It seemed that only Antonia was prepared to accept her, and welcome her into their lives. Refusing to succumb to his dark looks any longer, she turned away, breaking eye contact with him, and pretended an interest in the conversation Metellus was having with another guest who sat on the other side of him.

Thankfully, the rest of the evening went without any more mishap, as Metellus never left Livia's side for the duration of the gathering, and towards the end of the evening she found herself relaxing for the first time in his company.

Perhaps, she thought, their marriage might not be the sham she first thought it would be. With time could Metellus come to like her? To love her even? She prayed that someday he would forgive, and forget, the vendetta he held against her family.

Maybe with time…?

CHAPTER 19

The next three weeks passed without mishap, the days following a set routine of sorts.

In the mornings, Livia spent time with Elisha, and in the afternoons, she and Antonia would venture out, either to the Forum to shop, or to go to the Baths, before going to Metellus's villa to see the building work in progress. The builders were progressing well; they had now half completed the kitchen and slave quarters. The villa still needed furnishing, as many of the rooms were still bare.

Livia enjoyed the time she spent with Antonia, both of them enjoying each other's company, and Livia liked to think they had become firm friends.

Verenus, thankfully, was absent from his villa, having left as planned the following morning after their wedding celebration. He was working on a huge project, Antonia had told her, building a new country villa for a rich Senator whose villa in Herculaneum had been destroyed when Mount Vesuvius had erupted last year.

As for Metellus, he left early in the mornings to go to his warehouses located near the port at Ostia, and didn't return to the villa until late in the evening. His businesses were varied and complex she had found out, as well as wine and papyrus paper, he had diversified into other desired commodities such as silks and spices.

This had all come about because of the trade routes which had opened up with India, now that mariners had discovered how to sail with the trade winds. It meant shipments of silk could now be done by sea all year round, rather than having to rely on the land route, which had been the only way to transport silk to Rome up until quite recently.

Livia found this all extremely interesting, and she had to fight the urge to go to the warehouses and see it all in action. She knew, as a woman, she had no role to play in the male dominated field of commerce. Being a merchant was strictly men's business, and she found this quite frustrating. When she'd lived at her father's villa she had helped run the household, organising everything which went with keeping a villa of that size going. She had found it a useful way of occupying her time, and unlike her friend Portia, she didn't like to spend the whole day shopping, or being fitted out for the latest gowns, much preferring to use her brain for more practical purposes.

"Do you wish for more wine, mistress?"

The slave's words jolted her out of her revere, and she shook her head. "No. No. You may retire now."

Livia hadn't realised how long she had been sitting there, until she noticed with a start of surprise that the moon had risen high in the night sky. Hopefully, Metellus would be home soon. She sighed, and getting up from where she had been sitting in the coolness of the *atrium* she wandered through the quiet villa towards their bedchamber.

As she sat on their bed a few minutes later she had to admit to being bored. The long evenings seemed to drag indeterminably. Elisha was asleep, and Antonia had retired to her rooms, or was still out with friends, and Livia often found herself growing more and more restless as she waited for Metellus to return from his work.

And as she thought of him she couldn't stop a small smile…

If the days had been predictable, then so too had the nights!

Metellus had made love to her every night so far, since they had come to stay in Verenus's villa, and he didn't seem to be tiring of

196

her. He had taught her how to enjoy her body – awakening desires and longings in her she never thought capable of.

They made love with an intensity which stunned them both. Time and time again she cried out her pleasure, her voice hoarse in the night's silence, as shifting pangs of pleasure hit them both until, he too, cried out his release, flinging back his head and arching his back as he spilled his seed inside her. And then afterwards, their heart beats still thundering, he would turn onto his side and pull her into his body, his chin resting on top of her shoulder, the heat of his breath whispering across the dewy coated skin of her neck-

A knock on the door cut off her heated thoughts. "Come," she called out and the door opened to admit a young boy slave.

The boy bowed, "Mistress, you have a visitor."

"Who is it?" she asked, frowning slightly, as she wasn't expecting anyone—

"The man says he is your brother, Mistress. He is waiting in the *peristylium* for you."

Livia's eyebrows shot up. *What on earth was Flavius doing here, and why?* Absently, she nodded her thanks at the slave, and he bowed once more before he took his leave.

For a long moment she sat on her bed, wondering what to do, and also remembering the last time she had seen Flavius; and the ugly words which had been exchanged between them. It was obvious something major must have happened for him to come here to see her—

Her father! Livia stood quickly as a feeling of foreboding came over her. She ran shaking hands over the silk of her gown, composing herself before she exited the bedroom and hurried down the corridor. When she walked into the *peristylium* her heart sank. Instead of seeing remorse, and grief on Flavius's face, all she saw was anger and frustration.

For a heartbeat they stood there, adversaries ready to do battle, and when she saw the look of distain cross his face, as if coming here was as loathsome as something he'd trod in as he walked along the rubbish strewn streets of *Suburbia*, she stiffened, her chin lifting in defiance.

"Flavius," Livia said, her tone wary as she came further into the room, determined not to let him intimidate her.

Flavius ignored her greeting, and snapped out, "Father wishes to see you. Now."

"Father has recovered?" she gasped, "B...but I thought—"

"He has started to speak," Flavius said, interrupting her, before he shrugged, "It is sometimes hard to understand him, but if you listen carefully you can just make out most of what he is trying to say."

"But why does he want to see me now? For years he has ignored me, denied my very existence. What does he want with me now?" Her voice, she noticed, was hoarse with anguish, but if she expected any sympathy from Flavius, she was very much mistaken.

Dark colour suffused Flavius's face, and she saw his hands fist with anger as he tried to hold onto his temper. "I do not know, Livia," he bit out. "And in truth, I do not care. He asked me to come here to pass his message to you in person, and I have done as he asked. Now come, the hour grows late."

Of course! Livia thought, anger replacing anguish. Flavius wouldn't have come here of his own free will! It had only been because their father has requested it, that he'd deigned to step foot in this villa.

Resolve hardened her, before she said flatly, "I will come tomorrow when—"

"Now, Livia," Flavius interjected, cutting off her words with a slash of his hand.

"But...I..." Livia's words trailed off when she saw the anger flare in his eyes. Sighing, she acquiesced to his demand, and said with quiet dignity, "Yes, of course. I will come right away. Let me get my *palla*, and I will be right with you." Without waiting for a response, she left the room and went in search of Antonia.

Unfortunately, there was no sign of Antonia, and a slave

confirmed Metellus's mother was out visiting an acquaintance. Indecision caused her to hesitate for a moment, then she gave instructions to the slave to tell Antonia where she was going. For some reason she was reluctant to tell the slave to pass her message onto Metellus, and besides, if she were quick enough she should be back in time before Metellus finished work for the day.

The journey to her father's villa was conducted in total silence, with Flavius ignoring her all the way as they walked the short distance from Verenus's villa to their father's. Livia bit back a sigh of resignation. It would appear any sign of a truce between her, and her half-brother was never going to happen, and she couldn't help but wonder what her father wanted with her. Now, for the first time in living memory, he actually wanted to speak to her. The daughter he had, for all intents and purposes abandoned at birth…

And with those dark thoughts lingering, Livia followed Flavius into her father's darkened bedchamber, once they arrived at the villa a few minutes later.

As she walked up to the side of the bed her eyes grew wide, and her heart lurched as she took in the pitiful sight of her father laying there. He was almost unrecognisable. Gone was the robust, portly man she'd known, now replaced by nothing more than flesh and bones. His face was sunken, hollow grooves where his round cheeks had once been. Looking up at Flavius she whispered, "I hadn't realised he was so ill."

Flavius grunted, "Of course you didn't. You never saw him as I did. He has not eaten for weeks now, he refuses to for some reason."

Livia looked away, thankful that the darkened room hid the surprise which must have shown on her face when she'd heard the soft tone of Flavius's voice. Never had she heard him speak so reverently. She swallowed a lump of emotion, to see this gentler side to his character was most unusual.

"Livia." The one word, spoken with a slight lisp, broke the silence in the room, and Livia looked down at her father.

His eyes were now open, as he stared up at her, and for a

moment she felt a jolt of fear, and had to fight the strange urge to run away from him. But she didn't. Instead she came closer to the bed. "Father, I have come, as you asked." She wanted to say "ordered" but she didn't. She had such mixed emotions as she stood there staring at him. Even though she had been virtually ignored by him her whole life, she still felt a hint of pity for him. Blood was certainly thicker than water when it came to familial emotions, she thought wryly.

"Your...your marriage. It isn't right."

His words weren't what she was expecting to hear either. Schooling her features into what she hoped was a neutral expression, she leaned forward, and whispered, "I had no choice, father."

"I know. Flavius told me everything," he gasped, taking short breaths, his thin chest rising and falling with exertion. Speaking was obviously taxing him, and Livia waited for him to continue, aware of the shifting of Flavius's body as he stood on the opposite side of the bed.

She glanced across at Flavius, meeting his impassive gaze, before he shrugged, "I visit with him every day, and tell him what is happening in the Senate, as well as other news. I had not realised that even though his eyes were closed, and he couldn't speak, he *was* taking in everything I said. And when he finally opened his eyes this morning, and spoke for the first time, no-one was more surprised than me."

This time Livia couldn't keep the surprise off her face, and again totally out of character, her brother smiled, "I am not such the beast as you think me to be, Livia."

Livia blushed, when she realised Flavius seemed to have read her thoughts accurately. Even though he had showed her no kindness at all, it was obvious he held their father in great esteem. Loved him even. Breaking eye contact with him, she once again looked down at her father.

He had now managed to get his breathing under control, and lifting a thin hand he placed it on his chest he stammered, "Not...

not...me who be…betrayed Lucius Quadratus Aurelius."

It took a few moments for Livia to understand his dis-jointed words, but when she did, she felt the room spin as she took in the importance of what he was saying. Seeking clarification from Flavius, she looked across the bed at him. But when she saw a look of shock pass over his face, she was convinced that what their father had just revealed, had taken Flavius completely by surprise too.

Flavius confirmed her suspicions by saying, "This is the first I've heard of this."

A long silence fell in the room as they waited for their father's breathing to return to normal again, and when it had Livia asked in a gentle voice, "If it wasn't you father, then who was it?"

It was a short while before he answered, "I…I don't know. But…not me. I…I swear it."

The full import of what he was saying hit home, and for the first time in her life, Livia took her father's thin hand in hers, "You are positive it was someone else was responsible for betraying Lucius Quadratus Aurelius to Nero, father?"

Her father nodded, and she saw the relief fill his eyes when he realised she had understood what he was trying to say.

"Yes," he rasped, "Nero thought…thought it was me. I…I was rewarded beyond my wildest dreams…"

As his words trailed off, shock lent a sharpness to her voice. "So who did betray Metellus's father to Nero? Why did they keep quiet, and let *you* take all the glory? Surely *they* would have wanted the wealth and privilege of gaining Nero's trust?" She knew she was being unreasonable in the rapidity of her questioning, but she couldn't help it. A sharp pain above her eyes made her feel nauseous, and she lifted a trembling hand to rub her forehead, desperate to ease the pain pooling behind her eyes.

She shook her head, speaking her thoughts out loud, "It doesn't make sense. No sense at all."

"I never found out. And…and I didn't care. I had everything I wanted. Money, power, status. Everything except—" He stopped speaking, his eyes clenching shut for a brief moment as he fought his emotions, and Livia watched mesmerised as she saw a tear trickle out of the corner of his eye. "Everything except your mother."

Again his breathing got the better of him, and it was a long while before he recovered sufficiently to carry on. "You are so like your mother," he rasped. "She was so very beautiful. I am sorry for the way I have treated you. But I could not bear to look at you. At…at first I resented you for living whilst she had died. And when you grew up you…you reminded me too much of her. It… it hurt so much to even look at you."

Livia had to choke back tears, as bittersweet emotions assailed her. Oh, how she'd long to hear her father speak so. For years she had yearned for her father's love. Craved it with desperation. And now, here, in the twilight days of his life, he had confessed to her why he had rejected her. He had loved her mother with a deep passion, it was obvious now. Maybe he had loved her too much, and after she had died, he hadn't been able to cope. It still hurt, cut her to the bone even, that he had rejected her, but at least she now knew why.

A feeling of calm came over her, and for the first time in her life she leaned forward and kissed his cheek, and whispered, "I understand father. Rest now."

It was as if he'd been waiting for her forgiveness, because he then closed his eyes and fell into a deep sleep.

"May I stay with him for a while?" she asked Flavius, a little later.

Flavius, who had been uncharacteristically quiet throughout the proceedings, nodded. He was about to take his leave, but stopped at the door and turned to face her. "Your mother was the love of his life. After she died he never looked at another woman." Then, with a short nod of his head he left her alone in the room. Livia sat with her father for a long time, watching him sleep, her thoughts a jumbled mess as she assimilated everything that had happened this evening.

It was late when she returned to Verenus's villa, and as she nodded her thanks to one of her father's slaves who had escorted her back, she couldn't stop a shiver of trepidation as she made her way through the front gate, and headed towards the sleeping quarters.

The sound of her sandals on the marble tiles was the only noise in the empty and silent villa. As she walked down the corridor, she couldn't help but wonder how in the name of all that was holy she was going to explain all this to Metellus!

If her father was telling the truth – and there was no reason for him to lie surely – how would he take such news? Metellus was so bitter, so twisted in his desire for revenge, she was convinced he wouldn't believe a word she said.

But then why should he? For years, everyone had believed it was her father who had implicated Lucius Quadratus Aurelius in the Pisonian conspiracy. Why now, after all these years should he believe the words of a dying man? A man who he'd hated for years?

Because he'd spoken the truth, that's why! Livia was convinced of it. She had seen it on her father's face, heard it in the tone of his voice. Why, even Flavius had believed him, as he had reacted with such shock when their father had revealed his secret it couldn't have been fabricated. And as Flavius knew their father far better than she ever would, *he* would have known in an instant if he had been lying.

No, her father was telling the truth.

Eventually, she reached the door to their bedchamber, but she hesitated before she opened it, biting her bottom lip as a flurry of doubts hit her. Maybe she should wait awhile before she told Metellus anything about what had transpired tonight? Perhaps she should make her own inquiries into the whole affair first, gather evidence so to speak, before she told him what her father had revealed?

A wave of fatigue hit her, as the questions chased through her mind, demanding answers she couldn't provide. But she realised she couldn't postpone the inevitable anymore, and biting back a shudder of trepidation, she pushed open the door to their bedchamber, knowing instinctively Metellus was waiting for her on the other side.

CHAPTER 20

She was right.

He *was* waiting for her. Lying in the bed, one knee bent under the silk covers; covers she noticed which were bunched around his hips, leaving his chest bare. His hands were folded behind his head, the muscles of his biceps bulging where they were propped up by silk cushions. The posture was one of relaxed indifference. But his eyes, and face, told a different story.

He wore a brooding expression, his eyes half closed as they watched her enter the room. For a moment, she was tempted to turn and run, it was obvious he was holding onto his anger by a thread. She saw it in the controlled way he held himself; the pulse that beat rapidly in the hard line of his jaw, the darkness she could see in the grey depths of his eyes.

But she refused to be intimidated. Instead, she firmed her chin and stepped into the room, closing the door behind her with a slight click, the noise deafening in the silence of the room, before she leant back against the wood and waited.

And she didn't have long to wait before he said in a soft, but deadly tone, "Where have you been, Livia?"

Livia realised there was no point in lying. Just by the inflection of his voice she could tell he knew *exactly* where she had gone. Antonia, or the slaves, would have told him of her brother's visit,

205

she was sure of it. So she met his gaze full on, and with a calmness she was far from feeling, said, "I think you know full well where I have been. My father asked to see me."

Anger flickered in his eyes, and his jaw clenched even more, before he hissed, "Why?"

For a moment she hesitated, tempted to tell him the whole truth. But she didn't, wisely she held her own counsel, wanting to be sure of all the facts before she told Metellus anything. So instead she said, "He has awoken from his coma, and he wanted to make his peace with me before he dies." It was the truth of sorts, and her voice hitched upwards, before she continued, "He does not have long to live."

Metellus lifted an eyebrow, somewhat surprised by her words, but she was relieved to see some of the tension in his face fall away.

"I see," he murmured, but then the brooding look returned, "You should have asked my permission to leave."

Anger hit her, as tiredness and fatigue gave way to righteous indignation. Placing her hands on her hips she hissed, "I am not one of your slaves to be ordered around, Metellus. I did not realise I had to seek your permission every time I want to leave this villa." Her eyes narrowed in suspicion as realisation dawned, "Do you have spies following me?"

Metellus sat up, his eyes flashing with barely contained anger, and with a swiftness which surprised her, he swung back the silk covers and vaulted out of the bed. As he stalked towards her, Livia felt her knees grow weak, and she couldn't contain the strangled gasp that escaped her dry throat.

Metellus was naked. Naked, and fully aroused, and heading towards her!

Blind panic hit her, and without thinking, she turned and pulled open the door. But she was too late. Two hands slammed into the door frame above her head, and she found herself trapped between the wooden door, and the hardness of his body.

She could feel the heat radiating off his body as he leaned into her, causing her to moan as she felt his erection press against her lower back. Her heart beat accelerated, and she closed her eyes, at the effect his body was having on hers. She felt the warmth of his breath against the soft skin of her neck, as he lowered his head, before his mouth moved upwards and his teeth nipped at the sensitive lobe of her ear. She trembled uncontrollably, knowing she had lost this particular battle.

"You are my wife, Livia," his voice was quiet, measured, "What kind of a husband would I be, if I did not care about your safety? Yes, I have a man who watches you. Rome is a dangerous place to go out carousing on your own."

He stopped speaking for a moment, and she felt him stiffen behind her, his muscles tensing as if something had just occurred to him. "You are not planning anything are you, Livia? Like seeking your own revenge for instance? Because if you are, you will rue the day you ever tried to cross me." This time the tone of his voice was harsher, demanding, as he growled into her ear.

A mixture of hurt and red hot anger once more coursed through her, as his words hit her. With a swiftness that took him by surprise, she pushed back against his body, momentarily gaining an advantage as she managed to cause him to step backwards, giving her the chance to twist around and face him.

"Revenge! You talk to *me* of revenge, when it is *you* who seeks to bring down my family for something which happened years ago. *And,* before you carry on with your self-imposed campaign, you would be well advised to seek the truth of what *really* happened all those years ago, before you lay the blame at my family's feet."

She heard his hiss of anger at her words, and cursed her wayward tongue.

Oh, why hadn't she kept her mouth shut?

He glared down into her upturned face, his eyes flashing, "What is this nonsense you speak of?" and his hand snaked out and gripped her arm, the strength of his fingers digging into the softness of her flesh, "What lies have your father, and brother, been filling your head with tonight?"

She tried to shake off his hand, but it didn't move. With a bravery she was far from feeling she looked him in the face, "Not lies, Metellus. The truth." Her tone was frigid, but she didn't care anymore. The truth had to come out one way or another, "My father told me he had nothing to do with what happened to your father. He had no connection with Piso, or any of the other members of the conspiracy against Nero," and her gaze never wavering, she met the icy coldness of his grey eyes, "And…and I believe him."

Metellus snorted, a derisive sound and Livia stiffened. "You believe him? Ha! After all these years of virtually ignoring you, on the strength of *one* conversation this evening, *you* have now decided to believe the words of a liar and a cheat, and the man responsible for the murder of my father! How typical of a *Drusii*!"

His face mirrored the disgust he obviously felt, and the pulse that ticked furiously along his cheek bone made the scar on his face stand out even more. In the silence following his outburst, he pulled her away from the door, before wrenching it open, and heedless of the fact that he was naked, stormed out without a backward glance. He pulled the door shut with such a force, Livia was convinced the whole of the villa must have heard it.

That night marked a huge change in their relationship. For two weeks now, ever since he had stormed out of their bedchamber Livia never saw Metellus at all during the daylight hours…and neither did she see him during the night either, for he'd not visited her bed since.

He left the villa before dawn, and didn't return until late at night, and then he retired to another bedchamber on the other side of the villa. It was only Antonia's company during the day and early evenings that kept her sane. Antonia never said anything about Metellus's long absences, but every now and then Livia would look up and see her watching her, a look of pity on her face. But Livia never said anything; pride kept her quiet.

But when Antonia left to visit friends in the evenings Livia had to acknowledge to herself that she felt lonely. She even stopped eating in the *triclinium*, preferring to take her meal in Elisha's room before the baby went to sleep. At least she was guaranteed *some* company there!

And when Metellus *did* arrive back at the villa, she was acutely aware of the change in his demeanour. Gone was the polite, if remote man. Instead he was a cold hard stranger, rarely saying anything to her, only occasionally asking after Elisha's welfare, but that was about all.

It was as if he were punishing her for believing her father's version of events. And no matter how many times she tried to convince herself she didn't care, she knew she was only deceiving herself. *Would this emptiness be her life now? Should she have spoken in defence of her father? After all, Metellus had the right of it – he had ignored her all these years hadn't he? She had been nothing to her father, merely someone…nay not even that…something… to be used, and used again…*

A sharp pain pierced her chest as she realised she *did* care what her husband thought of her. Desperately. She wanted Metellus's affection, his respect, but above all else she wanted his love.

And the cruellest thing of all, now that he didn't want her in his bed anymore, he'd effectively abandoned her, and with it his desire for a son.

These past two weeks had torn her feelings asunder and she didn't know how long her ravaged emotions could endure the treatment he meted out.

Grim faced, Metellus stared with sightless eyes out of the window of his office, oblivious to the sights and sounds of the men working on the dock below him. Raking a hand through his hair, he rubbed the back of his neck to ease the tension there. Tension, which had increased day by day, ever since Livia had met with her father.

His actions these past weeks had left a sour taste in his mouth. He knew he was treating her abominably. Ignoring her – and Elisha – only returning to the villa late at night. They had become so distant ever since he had stopped making love to her...

It was as if he had somehow become two people. One was still bound to the promise he'd made to his dead father. And the other...? Well the other, was a man who had become a slave to the feelings he felt for Livia. Not making love to her was making him lose his mind. He wanted her with a force that left him aching.

She obsessed him. His mind. His body. His every waking thought seemed centred around her. All he could think of was being alone with her again, burying himself in the warmth of her body, making her cry out her need for him, before they took each other to the ends of the world and back.

"But it isn't supposed to be like this," he said to himself.

"Pardon, sir. I did not hear what you said."

Metellus turned to see his aide, Grasus, looking across the room at him, from where he sat at his desk a questioning look on his lined face.

Seeing Grasus also reminded him his work was suffering too. Even though he spent hours here in his office, he'd been unable to concentrate on important matters, such as planning new trade routes so he could expand his wine and olive oil businesses. And he'd been making stupid mistakes too. A small smile lifted his mouth. If it wasn't for Grasus pointing out all his errors, he would have ceased trading weeks ago!

"I want you to bring Spurius Proba here."

Grasus's eyebrows shot up, "The lawyer?"

"Aye, the lawyer," he said nodding, "I've heard he is honest, and loyal, but above all, he is discreet."

If Grasus thought the request strange, he never said anything. Doing as Metellus bid, he left the room with a small bow, and Metellus once more turned to stare out the window.

"You do not seem to like Metellus, Portia. Is there a reason?"

For a moment Portia said nothing, her shoulders slumping as she turned to her friend, a haunted look on her face. "I...I have heard things."

Livia stiffened, before a sense of foreboding came over her. Her hands started to tremble, so she hid them in the silk folds of her *stola* lest Portia see them.

"I...I have heard he is a womaniser. He has left a string of broken hearts from Rome all the way to Baiae. He refuses to commit to any woman apparently and—" Portia broke off her hurried words, her hand clamping over her mouth, distress etched on her face. "I'm sorry, Livia. Truly. It...it is what I have heard, 'tis all."

Livia took her friend's hand, "It does not matter, honestly."

Liar! It did matter. A lot. But what could she do about it? Nothing. If Metellus had a string of women from here, to the far corners of the Empire, there was absolutely nothing she could say, or do, to stop it.

Livia smiled at Portia, and if it was a tad forced, what did it matter? "Now enough of this idle chatter, can you help or not?"

Portia squeezed Livia's hand, "Are you sure you want to do this? Raking up the past is never a good thing in my opinion. Best let sleeping dogs lie I would advise."

Livia bit her lip, nodding, "Yes, I am sure. I need to do this for my own peace of mind, for my sanity even, and I need to do it quickly. I don't have much time, I'm supposed to be at the Bath house later this afternoon, Antonia is meeting me there."

Thankfully Portia never said anything further, and they left Verenus's villa and made their way down the road to Portia's maternal grandmother's villa. The villa wasn't too far away from Verenus's villa, and five minutes later they were in the *atrium* of the older woman's villa, waiting to be received by one of the most powerful women of her time.

Octavia Maximus was the widow of one of the most influential Senators during Nero's reign, and Livia was sure she must be able to shed some light on what had happened around that time.

"Portia! What a surprise. Come in, come in and introduce me to this lovely young woman," Octavia said a few minutes later, as she swept into the *atrium*, before taking a seat on one of the long couches.

"Grandmother, this is Livia a very good friend of mine. She has come to speak with you about something which happened many years ago."

Delight tinkled in the old woman's eyes. "Really? How intriguing. I do love a mystery. Come, sit next to me my dear," she said patting the silk cushion next to her, "And tell me what you want to know."

Once Livia had briefed her on who she was married too – although Livia suspected the older woman already knew, and was just being polite – she asked Octavia what she knew about the conspiracy against Nero.

"Of course I remember it," she said, warming to the subject, "It was all everyone talked of for weeks. The men who conspired against Nero were dealt with swiftly, they either died by their own hand, were executed or were exiled. It was a nervous time for all of us, never knowing if the Praetorian Guard would come to your villa or not."

"I was wondering if you knew of Lucius Quadratus Aurelius, and his involvement in it?"

"Well, yes, of course. Although at the time we were all amazed when he was arrested. He had not long returned to Rome you see, barely a year. He was a rich merchant, that was true enough, but he wasn't interested in furthering his political ambition, not like some merchants were. He seemed to be content just to ensure his wife and son were well cared for…" Her words trailed off for a moment, before she continued, her mouth twisting, "The gossip was rife at the time as I recall. There was much speculation as to why he'd come to be involved in the plot in the first place. He had no real reason to want Nero dead. Having lived for so long in Africa he had no axes to grind so to speak. Not like some in Rome. Yes, it was most strange. Most strange indeed."

Livia frowned, "Do you know why he left Rome in the first place, and why he returned?"

"Well, now that is a story I *do* know something about. And I remember it well. The scandal rocked all of Rome at the time." Leaning forward, the old lady's eyes lit up with the memory, "About eleven years before the conspiracy, Antonia had been promised to another – an arranged marriage of course – as the daughter of one of Rome's richest merchants she was betrothed in order to strengthen two already strong families and thereby enhance her father's standing. But hours before she was due to marry she eloped with Lucius. The repercussions were felt around Rome for weeks I can tell you. No one knew where they had gone. It was as if they had disappeared off the face of the earth. It turns out they went to Alexandria."

Livia started. *Alexandria!* How coincidental that it was on a ship to the same destination that *she* had met Metellus. "Metellus was born there?" she asked, a moment later.

Octavia nodded, "Yes. He was born two years after they eloped. I understand that his mother and father settled quite well in Alexandria. As a successful merchant before they eloped, Lucius found it easy enough to live and work in what is undisputedly one of the largest trading ports in Africa."

"So why did they return to Rome?"

"I heard it was Antonia's doing. She missed her family here in Rome. She also wanted to make peace with Lucius's family, as well as wanting a more settled and secure upbringing for Metellus. After ten years of being in exile, a self-imposed exile mind you, Antonia was convinced there had been enough water under the bridge, and it would be safe to return. And it was at first. Enough time *had* passed for them all to settle with remarkable ease back into Roman life.

Lucius, already a rich merchant in Alexandria, merely exchanged one trading port for another." Portia's grandmother sighed, "But of course the idyll didn't last. Within a year of their return Lucius

213

was dead, and Antonia and Metellus found themselves exiled again. This time by Nero. He'd confiscated all of Lucius's worldly goods, and left Antonia destitute." Octavia shook her head and tutted, "The rest, as they say, is history."

Octavia fell silent, and her eyes took on a faraway look before she continued, her head shaking, "But, considering everything that had happened between Verenus and Lucius, at least he didn't hold a grudge against Antonia and Metellus. We all thought very highly of him when he took in Antonia and Metellus after Lucius's death, offering both his protection and patronage."

Livia frowned, "But I don't understand, Octavia? Why did Verenus have a grudge against his own brother?"

"Well," Octavia said on a deep breath, warming to her story, "Because Antonia had been promised to him in marriage that is why. It was *Verenus* who was jilted on his wedding day. Antonia was in love with Lucius all along, and he with her apparently, although no one knew it of course. They had managed to keep it a secret. As I said earlier, they eloped, just hours before the wedding ceremony. Verenus was beside himself with anger and grief – he was very much in love with Antonia it seemed."

Octavia leaned across and patted Livia's hand when she saw her stunned expression. "The shock I see on your face, very much reflected the shock *we* all felt at the time my dear."

CHAPTER 21

"Are you sure? When?"

"Yes, Master. Yesterday—"

"Yesterday," Metellus shouted, interrupting his slave. "Why wasn't I told sooner?"

"I…I do not know Master. I…"

Metellus sighed, cutting off the stuttering words before waving his hand in apology, "It is not your fault, Titus. Thank you. You may leave now."

Once the slave had left, Metellus went over and sat at his table, leaning his head back against the wooden headrest. He closed his eyes for a moment, and assimilated what he had just been told.

Livia's father was dead.

Augustus Drusus, the man who had dominated his entire life since the age of ten was finally dead. *He should be pleased shouldn't he? Shouting his thanks from the rooftops of Rome, giving a huge offering to the gods for bringing him such good news about his death.*

But he wasn't. Instead he felt nauseous, as if he had just swallowed a flagon of rancid wine. Rubbing the back of his neck in frustration he stood up, the force of his movements causing his chair to tip over, as he paced the floor of his office.

He hadn't seen Livia in over a week, not since he'd asked Grasus to secure the services of Spurius Proba. Instead, he'd been staying here in his office, sleeping on a pallet, which had been hastily obtained for him.

He'd done so because he needed time to think. Time to rationalise what Livia had told him about her father. He knew, deep down, he *had* to get to the truth once and for all. Which was why he'd employed Spurius Proba to dig up the past and get to the truth – no matter how long it took.

But it had been so hard keeping away from her this past week. Night after night, he tossed and turned on the thin pallet, as temptation clawed at him, testing his resilience, goading him to return to Livia, and the pleasure he found in her arms. But he had resisted. Until now…

The room was in darkness, and for a moment Metellus thought the bedchamber was empty, but a slight movement near the window drew his eyes towards it like a moth to a flame.

Livia! She was sitting on the window ledge, knees drawn up to her chest, staring out into the darkness of the *atrium* beyond.

"Livia," he whispered, walking towards her, not wanting to startle her. He saw her shiver and Metellus winced. Maybe he shouldn't have come. But it was too late, so he continued, his voice quiet, "I only found out a short while ago about your father."

He saw her body stiffen before she turned to look at him, staring at him for a long time before she said, "Of course you did. I wouldn't have expected anything different."

Her voice was flat and emotionless, her face as white as marble. It was only her eyes which showed any emotion. They were haunted, the hazel of her eyes so dark, he felt himself drowning in them. As he approached her she turned away to look back out of the window. For a few moments indecision plagued him. Livia seemed so helpless, so vulnerable, all he wanted to do was take her in his arms and kiss the pain away.

"I'm sorry—"

"No!" The word was loud in the stillness of the room, and

Metellus heard the anger in her voice as she turned to face him once again. It blazed out of her eyes, and was evident in the rawness of her voice.

"No, Metellus. Do *not* say you are sorry. You are not sorry at all. My father is dead. You should be offering untold prayers and offerings to the gods."

He could hear hysteria replacing anger, rising in its intensity with every word she spat out at him. She was right. He wasn't sorry. He couldn't be. But he realised he *did* care about Livia, about how *she* was feeling. He cared very much—

"I want a divorce."

Metellus clamped his jaw shut as he bit back a retort. He realised he needed to be calm before he answered her, and so for several long moments he said nothing. Eventually he replied in an even, measured, tone, "There will be no divorce, Livia."

"But why?" This time her voice was anguished, and she jumped off the window ledge and approached him. The sound of her sandals on the marble floor the only noise in the room as she walked towards him.

"Why?" she repeated, when she stood next to him. "You've got your revenge. My father is of no use to you anymore. You've ruined our family. Flavius is in your debt for a lifetime. As am I—"

"No!" Metellus interrupted her heated words. "There will be no divorce, Livia. You will give me a son."

He heard Livia gasp, saw the haunted expression appear on her face once more as she stood paralysed to the spot.

She shook her head, the movement slow, before she whispered, "I do not want children."

Metellus clenched his fists, "Why?" The word was pushed past tight lips. "You may already be pregnant."

"I'm not." This time the words were firm, her chin lifting with resolve, as she met his gaze without any expression on her face.

Metellus nodded slowly, "I see."

"No, you don't. I do not want children, because my mother died in childbirth having me." Pain was etched all over her face as she spoke, and Metellus swallowed hard, fighting his emotions before she carried on, "I do not want to bring a child into this world, to be raised by a father who only married to satisfy his sick desire for revenge. And who, if I were to die, would abandon my child."

A long silence fell between them, until Metellus said softly, "I wouldn't abandon our child, Livia. And I wouldn't abandon Elisha either."

He saw indecision flicker across her face before she turned her back on him, and walked back to the window to stare out into the inky blackness beyond. He stood there for a long time, battling with his own emotions, before he said, "There will be no divorce, Livia. Ever." He saw her back stiffen, and without another word he left her alone with her troubled thoughts.

Livia rubbed her forehead, trying to ease the headache she'd woken up with these past two mornings ever since she and Metellus had argued the other night. She'd hardly slept at all, tossing and turning most of the night as Metellus's words had churned around in her head, over and over again.

Her demand for a divorce had been met with his blunt refusal, but truth be told, she shouldn't have really been surprised. Of course he wouldn't want a divorce. To do so would have made all his plans of becoming one of Rome's elite turn to dust. If he divorced her she would return to her *paterfamilias* – and she would, once again, be under Flavius's control.

But it wasn't just the issue of divorce that had plagued Livia and had caused her to lose so much sleep these past nights. It was also the fact that she had blatantly lied to her husband when he'd questioned her about being pregnant.

Even now she couldn't quite believe how brazen she had been when she'd looked him the eye and told him that she wasn't pregnant; when the truth was the complete opposite. She'd not had her monthly flow for over two months now; and if the slight swelling and soreness of her breasts were any indication, not to mention the nausea she felt on awakening in the mornings, then she *was* definitely going to have a child. Metellus's child. She knew she should have told him, and the guilt had eaten at her ever since. But she had been too raw, too hurt to tell him the truth.

She was also scared. Her outburst the other night *had* been a cry from the heart. She *was* terrified of dying in childbirth, just as her mother had. Maybe she wasn't being rational about it, but it was something she had been aware of ever since she had been a small child, and had first asked her father where her mother was.

His abrupt words about her dying in childbirth, as she gave birth to Livia, had impacted hugely on her. She'd never forgotten the stark pain she'd seen on his face, not to mention the underlying implication that it had somehow been *her* fault. The words, and her father's reaction, was something she'd carried with her every single day since. And even though Metellus had said he would look after any child she might have if she were to die, there was always the real possibility that he could change his mind—

"Are you all right, Livia?"

The whispered words intruded on Livia's thoughts and returned her to the present with a jolt. The fact that she was sitting next to Portia, and was in the middle of her father's funeral was testimony to how much guilt she was holding inside that she had forgotten where she was! Nodding slightly, Livia turned to where Portia sat next to her. Giving her friend a brief smile she said, "Yes, I think so. I just wish this day was over, that is all."

Portia never said anything, just smiled at her friend in agreement and squeezed her hand in sympathy. Thankful for her friends support, Livia turned back to concentrate on what the magistrate was saying as he delivered another eulogy in memory of her father.

The death of such a prominent man, as her father had been, warranted all the pomp and ceremony Rome could provide, and Livia knew she still had several hours to go before she could leave.

As she listened to another Senator praise her father for all the good works he'd done for Rome, she couldn't stop the small pang of envy that curled inside her.

Envy, for all those unknown people of Rome who had benefited from her father's hard work, and dedication, in making it the great city it was. It was as if he had lavished all his love, all his attention, on the city and had none left over to give to her.

Oh, how she'd longed for a small part of that love to be given to her, to sustain her throughout the lonely childhood she'd had. Only it hadn't. Day after day, ever since she was old enough to understand human emotion, she had craved it, yearned for it. And it had never come – well not until last month when her father had finally opened up to her whilst on his death bed.

Livia sighed. And now it was too late. Her eyes glanced across the room to where Flavius stood, his face impassive, emotionless, as he listened to the Senator speak.

There was no doubt in Livia's heart her brother would want nothing to do with her ever again. He'd made his intention clear enough on the day of her marriage to Metellus. But it still hurt. Even though they had never been close, her half-brother was still the only family she had left. And, she realised, her false bravado the other day to Metellus about getting a divorce had, in hindsight, been stupid.

Even if Metellus *had* consented to giving her a divorce, she knew with a certainty Flavius wouldn't have taken her back. *Why should he?* In his eyes she would have brought shame to the family for a second time, *and* she would have had to rely on his charity.

And charity had always been in short supply when it came to Flavius's feelings towards her. She knew why of course. It was hardly a secret within the household. Livia's mother had been her father's lover for several years before they had married; and when Flavius's mother had died when Flavius's was eight, their father had married Livia's mother barely two weeks after Flavius's mother had been buried.

Six months after they had married, Livia had been born. Her

birth must have been salt in a festering wound for the young Flavius, and even though her mother had died in childbirth, as far as he was concerned, *she* was the product of his father's affair, and the betrayal of his own mother's memory. His only consolation was that her father, too caught up in his grief for the only woman he'd ever loved, had abandoned his new born daughter, and Flavius had once again become the most important person in her father's life.

Livia sighed. No, she was under no illusion that Flavius would want anything to do with her now her father was dead. She had bartered, given to Metellus, to pay off her father's, and Flavius's debts, and was, in reality tied to Metellus for life.

She had no money. No status. No power. A woman, even one married or living in a rich household, was at the mercy of either their father's or their husband's will. Roman Society was very much a male dominated world...

As she watched Flavius, she saw him stiffen, and his eyes narrow, as he looked over to the doorway of the Senate building. She glanced over to see what had caught Flavius's attention, and when she saw Metellus standing in the doorway she couldn't stop her small gasp of surprise.

Portia must have seen him too, because she leaned in and whispered, "Did you know he was turning up?"

"No." She felt a myriad of emotions flood through her. Anger. Annoyance, but mostly confusion. *Why had he turned up? It made no sense.* She watched in stunned surprise, as he took a seat directly across the Senate from her.

"I think he has come for you," Portia whispered, "If his demeanour is anything to go by."

Livia felt a burning heat suffuse her body, as embarrassment surged through her when she met Metellus's bold gaze. His gaze was trained on her, and her alone, as if they were the only two people here in the massive Senate building. After what could have been seconds, or minutes, Livia finally broke eye contact, and looked back to the Senator who was still talking, trying to concentrate on what was being said.

It was over an hour later when the service finally came to an end, and Livia stood up, desperate to take her leave. She had only managed to take a few steps when a hand snaked its way around the slimness of her wrist halting her progress.

"Do you have no shame? Bringing him here."

Livia's face flushed with anger, as she met Flavius's angry gaze. Lifting her head with quiet dignity, she shook off his hand, and said with all the haughtiness she could muster, "I did not know he was coming."

"I can vouch for Livia," Portia said. "He was not at the villa this morning when I called for your sister."

Flavius's jaw clenched as he glared at both women. He grunted, the sound one of disbelief, before he stalked off.

"Livia."

The one word, spoken directly behind her, made both women spin round to face Metellus. Again he was staring at her intently, and Livia blushed.

"I have come to escort you home, Livia." Metellus said by way of an explanation for his presence here. "Our villa is finally habitable. We can retire there after you leave here."

Livia's stomach dropped, and she felt the colour drain from her face.

"I'm sure you are as keen to have your own home as I am, Livia. Living with one's relatives is not to be recommended for a newly married couple," he hesitated for a moment, his gaze going to someone who stood behind Livia, a twinkle lightening up his grey eyes, "Do you not agree Senator Amanius?"

Livia closed her eyes in mortification, and had to bite back the urge to groan. Turning she saw that the elderly Senator was standing behind her. *The Fates must surely be laughing at her, could the day get any worse?*

Senator Amanius laughed heartily, "I fear you are embarrassing

222

your lovely wife, Metellus. But yes. Young couples such as your-selves, need their own place, and their privacy."

She saw Metellus smile, and for a few moments the two men engaged in banal conversation. She remembered seeing the older man at Verenus's gathering the evening she had returned to Rome, and it was obvious he and Metellus were well acquainted. Once he had finished talking, Senator Amanius turned to Livia to offer his condolences, and then with a slight chuckle he walked off, leaving the three of them standing there.

"So are you ready to leave? I thought it would be nice to walk there. The heat of the day is finally abating, it is going to be a pleasant evening." His words were cordial, his eyes sparkling with amusement, as if he knew the inner turmoil she must be experiencing.

"Nice" wasn't quite the word she would have chosen, but Livia realised she didn't have much choice in the matter.

"Would you like me to come with you?"

Livia started. She had forgotten all about poor Portia's presence! "I…I will be fine," she stuttered, "But thank you, Portia. You are a true friend."

Portia never said anything else. Shooting a dark warning glance at Metellus she took her leave, leaving them alone, and Livia couldn't stop the tremble that went through her when Metellus took her hand and led her out of the Senate.

For the next few days Livia was kept busy. As the mistress of the new villa – their villa – she was kept occupied with its day to day running. Initially, she had found it daunting, and yes, she made mistakes, but she'd also learned from them.

Pride also stopped her from asking for help. Either from Metellus, or from Antonia, and she had been steadfast in her resolve to do it all by herself.

And she'd succeeded. Now the villa ran with smooth efficiency, and she was able to devote more time to Elisha, rather than relying so much on Addie the wet nurse who had spent so much time looking after the baby.

Livia sighed. Yes, to all intents and purposes she had an enviable lifestyle.

A beautiful villa, the envy of many of the *patricians* she met at the baths, a chest full of beautiful clothes, more jewels than she had ever had in her life and a healthy child *and* a handsome husband who provided for Elisha, and her every needs.

So she should be happy shouldn't she?

But she wasn't. And why? Because the husband whom she loved, *still* treated her in exactly the same way as he'd done when they stayed at Verenus's villa.

Like before, he was conspicuous by his absence during daylight hours. He only returned to the villa late in the evening, and beneath his polite demeanour and his brooding looks, there was an icy resolve.

"Livia, you are well?"

The words startled her, and she snapped out of her brooding thoughts, turning from the window she had been staring out of, to see Antonia walking towards her, a worried frown on her face.

Livia smiled, "Yes, I am well. It is good to see you, Antonia. I haven't seen you for a while."

Antonia waved a hand, "I didn't want to intrude, this is your home now. You don't want an old woman interfering in what is in effect your domain. I only came to tell you Verenus has finally arrived back in Rome last night, and is planning a feast to celebrate his return. It is to be held next week sometime. You are both invited of course."

Livia started, her heart racing erratically. *Verenus had returned!* She had been wondering when he would get back, as she had so many questions she wanted to ask him ever since she had spoken with Portia's grandmother. Smiling, so Antonia didn't suspect anything amiss, she replied in an even voice, "Thank you for the invite, we would be delighted to attend." She took Antonia's arm in hers, and led her towards the *atrium*, "Now come and partake of some refreshments. And before you protest, you are welcome here anytime. You could never intrude, Antonia. I value your kindness and judgement so much."

Antonia smiled, and as they walked she asked, "You have all you need?"

"More than enough. Metellus is most kind." Livia couldn't help the slight tinge of bitterness that crept into her voice, and was annoyed with herself for allowing it. After all, Antonia wasn't responsible for her son's behaviour.

But the older woman was too astute not to pick up on Livia's tone, and the underlying problem, and she stopped, and turned to face Livia a frown of concern on her face, "Metellus still refuses to forget this vendetta against your family I take it?"

When Livia nodded, Antonia sighed heavily, "I had thought with your father's death, he would forget all about it. Sometimes, I feel I do not even know my own son."

Emotion suddenly welled up in her and she burst out, "Why do *you* not hold a grudge against my family, Antonia? If *anyone* should hate the *Drusii*, then it should be *you*."

Antonia took Livia's hand in hers, "Child, please don't distress yourself. I *was* angry for a long time. But anger cannot change the past. I decided to remember the good times I had with my husband and be grateful for them," she lifted her shoulders in a helpless gesture, "Metellus could not understand, or forgive what happened I'm afraid, and for that I have borne his hatred with a heavy heart."

Antonia gave a bittersweet smile, "Now enough of this morose talk. Let us have some honey water, and enjoy spending some time with Elisha. I have missed both your company."

Later, as they lounged on cushions in the coolness of the *atrium*, Antonia put down her goblet and leaned forward and took Livia's hand once more, "I could not help but notice that you look ill, Livia. Are you unwell my dear?"

Livia's eyes widened as she met Antonia watchful gaze. "Why... why do you ask?"

Antonia smiled slightly at her hesitant answer, "You look fatigued. Pale even."

Livia looked away from her all seeing gaze, and whispered, "I was ill this morning."

For a few moments a long silence fell, before Antonia asked, "Are you with child, my dear?"

Livia blushed to the roots of her hair, but unable to lie she nodded, "Yes. I...I think so—"

"Oh, Livia, what wonderful news!" Antonia exclaimed, "Metellus—"

"No!" Livia interrupted, and agitated she rose from her couch and walked over to the small fountain, trailing her hands through the cool water, stalling for time, unable to face Antonia, "I...I haven't told Metellus yet."

"But he has a right to know," Antonia reasoned, "He is your husband. Maybe it will be just the news to bring an end to this vendetta he seems so intent of pursuing."

Livia shook her head, and turned to face the older woman, "Do you think so? I...I am not so sure."

Antonia opened her mouth to say something else, but before she could, Livia spoke first, "I will tell him. I promise. But not just yet. *I* am still coming to terms with the news myself."

She heard Antonia chuckle, and was thankful that the tension had now eased between them.

It was only later, after she had retired to her bedchamber that the full implication of the afternoon's conversation with Antonia impinged on her mind.

She was pregnant. And Antonia was right. Metellus had the right to know the truth. She shouldn't have lied to him when he'd asked the other day, but she hadn't been ready to reveal the truth to him then. As she sat on the edge of the bed, combing her long hair, she thought about what she had to do first, before she told Metellus she was carrying their child. She owed it to herself, her unborn child, and to Elisha. And…and she also owed it to Metellus.

Getting up from the bed, she went over to where a table and chair stood along one of the walls and sat down. Pulling a piece of papyrus paper towards her she picked up a stylus and started to write…

CHAPTER 22

"I've been expecting you," Verenus said, the sarcasm evident in his voice as he waved the missive she had written to him yesterday afternoon in front of her, "I had expected to see you here sooner."

The words weren't *quite* what she had been expecting to hear, and Livia instantly went on the defensive. Saying nothing, she followed Verenus as he escorted her through his villa, before leading her into the *tablinum*. With a curt nod he invited her to sit in a leather *curule* chair, before he positioned himself behind a large marble desk.

For a few moments a stilted silence fell between the two of them as they each took the others measure.

"You know why I have come?" Livia finally asked, breaking the uneasy silence between them, and refusing to be intimidated by him.

"Of course. It is obvious really. I know you have been speaking to people who were alive at the time of the conspiracy against Nero. You are a clever woman, who no doubt has put two and two together."

Livia sat in stunned silence, her face draining of colour as a knot of fear cramped her stomach. Verenus had been away from Rome for weeks, yet he *still* seemed to know everything that had been going on. She had seriously underestimated how far his tentacles reached here in Rome. But she refused to succumb to his domineering ways, and in a fit of defiance she raised her chin, showing him she was unafraid of him, "So you have been spying on me have you, Verenus?"

Verenus raised an eyebrow, derision stamped all over his face, "Of course. It is a wise man who keeps his friends close, but his enemies even closer. And my spies have been busy these past weeks, watching you and Metellus—"

"But why have you been watching Metellus?" she said, interrupting him a frown on her face.

Verenus lifted a shoulder, "It seems that it is not only you who has been asking questions of late." Then before Livia could ask what he meant, Verenus snapped, "So, why don't you just ask me?"

His face was expressionless, and she felt hers flush in vexation, and she had to bite back the words she wanted to say to the hateful man!

Instead she schooled her features and sat up, her back ramrod straight. "I think you probably know what I want, Verenus. But because you want me to say it, then I shall." Taking a deep breath, and with what she hoped was a determined look on her face, she said, "I want you to tell Metellus, and Antonia, that it was *you*, and not my father, who deceived Metellus's father. That it was *you* who betrayed your own brother to Nero. And it was *you* who told the Emperor a pack of lies that led to your own brother being executed."

The words, spoken in such a rush caused her breath to whoosh out of her suddenly tight lungs. There! At last she had said what she had been keeping to herself for days now, and she felt a great sense of relief now it was finally out in the open.

Verenus leaned back in his chair, and lifted his hands and started to clap, a slow deliberate clap, which spoke volumes. "I was right. You *are* a clever woman." Leaning forward he pinned her with his frigid eyes. "Now, tell me, how did you come to your deduction?"

Livia tried not to show the relief she was feeling. She had been right, it *had* been him all along! "My father told me he had nothing to do with bringing down your brother. He'd nothing to do with the Pisonian conspiracy. But, more importantly, he never found out who the person was that betrayed your brother to Nero. And why that person did not take the glory for themselves. My father grew rich off his supposed loyalty to Nero. Rich and powerful. It made no sense as to why my father should have been allowed to claim all the glory. Unless…"

Verenus quirked his head, a mocking smile playing at the corner of his mouth, "Unless? Do enlighten me, Livia."

Livia fought the sudden rush of nerves pooling in her stomach. She had to be firm, strong. Meeting his eyes with a directness she wasn't really feeling, she continued, "Unless…unless the man who betrayed him *already* had immense wealth, and power, *and* he wanted to keep his true reasons secret." She paused for a moment. "And that man was you, Verenus. *You* were already as rich as Croesus, *and* as Nero's chief architect, and advisor, *you* also had his trust. But you also wanted to exact your own revenge. Revenge against the brother who had taken the only woman you had ever loved." She waited for a heartbeat before whispering, "And the woman you still love to this day…"

Verenus laughed, a hollow, false laugh which caused Livia to shudder. "I am immensely glad women can't sit in the Senate. You, my dear, would be formidable."

He stood up, the movement sudden and violent, and the scraping of his chair on the marble floor, made her nerves scream. Livia watched him walk over to a sideboard and pour himself a goblet of wine. Lifting it to her in a silent mocking salute he drank it all in one swallow before asking, "So now you know my dirty secret, what are we going to do about it?"

Livia narrowed her eyes at the bitterness she heard in his voice. "I want you to tell Metellus, and Antonia, the truth. They have the right to know. And I, as Metellus's wife, have the right to be married to a man who can finally lay to rest the ghosts of his childhood."

Verenus broke eye contact with her, and she watched as he poured himself some more wine. Surprisingly, she saw his hand shake as he lifted the goblet, and she took comfort, and strength, from the small betraying gesture. Emboldened she carried on, "Well? Will you do as I ask?"

For several long moments he didn't answer her, as a myriad of expressions flashed across his face before he nodded abruptly, "I will tell Metellus tomorrow—"

"No!" Livia interrupted, her tone decisive, "You will send a message to Metellus, now."

For a long moment he stared at her, then she saw his shoulders slump, as if the weight of defeat had finally conquered him. "Very well." Walking over to his desk he took out some paper and wrote.

Once he had finished, he showed Livia what he had written, "Is that acceptable?"

Livia scanned the short missive, and satisfied with what he'd written, she nodded, Verenus then called for a slave and told him to take the note to Metellus's offices at once.

Once the slave had departed, Verenus leaned back in his chair, his hands clasped behind his head, "Now we wait."

Livia swallowed, her eyes meeting his. "Yes, now we wait."

Metellus slammed his fist down on the wooden desk in front of him. The force of which made the wooden planks groan in protest, and the young man who stood in front of it jump in fright.

"You are sure Spurius Proba? Because if you are not, and this information proves false, I will personally ruin you. Do you understand?" Metellus said, his eyes piercing the young man with an intensity which was frightening.

Spurius Proba swallowed, "I...I am quite sure, sir. I have been most thorough. It's why I have taken so long to come back to you. All the documents in front of you have been checked, and checked again. I am as certain as I can be that the information is correct."

Metellus said nothing, but continued to stare at the younger man. Although young, he knew Spurius Proba's reputation as a good lawyer had spread throughout Rome. He had the rare privilege of being known as an honest lawyer – a highly unusual occurrence – and it was for this reason Metellus had hired him. Spurius Proba had, and continued to be, in great demand and it had taken a lot of money, and influence, for Metellus to jump the queue and gain his services.

But it had been worth it. Now he had the proof in front of him. Proof his father had been betrayed, not by Livia's father as he had always believed, but by his own uncle.

Verenus! He could still not quite believe it. But, as he once again scanned the documents in front of him, he *had* to believe it. Because it was there in front of him – the full unadulterated truth.

It had been his uncle who had been the one to spread false rumours against his father. Verenus had been the one closest to Nero, the man whom Nero had trusted the most – and Nero – as mad as he was at the time, had believed everything Verenus had told him.

Verenus had betrayed his father, his mother and himself for years. It was *he* who had wanted revenge. Revenge against a brother who had stolen his bride-to-be, eloped with her on the morning of what was supposed to have been their wedding day...

As he flicked through the sheaf of papyrus papers laid out before him, he had to acknowledge Spurius Proba had been remarkably thorough. He had obtained written testimony from many people – influential people – who had been around at the time of the conspiracy against Nero, and it was abundantly clear that his father had had nothing to do with it. He had only been implicated because of well-placed lies given to Nero by Verenus.

How could he have been so stupid? So blind for all these years not to have seen through his uncle? And what of his mother? She had been invited to stay on permanently at the villa after his father's death. Distraught after the execution of her husband, and having nowhere else to go, Antonia had accepted his invitation to stay. Had she not suspected? He doubted it. Verenus had been nothing but welcoming.

It would appear they had both been duped by the one person they never thought would be capable of doing such a thing. But one thing puzzled him, and he lifted his head and asked, "Do you know how Verenus managed to keep this a secret for so long?"

Spurius Proba nodded, "Money. It would seem he bribed his way to keeping people quiet. I understand he paid enormous sums of money for doing so. And don't forget of course, once he had implicated Senator Drusus, the focus of attention was shifted onto him and not your uncle."

"Thank you, Spurius Proba," Metellus said a few moments later, after he had taken in the enormity of what he had learned, "You have been most thorough. I can, of course, rely on your discretion regarding this matter?"

"Of course."

Metellus knew he was telling the truth, and he nodded his thanks before reaching into a small chest which stood on his desk, taking out a small cloth bag he handed it over to the young man. "Here is the agreed fee, and something extra in recognition of all your hard work."

Spurius Proba took the cloth bag and bowed slightly. "Thank you, sir." As Spurius Proba turned to leave the office he hesitated and turned back to face Metellus, a frown on his face, "Forgive me asking, but what do you intend to do next? As a lawyer, I have to strongly advise you against seeking any sort of retaliation."

Metellus laughed, the tone harsh, his face an impassive mask. "Rest assured, I will not take the law into my own hands, it is not worth it. I have a young wife and daughter to consider. But thank you for your concern. It is most appreciated."

Spurius Proba flushed at the hard tone of Metellus's voice, but he didn't take offence. After all, Metellus had every reason to be angry.

Once Spurius Proba had left, Metellus sat at his table for a long time taking in everything he'd discovered this morning.

Livia had been right. Her father had been innocent all along. With a suddenness that shocked him, he felt an enormous weight lift from his shoulders as what had just been revealed to him, hit home. Livia had told the truth after all.

He'd been blinded by his past. He had taken everything she had to offer, giving her nothing in return. He had been ruthless, uncaring, and he definitely didn't deserve her love. She'd never asked for anything. All she'd yearned for were the things that *couldn't* be bought. For love. For family. For happiness.

When had it become more than just the taking her body? *Always*, his mind screamed at him. She was the only woman who had consumed his every waking moment, and the only woman he'd ever wanted…and the only woman he'd ever loved…

He'd only been fooling himself. For months now he'd refused to acknowledge what had blatantly been staring him in the face. What they shared together went deeper than just lust, just desire.

It was love. He was in love with Livia. He'd fallen in love with her compassion, her gentleness, her kindness – all he'd seen on the island. What other woman would have taken in the baby of a leper? And she had also been honest with him from the start.

She hadn't tried to hide her love for him. Instead she had been open, honest, challenging him to love her. Defying him to stop his revenge against her father. But he had refused to accept it, too blinded by his past, and had carried on regardless, hurting her, treating her abominably. The thirst for revenge too strong to slake.

"Fool," he ground out through clenched teeth. Anger surged through him and he thumped his clenched fist down onto the hard wood of his desk, relishing the small amount of pain it brought. He had to put things right. Now. He just hoped he hadn't left it too late…

With resolution firming his spine, he stood up and shuffled up the papers Spurius Proba had left for him. As he walked past his scribe, who worked in the adjoining room, he said, "I am leaving early, Grasus. I have important things to attend to at my villa. I need to undo the past. I just hope I'm not too late…"

"Mother? I hadn't expected to see you here. Where is Livia?"

Antonia frowned, "She has gone to Verenus's villa. I came here at her request. She asked me to sit with Elisha as she has something to discuss with him. I thought it had something to do with the villa-" She stopped speaking when she saw a look of anguish pass over his face. Rushing forward she placed her hand on his arm, "Why, what is wrong?"

A black look crossed Metellus's face, "When did she leave?" He asked, ignoring his mother's question, "How long ago?"

Antonia gasped when she heard the anger in her son's voice. "An…an hour ago at the most. Metellus tell me what is wrong?"

Metellus shook off his mother's hand, "Verenus is up to no good—"

Antonia's face paled, "What are you talking about, Metellus? Have you gone mad? Verenus has been so good—"

"Verenus killed father," he interrupted forcibly, "*Not* Livia's father. She was telling the truth, but I refused to believe her."

Antonia lost all colour from her face, and sat down before her legs gave way, raising a shaking hand to her temple. "I…I don't understand, Metellus. What are you saying?"

Metellus realised the shock was too much for his mother, and he cursed himself for being so blunt. He should have explained everything to her later, when he had the time. "I don't have time to explain now, mother. But believe me it is true."

"But—"

"Not now, mother. I'm sorry, but I need to go now! Livia might be in danger."

Antonia's cry of distress was the last thing Metellus heard as he ran out of the room.

"Would you like a drink? Some honey water perhaps? It is very hot today and you look a little piqued."

Livia bristled at the supercilious tone of Verenus's voice. He really was a horrible man she thought. It just amazed her that neither Antonia nor Metellus were able to see through him. But then why should they, when he had only ever shown them nothing but kindness? It was only with *her* he'd revealed his true colours. Right from the very first moment since they were first introduced. Sometimes it took an outsider to discover the truth; to expose the underbelly of a serpent lurking inside a family.

"Thank you, some refreshment would be most welcome," she was amazed at how cordial they were being, considering what was going to happen soon. Wisely, she said nothing about the nausea she was experiencing, the less he knew of her condition the better, and accepting the goblet of honey water he handed her with a small nod, she moved away from him and sat on one of the silk covered couches before taking a sip of her drink.

As the minutes passed, the tension in the room grew more palpable as they waited, and Livia prayed Metellus was in his offices, and not down on the dockside, when the message was delivered. As she sat there waiting for him to arrive she laid back on the couch, content to close her eyes for a moment. She hadn't realised how tired she was. Obviously, her recent lack of sleep was beginning to take its toll. Maybe if she just closed her eyes for a moment...

Livia woke up slowly, her hand lifting to her forehead as an intense pain shot through her temple. She felt so tired, so lethargic. What was the matter with her? She needed—

Groaning, she forced her eyes open. As she focussed on her surroundings she realised she was in a darkened room lying on a bed. Had she returned to their villa? If so, she hadn't been aware of it. The last thing she remembered was sitting with Verenus, waiting for Metellus—

She gasped and sat up, the pain in her head making her feel nauseous. As her eyes adjusted to the dimness, she realised she wasn't in her own bedroom. The room was very small, the bed no more than a cot with a straw filled mattress, bare of any other furniture. If she wasn't mistaken, it very much appeared as if she were in one of the slave's quarters. But why? She tried to get her whirling thoughts into some sort of order, to piece together exactly what was going on.

She remembered being in Verenus's villa in the *triclinium*, drinking his wine waiting for Metellus.

Then what? Nothing. That was the last she remembered. *What on earth was going on?* Swinging her legs over the side of the bed she stood up gingerly, unsure if she had the strength to stand. For a moment the room swam before her eyes, and she had to steady herself by resting a hand on the stone wall. Once the room had stopped spinning, she made her way to the door. *Had she become ill, and Verenus had taken her to rest in one of the rooms? But why a room belonging to a slave? Did she mean so little to him?*

When she got to the door she turned the handle. Only it didn't move.

The door was locked. Livia frowned, trying to think logically, but her head felt heavy, as if mud, instead of blood, was flowing through it, and for a second she thought she had made a stupid mistake. So she tried the door again. But the door didn't move. It was definitely locked.

Lifting her fist she banged on the door and shouted, "Verenus! Verenus! Let me out at once. This is madness."

Nothing. Not a sound could be heard from the other side of the door. Livia stood there, her head resting against the thickness of the wooden planks trying to collect her thoughts.

Verenus, she realised, was up to no good. It was obvious he had put something in her drink, a drug of some sort to make her sleepy.

Lifting her head away, she once again banged on the door. But as she did so she realised it was pointless – no-one was there. Glancing behind her to the back wall she spotted a small window; its wooden shutters closed, but she knew that with a small push they should open easily. She should be able to climb onto the window ledge and jump out. The slave quarters were at the back of the villa she knew, and not too far from the *atrium*.

With a renewed sense of relief, she walked over to the window and pushed the shutters open.

Only they didn't move. Livia shook them again, but it was no use they were closed tight. Leaning forward, she squinted through the small slats, and saw that a large plank of wood had been nailed across the shutters sealing them shut.

She was trapped with no way out. Her breath caught in her throat as she bit back a sob of panic, and the pain in her head returned with renewed vigour. Swallowing hard she fought back the waves of nausea that threatened.

Rushing back to the bed, she laid back down on the mattress and took in several large breaths to calm herself, her hand moving to rest on her still flat stomach, in an unconscious gesture of protection.

She needed to collect herself, steady her thoughts. She needed to be strong, not succumb to panic, and for a few minutes she lay on the bed, the silence of the room helping to soothe her nerves. But then she heard a noise from outside the door, and with lightning reflexes, and ignoring the protests of her body, she flew off the bed and ran to the door, her small fists pounding on the door.

"Verenus! Verenus! Open this door at once. If you don't I'll—" *I'll what?* She thought. There wasn't anything she could do about the situation she currently found herself in. She was trapped, and at the total mercy of a madman!

The smell of acrid smoke hit her senses, and glancing down, she watched in horror as thick black smoke seeped through the small gap under the door. For a moment disbelief held her immobile at what she was witnessing, but then her survival instincts kicked in, and she rushed over to the bed, and pulled the straw mattress off the wooden frame. Dragging it across the floor she pushed it against the door, praying the makeshift barrier would prevent the smoke from filling the room too quickly.

But she knew it was only a stalling tactic. It would be only a matter of time until—

Livia bit back a hysterical sob. "No." She moaned, unable to believe what was happening; unable to comprehend that Verenus wanted her dead. The pounding in her head intensified, along with the terror which was threatening to consume her. Feeling nauseous once more, she rushed back to the bed and sat down on the bare wooden boards, trying desperately to calm herself, as she watched the smoke starting to fill the small room. With a feeling of helplessness and dread she knew there wasn't a thing she could do about it.

Tears fell unheeded down her face. "I'm sorry Metellus. I tried. I really tried." Her hands fell across her stomach as if to say sorry to her unborn child. Closing her eyes she blanked out what was happening. She needed to sleep. She needed to block out this living nightmare…she needed to take herself to a better place.

So with a small smile on her face, she remembered the time she'd spent on the island with Metellus…and the night she had made love with him…

CHAPTER 23

"Where is he? Where is Verenus? And where is my wife?"

The slave stepped backwards, recoiling at the ferocious tone, before stammering, "I do not know, Master."

Metellus hissed, his eyes frantic as he searched the empty courtyard looking for any evidence as to where they could be. He'd already searched every room in the villa, but there had been no sign of them. The only evidence of Verenus and Livia having been there, were two empty goblets of wine and the remains of a small meal.

"Have they left? Where did they go?"

"No...nowhere, Master. I swear. I have not left my post here at the gate. If they'd left, then I would have seen them."

Metellus frowned, thinking quickly. "What about the slave quarters? Isn't there a gate that leads out the-?"

He stopped speaking, when he heard a shout coming from the rear of the villa. With every instinct on alert he started to run towards the raised voices. But as he ran he heard the words "fire" being shouted, and his heart beat accelerated as a feeling of dread came over him. It was only when he rounded the corner of the villa, and came to the single storey building which comprised the slave quarters, that he saw the evidence for himself. Thick black smoke and huge flames of fire emanating from the furthest of the slave quarters. In an instant he realised what was happening. What Verenus had planned…

"Livia," he shouted. "Livia…"

Metellus ran towards the scene of destruction as if all the gods of the Underworld were after him. Slaves were frantically trying to put out the fire, forming a human chain as they threw endless buckets of water over the inferno.

At that moment a total sense of helplessness washed over him. Was he too late? Could Livia survive such a fire – or more importantly the deadly smoke – which was engulfing the small room?

Refusing to be defeated he rushed to the front of the human chain of slaves, and immediately took charge.

"We need to get the door down. The smoke will be too intense." He yelled the words at one of the slaves – Isis – he recalled, Verenus's overseer.

"But…but the door is too thick, Master. We have tried. That is why we are using the water from the pond in the *atrium*."

Metellus thought rapidly. They had to get the door open. It was the only way to save her from the smoke. Twisting his head, he searched frantically around the courtyard that led from the main villa to the slave quarters before he spotted a marble bench which sat along one of the back walls of the villa.

Running toward it he shouted over his shoulder, "Isis! Get some of the male slaves over here *now* to help me lift this bench! We will use it as a battering ram!"

Isis, thankfully, comprehended what Metellus was planning, and ordered five of the other slaves to break the line and help him. Once they had lifted the marble bench, Metellus shouted at the other slaves to move away from the door, and with a clear path the six men rushed towards the door, hitting it with all their strength. At first the door didn't move, and Metellus shouted, "Again! Hit it again."

This time the door burst open, the hinges flying as the marble bench obliterated the wood. "Thank the gods," Metellus whispered,

241

before he rushed into the smoke filled room…

The sight of Livia lying there was the worst moment of Metellus's life. Worse, he realised, than watching his father being arrested by the Praetorian Guard and dragged away from their villa never to return.

Blood rushed in his ears, thundered through every vein of his body as he ran over to where Livia lay on the bed. With gentle movements he lifted her, noticing how so slight, so slender she was, barely weighing anything as he carried her out of the smoke filled room. Her head lolled as he carried her, her arms dangling as they hung lifelessly from her body, and Metellus couldn't hold back his moan of anguish.

"Please." It was all he could whisper, his brain refusing to let him utter the words *'don't die'*, and it wasn't until he'd lowered her onto a marble bench in the *atrium*, bent his head to her chest, that relief surged through him when he felt the flutter of her heartbeat against her ribs.

"Thank the gods," he breathed, before he lifted his head and looked at the group of slaves who all stood there watching in varying states of shock. "Run," he barked at one of the slaves, "Get me some water, and some wet cloths."

As he waited for the slave to return, he tapped Livia's cheek, trying to stimulate a response from her. "Livia. Livia wake up. It is I, Metellus."

He kept his tone gentle, even though his heart was hammering, threatening to burst out of his ribs as anger clamoured inside him, and every instinct he possessed urged him to go after his uncle. Verenus was responsible for this. Verenus had nearly killed Livia!

He leaned forward, stroking the smooth skin of her cheek, noticing how much his hands shook as he pushed back the dishevelled hair from her face. She looked so beautiful, so vulnerable. And he'd never loved her more.

"Livia," he breathed, lowering his face so his mouth came to rest against her ear, "Livia wake up. Wake up my love. Wake up so I can tell you how much I love you…."

"Livia. Livia. Wake up."

The words sounded so far away as they permeated the cloudy fog of Livia's brain. At first she ignored them, wanting to go back to sleep, needing to go back into the arms of Morpheus. *Go away. Leave me alone.*

"Livia. Livia. It is I, Metellus. Wake up my love. Come back to me, don't leave me."

Livia smiled. *Metellus wanted her. How lovely.* Slowly she opened her eyes, needing to know that what she'd heard *wasn't* a dream; that Metellus *did* want her.

Unfortunately, her inner peace was shattered when she was seized by a violent burst of coughing, that caused her eyes to start streaming, and all thoughts of Metellus faded.

"Here. Take a sip of water."

A hand lifted to cup the back of her head, lifting it slightly before she felt the metallic rim of a goblet press against her lips. Greedily she sipped the welcome liquid as it soothed her burning throat. She recalled another time when someone had given her water, tended to her needs and instinctively she knew that it was Metellus who administered to her. But before she could open her eyes to thank him, she felt the cool comfort of a wet cloth being placed over her streaming eyes.

"I'm going to wash your face. It is covered in soot." The soothing words became action, as the cloth skimmed over her skin, and it was only when the cloth was removed she was finally able to open her eyes. What she saw caused her heart to pound. Metellus was kneeling next to her, watching her with a concerned look on his face, lines of fatigue, and something she couldn't define, etched on it.

"What happened?" Her throat still hurt, and it was an effort to get the words out. But she needed to know, "Verenus. He…he…"

"I know," Metellus said interrupting her faltering words, taking both her hands in the warmth of his, "I know everything. Now, please do not distress yourself. It is all over. You are safe now."

"Safe? Are...are you sure? He...he tried to kill me."

Metellus's mouth pulled tight with anger, "Shh, Livia. Trust me it won't happen again."

Livia stared up at him, saw the determination in his eyes, the truth reflected in the fiery depths, and a huge surge of relief came over her. Metellus would protect her.

"Thank you," she whispered, smiling up at him before she closed her eyes as a wave of fatigue suddenly overwhelmed her. She needed, wanted, to sleep so badly...

"No, Livia! You must not go back to sleep."

His voice held a tinge of panic, and Livia felt something tap against the side of her face. Frowning in annoyance, she shook her head trying to dislodge the worrisome touch.

"Livia. Wake up please. Elisha needs you."

Elisha! The baby's name was enough to bring Livia out of her stupor, and she once again opened her eyes, blinking against the bright light from the afternoon sun. Squinting, she focussed on the man in front of her, "Elisha? She is well? Unharmed?"

She saw Metellus smile, a slight lift of his mouth, "Aye, she is well. But I am worried about you. You must sit up."

He leaned forward, and placed a hand under the small of her back, exerting enough pressure to lift her up. With his other hand he swung her legs so she came to a sitting position. She noticed, rather absently, that they were in Verenus's *atrium*.

A shiver of fright assailed her, and she looked around her, "Verenus? He...he is gone?"

Metellus nodded. "Gone. And he will never return. I promise you. He can't hurt you anymore."

She heard the earnest tone in his voice and nodded. The small movement set off another coughing fit and she gasped for breath, relieved when Metellus passed her the goblet of water once more.

She took it from him, her hand touching his, feeling the tension in it. Looking up at him she saw the worried look on his face as he watched her. Her insides clenched with something she couldn't identify, and her eyes locked with his. For a moment neither of them moved, as they both stared at each other.

"Take a sip." The words were whisper soft, and Livia shivered at the intensity of his voice.

Once she had taken some more water, she handed the goblet back to him, "Thank you. You are most kind."

A ghost of a smile flitted across Metellus's mouth. "I think I once told you, kindness is not one of my strong traits, my love."

"Did you rescue me? All I remember is being in a small room and there was smoke." Her head shot back up and her eyes once more met his. "Oh! You just called me your love."

"Yes. Yes, I did, didn't I?" His eyes bored into hers, dark with intensity, with a passion she hadn't really seen before. "I've been a fool, denying the love I feel for you. Rejecting yours. I'm sorry Livia," he said, his voice low, unsteady. "I'm sorry for not believing you. This is all my fault. My fault for pursuing revenge which was outdated and wrong."

"It doesn't matter."

"It does matter," he said forcibly, "It matters a lot. But I'm asking for one more chance. The chance to make things right between us."

Livia looked deep into his eyes, knowing his words were heartfelt. His hands were warm where they held hers in the strength of his. Mesmerised she smiled, "I love you Metellus, I have since the first moment I saw you."

He nodded, and she saw him swallow with difficulty before he said, "I love you, Livia. You make my life whole. You give me purpose, a reason to live. I thought I'd lost you, and I never want to feel that sense of despair, or hopelessness, ever again. My pride stopped me from telling you how I really felt. And my desire for revenge blinded me to everything."

Metellus leaned forward, and pulled her head closer to his. "Can you forgive me?" he whispered against her mouth, "Forgive me my stubborn pride and arrogance? Give me one more chance to let me show you how much I want you? How much I love you. How much I've *always* loved you."

Livia lifted her head, her lips whispering across his, "Kiss me, Metellus. Show me how much you love me."

It was all the inducement Metellus needed, and he lowered his lips to her. The kiss was soft, warm and of such sweet tenderness it communicated a lifetime of promises, and Livia's heart soared, before her free hand slid around the nape of his neck pulling him even closer.

Eventually, Metellus pulled away from her, looking at her with an intensity that caused a flood of longing inside her. Pulling her into his embrace he held her tight, his mouth next to her ear as he whispered, "Livia. My love. My life. You make me whole."

EPILOGUE

Metellus stopped pacing the corridor and rested a hand on the cool marble of one of the columns. With the other he rubbed the back of his neck in weariness, before he brought it round to rub his face.

The two day old growth on his face told him everything he needed to know.

Sudden silence from the room in front of him caused him to still, and his heart pounded in fear and trepidation. At long last Livia's cries of distress had abated. He wanted to barge through the door, take Livia from the bed and ride away with her, taking all the pain she was going through away from her.

But he couldn't of course. He was a man, and she was a woman. A woman who was trying to deliver their child.

Only the babe hadn't come. Metellus refused to think what might happen, what had happened to Livia's mother; although he had promised her he would look after the child if—

"No!" he shouted in the stillness of the corridor, and refusing to heed his mother's warning not to enter the bedchamber, he pushed open the doors and strode in. He stopped midstride when he heard a loud wail. At last! The baby had come, and relief shot through him. But relief turned to guilt when he encountered his mother's censorious frown.

But he ignored it, and walked over to the bed. Livia lay there, holding a red faced bundle in her arms. She lifted her head and smiled up at him. "We have a son, Metellus. A healthy son."

Metellus swallowed the lump of emotion which suddenly appeared in his throat. All he could do was nod. He'd never felt so powerless in his life, and Antonia took charge once more, shooing him out of the room.

"Leave. We need to finish off in here."

Heeding his mother's orders Metellus left. Once again he paced the corridor outside the bedchamber for what seemed hours, but could only have been minutes, until, finally, his mother came out of the room.

With a smile she said the words he'd been longing to hear, "Livia is asking for you."

Metellus found himself unable to speak, so he just nodded before entering the bed chamber once again...

"He looks like you."

"Really?" Metellus looked down at his sleeping son, who was cradled in the crook of Livia's arms. "He looks all crumpled and red."

Livia laughed softly, not wanting to disturb the baby. "Like I said, he looks like you."

Metellus grunted with humour, a smile on his face before his expression sobered, and he looked deep into her eyes. "I...I thought I was losing you. You were in so much pain."

"I know. It was a long hard birth. The midwife was worried I think. But I got through it, and we have a fine healthy son. A beautiful brother for Elisha."

"I never want to put you through that again. I couldn't live with myself if—"

"Don't torture yourself, Metellus," Livia said, lifting her hand and gently cupping the side of his face, "I am fine, truly. And in all honestly we will probably have more children. Unless you have grown tired of me of course…" Livia asked, an impish smile on her face.

"Never!" Metellus growled, leaning forward to repeat against her lips, "Never."

Livia smiled up at her adoring husband. "Good. We have our whole lives ahead of us. Now kiss me husband."

Later, when the baby was fast asleep, and Livia and Metellus were wrapped in each other arms, Livia asked quietly, "Have you thought of a name for him?"

Metellus nodded, "I thought of Lucius Augustus. In memory of both our father's."

Livia nodded her approval, not moving her head from where it had been resting on Metellus's chest. "That is very noble of you. It is a fine name."

"I have something to tell you."

Livia stiffened when she heard the serious in his voice, and lifting her head she looked up into his face, her eyes questioning.

"Verenus is dead."

Livia gasped, raising herself up onto one elbow to look at Metellus fully. "How?" she whispered.

Metellus shrugged. "I do not know the full details. His body was found on some rocks. It appears he fell off a cliff."

"Where?" Ever since that fateful day, when he had tried to kill Livia, there had been no sign of Verenus. It was as if he had disappeared from the face of the earth. Livia knew Metellus had paid people to try and find him, but it had been a futile exercise. Verenus's wealth had paid for his disappearance it had seemed. And even though she had begged him to forget about his uncle, Metellus had refused to stop looking for him.

"The man I hired – Spurius Proba – found him living on Capri."

"Capri!" Livia exclaimed. "So that's how he was able to remain undetected." Living so far away from Rome, and on an island as well, he would have been virtually impossible to find.

"You…you said he fell from a cliff?"

Metellus nodded, "His slave told Spurius Proba he'd found him lying on the rocks late one afternoon. He'd gone for a walk in the morning, and when he hadn't returned for some time they went in search of him." He shrugged, "The slave said he was ill, his mind gone. Had been for weeks apparently."

"Do you think he took his own life?" Livia asked, after a long silence had fallen between them, each of them caught up in their own thoughts and memories.

"Yes. I think so." His voice was flat, emotionless.

"Does Antonia know?"

Metellus's lips pursed, "Yes. I told her earlier."

"And how did she take it?"

Metellus looked away for a moment, deep in thought, before he returned his gaze to hers. His grey eyes met her anxious ones, his lips lifting in a slight smile before he answered, "She took it all rather well, considering."

Livia nodded. "Good." Livia released the breath she hadn't been aware of holding, relieved to hear Metellus's words.

For a while, after Antonia had found out that it had been Verenus who had effectively murdered her husband, the older woman had been eaten up with guilt, blaming herself for persuading her husband to return to Rome. She had been convinced that if they had all stayed in Alexandria her husband would still be alive.

She had begged Metellus's forgiveness, never suspecting Verenus capable of doing such evil. She had, she told them, been so grateful to Verenus for helping her after Lucius had been killed that she had trusted him implicitly, blindly accepting his offer of a home and stability for them both. She'd never for one moment realised the depth of Verenus's anger and hatred toward her, and Lucius, for causing him the humiliation of being jilted on his wedding day.

It had taken a considerable amount of time and effort on Metellus's and Livia's part to convince her that she was not to blame for Verenus's actions. Thankfully, Livia's advancing pregnancy had also helped ease some of Antonia's guilt, as Livia had

250

begged Antonia to help her when it came to the birth.

Livia sighed, "I'm sorry, Metellus. I know what he did was wrong. But he was good to you, and your mother, for many years."

Metellus smiled, taking hold of her hand, his thumb rubbing the sensitive underside of her wrist in an unconscious gesture, "Trust you to see the good in people, Livia. But it was all false wasn't it? A lie. For whatever reason his sick mind conjured up it suited him to keep my mother and I under his protection. But thanks to you, I was finally able to see through my blind loyalty to him and see him for what he really was – a man eaten up by jealousy – revenge. As I was before your love healed me. I could never forgive him for what he did to you – to us."

"I know Metellus. I know. But we have our whole lives ahead of us. Nothing can come between us now. Nothing."

Livia felt the tension leave his body at her words, and leaning forward she took his face between her hands and kissed him, wanting, needing, to take away the pain he was feeling deep inside.

"Ahh, Livia. What would I do without you," he said breaking away from her loving mouth and hands. "You are my love, my life. Never change. Never." And then he leaned forward, pulling her compliant body to his and kissed her deeply, expressing his love for her without the need for words.